'One of the most beautiful *New Woman*

'*The Broken Book* is wonderfully rich, complex and compelling. Susan Johnson has created an audacious and original novel with an awe-inspiring ability to explore emotional truths.'

*Daily Advertiser*

'A novel of great creative and emotional perspicacity that conveys in equal measures the vivaciousness and tragedy of Clift's life.'

*Sun Herald*

'A bold narrative, in which we're constantly reminded by the quality of her prose that this is an imaginative work ... It's a kaleidoscope of memory, jagged and disordered as the artist's tragic life.'

*The Canberra Times*

'Every word is given its proper weight and every idea its own space.'

*Vogue Australia*

'Like some of the greatest writers of our age, Johnson weaves her narrative with fragments of memory, loss and longing ... It is the best piece of literature I have read this year.' *Manly Daily*

'*The Broken Book* pulses with the stark emotion and ring of truth that characterised Clift's work ... a beautiful book by a beautiful writer.' *Who Weekly*

'I believe this to be a significant new novel, to be recommended to all who enjoy tales with depth, passion, conflict and believable, compelling yet flawed characters.' *Australian Bookseller & Publisher*

# the Broken Book

Also by Susan Johnson

FICTION

*Latitudes: New Writing from the North* (co-editor, 1986)

*Messages from Chaos* (1987)

*Flying Lessons* (1990)

*A Big Life* (1993)

*WomenLoveSex* (editor, 1996)

*Hungry Ghosts* (1996)


NON-FICTION

*A Better Woman* (1999)

the
# Broken Book

## SUSAN
## JOHNSON

ALLEN&UNWIN

This edition published in 2005
First published in 2004

Allen & Unwin
83 Alexander Street
Crows Nest NSW 2065
Australia
Phone:   (61 2) 8425 0100
Fax:      (61 2) 9906 2218
Email:   info@allenandunwin.com
Web:     www.allenandunwin.com

National Library of Australia
Cataloguing-in-Publication entry:

Johnson, Susan, 1956 Dec. 30– .
   The broken book.

   ISBN 1 74114 664 X.

   1. Women novelists, Australian—Fiction. I. Title.

A823.3

Set in Adobe Jenson Pro by Bookhouse, Sydney
Printed in Australia by McPherson's Printing Group

10 9 8 7 6 5 4 3 2 1

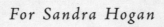

*For Sandra Hogan*

*I was conscious that not only my remarks but my presence was criticised. They wished for the truth, and doubted whether a woman could speak it or be it.*

VIRGINIA WOOLF, JOURNAL, 1909

*Beauty is only the promise of happiness.*

STENDHAL

*Life is easy to chronicle, but bewildering to practise . . .*

E.M. FORSTER, *A ROOM WITH A VIEW*

# Part One:

## Katherine

National Library of Australia

Papers of KATHERINE ANNE ELGIN, 1923–1969

Date Range: 1941–1969

Size: 1.82 m (13 boxes)

Location: National Library of Australia, Manuscript Section.

Access: Partly restricted. Not for loan.

Immutable: 11568464

Correspondence, juvenilia, journals, journalism including: *Katherine Elgin's World*; handwritten drafts, literary transcripts of poetry, short stories and novels including: *The Broken Book*—Na—106 leaves. *The Broken Book* is a fragment from an unfinished autobiographical novel that Elgin was working on before her death.

Born August 31, 1923 in Kurrajong Bay, New South Wales, Elgin lived in London and Greece in the 1950s and 60s before returning to Australia in 1965. She died in Sydney on October 27, 1969.

She was married to the poet and novelist DAVID MURRAY (1912–2002) with whom she had two daughters (Anna, 1947–; Elizabeth, 1949–1972). The papers of David Murray are located in the Archive Section, Harry Ransom Humanities Research Center, The University of Texas, Austin.

*Sydney, 1969*

'I'll tell you why I'm not writing,' I said.

But his attention had begun to wander, as it often does these days, and since he was no longer listening, I didn't tell him. He was reading the paper but pretending not to in that infuriating way he has, half smiling, his eyes flitting absent-mindedly back and forth between my face and the newspaper. I stopped speaking and waited to see how long it would take him to notice. After several minutes I gave up and pushed back my chair. 'Mmm,' he said, 'what did you say, darling?'

If he had listened I would have told him that creativity is energy, which, if he had cared to hear, he would have understood.

Creativity is a bodily energy, I would have said, 'And I no longer have the muscles for it.' I would have added: 'I have lost my nerve.'

I might have said: 'I no longer have the energy to pull out the proper length of gut and hammer it to the page.'

And: 'I'll tell you why I'm not writing. It's because I no longer have the necessary energy to grow my own hair.'

Once, he might have laughed.

Actually, I am too tired to explain anything.

I wonder how I grew so tired, so muscleless. I am so very tired. I wish to sleep and never wake up.

Once I had the energy of a thousand girls at play. I could demolish time, run through space, eat up the world. I kept the pulse of movement along my legs; the backs of my calves were full of waiting motion. I remember my body being perpetually braced, as if everything inside me was primed and ready to spring. My body was my gift, a seam of girlish courage ran the length of me, lighting my days.

This inexhaustible energy was also in my head, in the ringing cells of my brain. I walked as if floodlit, alive with ideas, blossoming with stories. This energy was a form of happiness, and for years and years I believed it was simply a matter of casting out a shapely net to haul it in. O, once I was a ball of fisted, happy energy, a roar of love.

I have been tired for so long. Somewhere I have always been waiting, and waiting is an enervating habit.

I have used up my teaspoon of hours.

I have lost my muscles.

I have lost my face.

I am forty-five years old and the dirt of the grave is fast upon my tongue.

Once I lived in some perpetual present moment, never

thinking of the future, wilfully refusing to imagine what lay ahead. Now I am stranded in my bleak future, everything behind me, everything spent, a clock that has used up all its ticks.

These thoughts passed through my head last night as I lay too long in the bath, idly watching the soap growing softer and more waxy, a bloom of cloud. The January heat sends me to the bath morning and night; last night I lay there for perhaps two hours, the water growing colder, knowing I should get up. Yet I could not rise and thought instead: I would like to stay here and slowly melt away. I understood that I was comforting myself with thoughts of my own extinction, yet the idea of melting away seemed exquisitely peaceful. I lay there fat and dumb in the cold milky water wishing I could pass away, without having to lift a finger to assist. *Pass away*. Such soft effortlessness, such dreamy pleasure.

A clock, a disappearing block of soap, I am sinking beneath my own metaphors. I cannot help myself—on the desk in front of me is a ball of twine and it occurs to me that my life is like that balled knot and I have come to its end. I can imagine the feel of the frayed, rough end of the string between my forefinger and thumb, pulling hard but finding there is no more string. David has always been scornful of my metaphors, his own writing is leery of them. I remember in London when I was learning French I was thrilled to discover that the French language was a sea of metaphors—for example, there is a phrase you can use when someone dies that translates as 'he felt the lead under his wings'. I suppose it prosaically refers to a bird felled by a hunter's pellet, but nonetheless I love the image of the translucent weightless wings of some breathless angel becoming heavy and cold.

David has always loathed, too, what he calls my air of 'restrained hysteria' and I thought of this as I lay in the cold bath last night dreaming metaphorically of my own death. Months ago, when I could still work on *The Broken Book* and it seemed for a fleeting moment as if that poor flogged character Cressida Morley had finally sprung into breathing life, I furtively passed him the first few chapters. I hate anybody reading my unfinished work and it is a measure of my despair that I gave them to him at all. He said he found its tone off-putting, florid, 'resonant with a beseeching quality', entirely too overwrought for his tastes. 'Your Cressida veers perilously close to purple,' he said, 'I'm not convinced the faux melodramatic tone works. And I think *The Broken Book* is a questionable title. It's too explicit.' Is he right? Should I change the tone? The character's name? After David's reading I looked at it again—Christ, what was I thinking? I planned to write an imaginary autobiography, a portrait of the artist as a young woman, a story that revealed a portion of our hidden selves. But where does autobiography end and fiction begin? Is Cressida only an etiolated version of myself when I wished her to represent the whole of evanescent, amorphous life?

I don't know any more. I seem to have lost the art of judgement, the ability to know my own mind. It was cruel of David to ask why I wasn't writing if he already knew the answer. He is still writing, he is still sailing on the ship, while my metaphors capsized long ago. His book is already safely bound for the shore, almost finished—his rendering of me, of the girls, of our shared life, all carefully stowed. *His* Cressida Morley has breath, muscle, gut; my Cressida has died upon the page. I don't know why, only that I cannot move the story forward. I should have changed her name. How did we end up both writing about a character with the same name?

Too late, too late, for us and for me. I am becoming undone, I am becoming beseeching—and I cannot imagine ever finishing a book again.

No longer can I attempt to unravel the knot, on the page, as I have always done. I cannot write, I cannot write to save myself now. I cannot even remember how it was that I came to lose my fists.

And this: once, on the island, Panayotis told me his most secret dream. We were drunk, it was late, and David had gone home in disgust. Everybody else had left the taverna and it was just Pan and me, drinking and smoking, telling each other everything. I remember he was wearing his blue fisherman's cap, even though he wasn't a fisherman, and that the first cold fingers of winter were upon the air. For some reason the thought of winter panicked me—I felt frightened, full of foreboding. It wasn't cold enough, though, to move indoors and we were at a table facing the harbour, a new bottle between us.

'Do you know, Katerina,' he said to me in Greek, 'my dream is to sit down at the table at lunchtime and eat a whole chicken by myself. I will not cut off the finest part of the breast for my wife, I will not slice off both legs for the children. I will sit at the table and eat every last bit up, the whole chicken, by myself.'

He looked at me with an expression of such longing that I was pierced by a vast, unfathomable grief.

Pan would be an old man now. I wonder if he ever realised his humble dream.

Did I ever eat the whole chicken?

# The Broken Book

(FROM KATHERINE ELGIN'S UNFINISHED
AUTOBIOGRAPHICAL NOVEL)

*Once there was a girl in a country at the far end of the earth
who thought she was not very good. In fact, she believed she
was stupid, bad on the inside, and everybody in the whole world
would guess. Sometimes she wasn't even sure she existed and
could not have said what her truest feelings were, or indeed
where she ended or began. The girl felt she had no proper shape,
no sides as it were, and she dreamed of being more fixed, more
clever, of winning the admiration of brilliant unknown people.
In the future, when she grew up, her life would be as beautiful
as a book, peopled by interesting and fascinating things, sweeter
than music or love. Everybody would love her and life would
be like a flower pressed between paper, perfect in outline, every
line careful as if etched. In this book of life no one would get
old or sick or scarred, no one would be found cruel or wanting,
and every husband would be perfect.*

*The not-very-good girl was called something plain like Kath or Mary or Joan. When she grew up to live in a book she promised to call herself Cressida, a name rich and strong in allusion, belonging to a different kind of girl altogether. A girl called Cressida might be fatally alluring, full of life and wit, a repository for a thousand men's dreams.*

*So it came to pass that the not-very-good girl grew up and became a writer and lived her truest life in a book. She lived her best life on the page, deep between the beginning and the end. Inside the book she was her own God and she made everyone do exactly as she liked. In the book she had everyone's attention, everybody listened, everybody had to pause to hear what it was she had to say. The not-very-good girl called herself Cressida just as she had promised and as Cressida she put all the glamour and excitement and adventure onto the page, all those flowers, all that life, compressed into a clear and final shape. In the book even pain could be said to have a meaning.*

*Cressida had colour in everything, cheer in adversity, passion, love. She travelled to exotic lands with reckless men, and imagined her life as one big risk that paid off. She had the children she wanted, a life other people envied, achievements of which other people only dreamed. She even became a character in other people's books and in other people's imaginations, for her reach was legendary and lasting.*

*And so it was that the not-very-good girl left behind her ordinary, more shabby self. In the book she perfected herself,* and its pages proved the safest place to hide. She buried herself so deep in the book no harm could ever find her.

It happened then that Cressida became the girl in the story who woke up one day and said, 'Every morning is the same. I place my feet upon the floor. I walk to the bathroom, wash my face, look at myself in the glass.

'I want to be the girl who sees the world, who marries the right man, who wakes each morning to something new and exciting. I want to be the girl who dared to dream, who flew so high she felt the breath of angels.'

Let Cressida say, 'I know! My book will be my boat, my wings. My book will be the engine of my hopes.'

So the newly created Cressida Morley, who was no longer ordinary, stupid or not worth listening to, went to her notebook. She took up her pen and wrote, 'Where to begin?'

Look upon the cloudless dome above our heads, the unblemished sweep of Australian sky. I am ten years old, invincible, standing on the bottom curve of the earth, the downward sphere of the world, already straining towards the blue feast of the sky.

Here are the things I love:

My father.

My mother.

My sister.

The sun.

*Lightning.*

*Mangoes.*

*Peeling off the wisps of transparent skin from my sister Hebe's sunburned shoulders.*

*The ocean.*

*Picking my nose.*

*Swimming.*

*The scent of jasmine.*

*Daytime.*

*Watermelon.*

*Doing a really big poo.*

*Dancing.*

*The smell of seaweed drying along the waveline.*

*That delicious moment just before I fall asleep.*

*Stroking that bright button between my secret lips down below.*

*Being admired.*

*The blowhole.*

*Here are some things I hate:*

*My father.*

*My mother.*

*My sister.*

*Being laughed at.*

*Not being taken seriously.*

*Steak and kidney pudding.*

*The smell in the dunny when the can is too full because the dunny man hasn't been.*

*Singing in the school assembly.*

*Peggy Gordon.*

*My big, slobbery lips.*

*Having to say, 'Very well, thank you,' when someone inquires after my health.*

*Wearing shoes.*

*Going to bed with my hair in onions.*

*Winter.*

*Night.*

*Fat white maggots on the wooden floor of the dunny.*

*The blowhole in the rocks next to the ocean shoots out a plume of furious water as if Neptune himself was spitting it out. Whoosh! Up it comes, over and over, a railing, contemptuous, frothing spume of sea, spat right in our faces. I am the only girl in the whole school to run through it: I took one great triumphant leap straight through its angry spout, getting pulverised, soaking wet, stranded. It almost knocked me over with the force of its hate, but I am a girl who went fishing on the rocks with her foolish father, was swept out to sea by a freak wave and came back, alive.*

*I am a girl who will gladly fight any boy who calls me names. It was me who kicked Stephen Asmus in the guts for calling me Brains; me who rolled with him in the dirt because he tried to put gluey red sap from a gum tree in my freshly cut hair.*

*Throw me the ball!*
*Hit me with sticks!*
*Come on, I dare you!*

*I am the second daughter of Percy and Dorothy Morley and I am living in a seaside town with a blowhole because my father hates the ubiquity of sport. More exactly, he hates the way in which sport in Australia is exalted, ranked high above every other human accomplishment. He believes sport in Australia is regarded as the greatest, most noble of human achievements, greater than any painting, any book, any piece of music you might think of. My father sees the worshipping of the accomplishments of the body as a sign of a culture dead to everything he most believes in, representing a world stripped of intellectual striving, where the only thing that truly matters is the curve of a human wrist in the act of swinging a bat, the line of a hand in the water as the hero gracefully digs his way to the end of the pool.*

*Before we moved here my parents lived in a tiny terrace house beneath the mighty shade of the Sydney Cricket Ground. The roar of the sports-loving crowd offended my father's ears every Saturday during the cricket season; my mother told me that during Donald Bradman's famous record-breaking run in 1930 he stood on the buckled square of concrete outside the front door, yelling abuse at passing sports enthusiasts.*

'You're a bunch of nongs!' he shouted. 'Mindless, the bloody lot of you! Why don't you go home and read Dickens? You might learn the sweet craft of humanity!'

My mother wondered whether a good game of cricket mightn't teach them the same thing, but she never said. My father's usual preference was for the English poets, Wordsworth and Milton and Marlowe, but perhaps he plumped for Dickens fearing the passing crowd might never have heard of them.

This practice of hurling abuse at innocent sports lovers ceased abruptly when Len Hatterstone, the local policeman, arrived to break up a scuffle. Someone had jumped the fence to give Dad a deserved walloping.

'Perce, it's a bit rich, mate, giving everyone a piece of your mind when they're only minding their own bloody business. Lay off, will ya?'

My father laid off by moving hundreds of miles away, as far as possible from the Sydney Cricket Ground. It obviously did not occur to him to move to another suburb, or perhaps another street.

It simply disgusts him, the way Australians lie down before the perfectly sculpted athletic form like Ancient Greeks, like Spartans, seeing God in the hard triangle of muscle in a back or a thigh. He predicts that when the Don finally pops his clogs he will swing his bat endlessly in Australian heaven; he says it's odds on that Bradman will be the first Australian saint. My father goes on and on about how Australians see something heroic in sport, as if a pure act of the body contains nothing

17

murky or ambiguous, and is unsullied by the dirt of an idea. Sport allows Australians to reduce life to all its banality and glory, he spews, the human body at the peak of its perfection, removed from all other mundane or weighty burdens. Raw life for idiots!

This is the kind of thing my father says when he is in full rant, for before anything he is a speaker fatally lost to hyperbole. He is a disastrous mixture of oaf and cultural fanatic; Australian colloquialism is his vehicle of speech yet he delivers it with religious fervour, Sturm und Drang, peppered with an odd literary flourish, frequently resulting in a kind of accidental poetry. In short bursts he can be a brilliant, charismatic speaker, words falling emphatically from his mouth as if ready-made with exclamation marks.

He is a secret Englishman. That is, he was born in Stoke-on-Trent, an only child, moving to Australia with his shopkeeping parents at the age of six. Forever after my father has been one of life's exiles, forever yearning for a better place. He keeps his Englishness hidden though, as is only wise, for like the Irish, Australians do not like the whiff of supposed superiority and are quick to take offence at any slight. Yet all his life my father has exalted anything English: we eat cream teas and learn Shakespeare and when he converted to communism he had the most difficult time trying to reconcile a classless society with the monarchy. 'I suppose it must go but, by jings, there's beauty in it.'

*The four of us then—Hebe, Mum, Dad and me—unbroken still, all piled in together in our tiny wooden house by the sea. If we walk out the back door, through the tough buffalo grass growing in the back garden, past the clothes line (one end of wire tacked to the back wall of the house, the other held by nails hammered into the mulberry tree; an old broomstick with a v-shape cut into its top holding up the wire in the centre), we reach the sand dunes and then the boundless sea.*

*There is no back fence, we walk up and over the sand dunes straight onto the beach. When we go to the beach for the day Hebe and I carry the woven beach bag between us, swinging it, but not so high that we disturb the contents of our picnic. Dad strides up ahead carrying the family beach umbrella, dressed only in swimming trunks—spindly legs on skinny body, broad shoulders, very tanned. Mum rushes up to catch him, takes his hand; she is plumper than him, dressed in a patterned sundress over her swimming costume. It is always a red-letter day for us if Mum joins us for a swim. Hebe and I are plunged into happiness by the fact that our mother is coming with us into the sea.*

*The beach is untrodden sand, white, silky, the sea a glinting, splashing spew of colour. Greens, blues, silver, the hat of the sky. No wind, no one else about, a school of dolphins rising and diving.*

*We walk far up the beach, right up past the point, near two fishermen. 'Fish running?' asks Mum, bending over to look in* the bucket. The bucket is full of silver twisting bream, the effortful pulse of gills, glassy eyes not yet clouded.

We pick a site miles from anyone. Once, memorably, Dad danced around the beach umbrella, pretending to do a Red Indian war dance as he pierced the pointed end of the umbrella into the ground. 'Humma, humma, humma, humma,' he chanted in mock Red Indian. 'Come on, girls, join in!'

And we stamped around in a circle with him. 'Humma, humma, humma, humma,' said Mum, joining in, the four of us in an impromptu family war dance around a twisting umbrella. Round and round we went, laughing, the mad Morleys: brown, tossed, worshipping the sun, the beach, the glory of the untarnished moment.

Dad loves scaring us and we love to be scared. Sometimes he sneaks into our room at night with a candle held under this chin, pushing out his lower jaw and exposing his bottom teeth. 'I am the Vampire of the Blowhole,' he whispers and we scream.

'I've come to drink your blood,' he cries, rushing towards us. We long for him to drink it.

Sometimes Dad pretends to sew his upper lip with an imaginary needle. He threads the invisible needle, miming the whole thing—tongue in one corner of his mouth, eye squeezed up in concentration, invisible needle held up between his fingers while he tries to thread the cotton—then he mimes putting the needle up through his upper lip. When the lip is supposedly caught by the knot at the bottom of the thread he pulls the needle up and his lip comes with it—one half of his upper lip, a curl, a funny sneer, a lip being dragged up by a thread.

We laugh until our stomachs hurt.

Our dad is a nong! A prize idiot!

Our dad is the funniest man in the world!

Once the four of us went up the Hawkesbury, to Dangar Island, to stay with Uncle Terry, and all four of us got bitten by bull ants on the same day. There was a sand toilet—a hole in the ground and a plank to sit on—and a beach house shackled together with fibro, slabs of corrugated iron which leaked when it rained, windows without glass. Dad was out the back on our first day, out near the pile of wood kept for winter fires, looking for the giant frilled-necked lizard called Shorty who lived beneath the wood pile. A bull ant bit him on the toe—you would think it was a shark from the racket he made. Then Hebe got bitten later that morning when she poked a long stick down a nest and an army of bull ants attacked her: all up her legs, and one bit her near her wee hole. Mum got bitten when she was hanging out the washing and an ant crawled into her shoe; as for myself, I was quietly reading David Copperfield under a tree after lunch when I got bitten on the bum.

*How we laughed, the jokes we made, which we told again and again, year after year. The Bull Ant Family: firm friends to ants the world over!*

*I will be madly in love with my father for a long, long time, forever trying to capture his kind opinion or even his momentary attention, but I will hate him too, for the great stain he spreads over my life, for the abrasive, harassing sound of his endless booming voice which follows me from room to sea.*

*He is always talking, talking at me, talking over me, and never, never listening. I am so used to going unheard that surely words would be stillborn in my mouth. I am so used to being told what I am supposed to think and feel that I am no longer certain who I am. My father is always telling me what to do, always issuing instructions or laying down the law, or else talking endlessly on and on about himself. He is a bully with a bully's sentimental streak; a crude thick streak of self-indulgent bullshit runs straight down his middle. His eyes invariably fill with tears when he speaks of his dead, saintly mother (pure Dickens), or when he tells of finding his dear old father dead on the floor, the sad egg he was cooking for his tea still on the stove, cracked and waterless in the burned pot.*

*But my father never cried when my adored cat Mordechai was bitten by a snake and died. Nor did he comfort me, being too busy heading off to some meeting about the world-wide*

Depression, all fired up with fresh ideas about communism. He doesn't care that my mother loves my sister Hebe more than me, for he doesn't seem to notice me at all. His nickname for me is Dopes, after Dopey in Snow White. 'Here she comes, old Dopes, old Dreamy Drawers,' he usually says when I come in the door.

My father didn't notice the day I came home from school crying because Peggy Gordon accused me yet again of being stuck up. 'You love yourself, Cressida Morley! Cressida Morley loves herself! Cressida Morley loves herself!' He only noticed when Miss Petersen came to see him the time I wagged school for a whole week because Peggy Gordon always sat behind me, laughing. He asked my mother to get the strap and took me into the bathroom. 'Please, Daddy, not the strap! I promise I'll be good!' My arm has instinctively begun to rise up to cover my face whenever I pass him.

My father will only begin to pay attention when I bring scandal down upon the family head, ruining everything.

When I am older, at the beginning of the war, before I wreak my personal destruction, all my friends will laugh at him, he is so strange: the worker's friend spouting Wordsworth! The worker's friend able to remember every single verse of Tennyson's In Memoriam! Everyone will think he is a loveable, funny old goat.

I know he is not. I know my father to be the whetted knife, sheathed.

⥲

*Hey, Peggy Gordon: I love myself!*

*I am delivered, walking fast along the sand. Look, my handsome brown feet, square at the toe, leaving hardly any prints as I walk. I am Cressida Morley and I love myself, I am Cressida Morley walking close to the shoreline, where the sand is hard as a road.*

*I am lifting off, into eternity. Soaring!*

*I am ten years old, unbuckled from the house of my father, the bully. I am free of the house of my mother, the clever sulker. I cannot hear his voice, or hers; the only thing I hear is the suck and crash of the ocean, that endless dance of sea and moon.*

*My body is waking up. I am alive, stretched and rustling to the very tips of my fingers.*

*I am a girlish triumph.*


*Sometimes in my father's house at night I creep out when I am supposed to be in bed. This is because my hair is tied up in onions, five perfectly spaced rags around which my hair is curled, causing the onions to bob like corks whenever I move my head. Without onions my hair is long and straight and the fashion is for curly hair like Peggy Gordon's. Onions are all right when I am sitting or standing but sleeping on them is like sleeping on a pillow filled with walnuts. Every night my head does a dance upon the pillow in its quest for lumpless space.*

*In the dark I feel my way along walls and doorways till I can safely crouch behind the chair in the living room and watch* my parents around the radio in the kitchen. My father is quiet for once, listening with the full force of his ears. What ears he has, live creatures on his head, big as my hand! My own ears are friendly at my temples, coyly composed. I fear, though, that I have inherited like a family curse my father's large and sensual mouth: to me his lips look ugly, squalid, as if they don't quite fit his face. My own lips are slobbery suckers, the bane of my life, the subject of teasing by Peggy Gordon, who has recently taken to calling me Lubra Lips.

I do not yet know that these very same lips will prove to be my face's most sublime invitation.

Hey, Peggy Gordon: I am going to grow up to be beautiful.

Hey, Peggy Gordon: I am going to grow up to command the eyes of every fucking man on the planet.

Put that in your pipe and smoke it!

*Sydney, 1969*

From my desk by the bedroom window I can see the length of the garden, with its English gardenias and roses and rhododendrons, its lilies and camphor laurels. In the early spring I planted a jasmine vine directly beneath the window because I wanted to be reminded of being ten years old and lying in a froth of flowers. The jasmine vine which kept up the back verandah of our house when I was a girl was wreathed with the breaths of flowers. I used to lie flat on my back, my head completely inside the vines, taking in the private exhalations of blossoms. I wish to lie among their scent again.

But, look, the push of reality. Look beyond the tame English roses, the trimmed hedge, and raise your tired eyes to the sky beyond the fence. Witness there the unruly clutch of native trees, the eucalyptus and ghost gums and waratahs and the frilled-necked lizards, look upon that straggly beauty which slipped the fence and broke the painting. Of course the first

English painters who tried to claim those trees could not literally see what was in front of their eyes, reproducing instead a painting already in their heads, some extract from an interior England. The beauty of the Australian bush does not easily compose itself for the brush or the camera: the tallest of those ghost gums beyond the fence stands like a fist pushed through the hard dirt of the earth, fully clenched.

I myself have lost entirely the memory of clench. My hand on the desk worrying its end of string is slack of muscle. I have lost the ability to raise my fists in my own defence. David has somehow worn me down, or I have worn myself down—whoever is guilty, here I am, at the end of myself in this curiously silent place among the trees and the birds, the wind moving the tops of the trees about like the sway of an airy sea. Beached, Katerina, surprised to find yourself on the manicured sands of the northern suburbs of Sydney, known to all Sydneysiders as the North Shore, as if it were the furthest stretch of some vast, encompassing beach. When I was a girl this area could only be reached by ferry until they built the Sydney Harbour Bridge; back then it was a curious mix of market gardens and small holdings, of occasional suburbs peopled by toffs who lived in grand houses and sent their sons to faux English public schools. The really big money was always in the eastern suburbs but some of it came here too, to build mock English houses and mock English gardens. England was the mother country.

I think my girls are dreaming of America. Lil is saving up to go to San Francisco; she is, I suppose, what is known as a 'hippy' and comes home clothed in fringed garments and woven headbands, her blond hair hanging loose all the way down to her bottom. 'Anaïs Nin is unbelievable, Mum. You've *got* to read her!' she says, bursting through the door, dragging in another new friend from university. Lil is dangerously beautiful, dangerously optimistic, full of innocence, unpeeled like a fruit. Greece has fallen away from her, as if that part of her life might never have been. She might be any other Australian girl, blithe and suntanned; she rarely speaks Greek now, and I am always shocked if I chance to hear her speaking Greek with Anna. Life has not yet pressed its weight upon her and when we are standing together in the same room I try not to breathe too heavily, lest I infect her. I carry the germ of melancholy, filled with the knowledge of life's sober mathematics, its cruel invisible subtractions. I am the diminished sum of my parts, an entire lived experience, and she is right to be leery of me.

'Mum, what's wrong with you? You're so cynical!' she said yesterday. She has decided she is going to be a poet and is putting together her first collection of poems (too many of them, I fear, are antiwar poems which will date); she wanted to talk to me about possible publishers. I felt tired just thinking about the long stack of words ahead of her, the money that will never come, the rewards she will never reap. A poem to the world is a pea to a starving man: too small, too inconsequential. Did I say this aloud?

'It's just that it's a very, very hard life, Lil. I want you to have an easier life than mine.'

She looked at me in all her cold and beautiful fury. 'I'm going to be a poet whether you like it or not.'

Anna came in then, Anna of the sad eyes, my stern maiden. Anna has already surely detected the whiff of life's decay, although she is barely older than her sister.

'I thought you'd be proud of her, Katherine,' she said, 'wanting to build another wall in the house of art.'

I raised my eyebrows. Like her father, Anna has always been quick of tongue, a girl who, unlike myself, never suffers from *esprit d'escalier*. 'The house is too cold,' I said, 'it has no running water.' I thought this was rather good.

Then David came in: the whole family, one, two, three, four. A rare occasion, the lot of us, in the same room, with no screaming.

'What's this?' he said, and Elizabeth rushed up to him with her golden hair and her beauty and her optimism and shone upon him like a personal sun. Their heads were together and Anna and I looked at each other.

I remembered Anna at seven or eight, in the rain on a beach in Greece, turning to me and saying, 'I don't care if I die, Mummy, because then I can go to heaven and sit on a cloud.'

I crossed the room and put my arm around her.

'Sweetheart, do you still want to sit on a cloud?'

She looked at me, confused. 'What are you going on about?'

I for one would like to feel the air's tender ministrations. My children are grown. All my rooms are empty.

Another fight with David—this time over a silly letter. The *Herald* insists on passing on these things—sometimes there is a great swag of them, from women who say they feel *exactly* like me, that my column somehow crystallises all the inchoate emotions inside them. They feel like they know me, they write, as if I am an old friend, moreover a wise old friend who can tell the secret at their centre. 'You are my oracle!' writes a Mrs Judith Watts of Kogarah, to which David snorted, 'Blimey, Sydney's very own Sibyl.' In her four page letter Mrs Watts told me everything—how many children she has, how she fell out of love with her husband, how sometimes she doesn't even know if she loves her sons. 'Do you ever feel like that, Katherine?' she wrote impudently, for it obviously did not occur to her that as a complete stranger she had no right to ask.

'Well, what do you expect?' David said when I got angry. 'You can't write about your private life every week in a column and then complain when people make assumptions.'

'Christ, David, you should know more than anyone the difference between real life and writing about life! My private life is private, the column is something I write for public consumption. It's not my actual, lived life.'

He looked at me with an expression I can only describe as distaste. 'Oh yes? And what is your real life, darling? What exactly is *Katherine Elgin's World?* I think you're so full of bullshit you wouldn't know. You mixed up reality and fantasy a long time ago.'

And so it went, growing nastier and more bitter. In the book of David I am some sort of sad old fantasist, growing cold in the ashes of my life. I should have stayed living in my fantasy world on a rocky island in the Saronic Sea because clearly I cannot live like everybody else in a real world stripped of illusions. I have lost my looks, my sense of humour, my *joie de vivre*, my charm to men. I drink too much and I should take more exercise. My act of sophisticated poise may fool the rest of the world but it will never fool him. 'I know all about *you*, my love,' he said, his mouth pulled down in a sneer.

I thought: no one knows me. I am a secret made of secrets, a locked door. I am a woman who makes her living offering up her life for public consumption, yet knows she gives nothing away. I am the most secretive woman I know.

Meanwhile, a young publicist arrived in the middle of the fight to take David to lunch to discuss his nearly finished book. I rushed to the bathroom to hide myself, the well-known columnist, wife of the husband, pressing a towel against her ugly, swollen eyes.

Meanwhile, every day is the same: fight after fight after fight.

Meanwhile, each week the cursed column grows more insurmountable than a book, 1000 blooded words which might as well be 1000 chapters. Such scattered, paltry words, so hard to conjure, so ultimately meaningless. How did I ever think there was a chance I might one day write a great book?

Perhaps David is right and I have confused art and life. I know that for a time my writing was where I lived my truest life—now the question is whether I exist at all if I can no longer write fiction. I seem to be slowly fading—the technical term is blocked but the feeling of no longer being able to write is one of having no outlines, of being blurred. I can't write because I can't bring something into focus. I don't know what that something is.

Meanwhile, I am remembering that many of our fights begin with David's question, 'Well, what did you expect?'

What did you expect, Katerina? Just exactly what did you expect?

*Sydney, 1941*

*Friday the Thirteenth—my first journal*

Actually it's Saturday now—I was preparing to write last night but, realising the date, didn't want to start. However, this book was opened and begun on that day, a day full of fears, superstitions—some sort of echo of my existence, I suppose. Fate, in a way.

I am seventeen years old (almost eighteen) and I fear mediocrity more than anything. Even my own father thinks I'm stupid. He calls me Sleepy because he thinks I'm like the sleepiest, stupidest dwarf, the goofy daydreamer—'Old Sleepy wouldn't know if her bum was on fire!' Mum and Ros always laugh, which only encourages him. He knows I'm good at English, but of course no one is allowed to be as good as he is at anything. And Rosalind is the *brains* in the family.

My whole life I have always been second best, the runner-up, never first—not as clever as Ros, not a hope of being as brilliant as Dad. To top it off, in my last year of school Elaine

Murphy won the school English prize and I came second, even though I tried my absolute hardest. When she stood up to accept her award I felt really sick, as though it was some sort of premonition about being an also-ran for the rest of my life—never good enough, never the best, always mediocre. Only Mrs Ford believed in me and even she ended up becoming an English teacher instead of a writer. (She gave me her copy of *Madame Bovary* which she's had since she was sixteen.)

Last year Mrs Hope (!!!) got us all to do some calligraphy. We had to choose a line of poetry or an aphorism. I chose this:

> *It might be easier*
> *To fail with land in sight,*
> *Than gain my blue peninsula*
> *To perish of delight.*
> *—Emily Dickinson*

'Kath, dear,' Miss Hope said, 'you are sixteen years old with everything in front of you. Why not aim for the blue peninsula?'

But what if I fail? What if I can't do it?

The blue peninsula of the world is so large, so unattainable, and I am so inconsequential. I am only a girl in boring old Australia, an unimportant country far from everywhere, and I don't know anything, not really. I don't understand how telephones work, let alone the difference between capitalism and communism. How does Dad remember all those things? How can I be more like that, able to present an argument or analyse something, instead of being diverted by the beauty of the oceanic sky out the window or the locked sadness in a passing boy's face? Everything I know is useless, useless—not very important. I need to read more, learn everything, PAY ATTENTION.

Instead I remember all the wrong things, everyone who was ever cruel to me, anyone who ever hurt me—the ugly man on the beach; fighting hard against that bitch Betty Gordon who made going to school every day such an ordeal, such a bloody misery—I remember all that *perfectly*. It's possible, isn't it, that everyone's life is made up of a string of feelings—that a feeling might be more real than a fact?

I must train myself to notice everyone; to take notes, make character sketches of people I know and people I don't—I MUST BEAR WITNESS. Already I have a sense of time slipping away, running through my fingers, and if I don't start now it will be TOO LATE!!

POEM
*One day*
*I will wake the ocean.*
*One day*
*I will rouse the sky.*
*One day*
*I will reach the blue peninsula—*
*In planting my flag,*
*I will learn the true art of delight.*

Oh, everything I do is so second-hand, so unoriginal. How can I train myself in perfection? *Please* let me do something perfectly. *PLEASE LET ME LEARN TO WAKE THE OCEAN!*

## Sunday

Now that the war is on everything seems shaken up, everything seems changed, even possible. It's like there's a giant crack in the wall and everyone is rushing through it. Everyone is secretly excited, no, *thrilled*, by the disruption to ordinary life but too guilty to say so, just like when the sandbank collapsed at the beach that time and all those people started drowning. Everyone on the beach was rushing around screaming, mad, crying, but *charged* with life, really intoxicated by being shown what truly mattered. This is what I think—I reckon people need drama in order to feel they are alive—everyone needs the brush of death every now and then to make us remember what it is to really live.

I know that people who have actually lost someone dear to them feel different—violently angry for a start—but for everyone who hasn't, like me, the war is sort of an unexpected holiday from ordinary life. It's as though all the old rules have gone and there are no restrictions any more. I know one thing for sure and that is that Mum and Dad would never have let me come up to live in Sydney if it hadn't been for the war.

We all know people are dying now. I am even starting to know some personally—Ruth Parker's brother John was killed last month and what happened to the family was incredible, so spooky and so very, very sad. When Ruth told me the story of how they heard he was dead, my whole body prickled with goose bumps.

All the Parkers played tennis—no one in our house played (Dad thinks organised games are for mugs and the only sport Ros and I ever played was school hockey). Anyway, Mrs Parker and John were particularly close—he was her only child until Ruth was born when John was nearly ten. Well, one Sunday last month Mrs Parker was sitting on that wrecked old cane chaise lounge in the back garden—half asleep, with a copy of the *Kurrajong Examiner* over her face, as it happened—when John walked around the back of the house in his tennis whites. BUT HE WAS FIGHTING WITH THE SECOND AIF IN CRETE!!! HE WASN'T EVEN IN THE COUNTRY!!

Mrs Parker sat up. 'John? Darling? Are you all right? What are you doing home?' Ruth said her mum was suddenly flooded with peace, she didn't even think to rush up to him, she just watched him and felt really calm and somehow happy. 'Mum, I'm fine, I'm really fine. I want you to promise you won't worry about me. Always remember that I love you very much.' He smiled at her, a really deep, loving smile, and then he turned and was gone.

Ruth said her mum walked straight back into the house, unruffled as you please, and said to Ruth and her dad, who were sitting in the kitchen, 'I'm afraid I have some awful news.

Our dear John has gone from us.' And then she sat down at the table and sobbed.

And do you know what? SHE WAS RIGHT! They got the telegram about three weeks later: Sergeant John Parker, 27, of the 2/1st Battalion, killed in action, Crete.

John used to write the most wonderful letters.

*Ruthie, when we manage to get into the villages, we often find cats tied to doorknobs by bits of string. Do you know why? When everyone is starving, they eat the cats, so cats are not allowed to go wandering. The question is: should one let them off, in the hope that they will make a dash for freedom? Are the ones tied to doorknobs destined for their owner's table? Or would they die faster if I let them go?*

At night I often lie in bed and think of John. I try to imagine how it was that he got home to his mother. What force of will allowed him to pass through air and time, through death itself, to bring comfort? Imagine the act of selflessness—at the moment of your own death, at your own perishing, that glad rush to the living, towards love.

I try and read everything I can about the war, and I ask every boy I know to tell me everything, but I still cannot feel it, how it must be, the noise, the smell. Funnily enough, hearing that story about John is the closest I have come to feeling the reality of it even though it sounds like a dream.

I remember reading somewhere that in the Great War, on

particular kinds of days when the weather was a certain way, you could hear the fighting in France from England.

I feel as though my ears are constantly straining for a sound that is too far off to hear. When we were kids Ros used to unexpectedly put her hand over my eyes, to annoy me—she knew it drove me crazy. I used to flail around, maddened, furious—it's completely shocking being made unexpectedly blind—it's much more unpleasant, more frightening, than you would expect.

I feel like that now—as if I can't hear anything or see anything, as if someone has got his hands in front of my eyes. I want to do something practical—train to be a nurse, ship out with the men, *act*. I WANT TO DO SOME GOOD IN THE WORLD, MAKE A DIFFERENCE. Oh, life is so wonderful, so interesting and strange—I want to feel every inch of it, live my life to the absolute fullest, see everything, go everywhere, LIVE.

I wonder what's going to happen to me. I wonder how old you have to be before you stop wondering what will happen to you?

# The Broken Book

*My father Percy Morley is the editor of the* Blowhole Examiner.
*He has a staff of four, supposedly journalists, but they also double
as secretaries, copytakers and advertising reps, taking down the
stock sale results and writing up the radio guide and doing up
advertisements as well. Mrs Hunter is the only real journalist—
she was once a copy girl on the* Argus *in Melbourne but she
gave it all up to marry Mr Hunter. But Mr Hunter is a
disappointment, being the town's Dirty Old Man, with hands
faster than Hopalong Cassidy drawing a loaded Colt. All women
have to give up their jobs when they get married, but my sister
Hebe and I believe Mrs Hunter gave up the wrong thing. That's
the thing about mistakes, you only know it's a mistake once
you've made it. Hebe and I reckon you should be able to tell
beforehand whether something is going to be a mistake or not,
then you could decide to do it anyway, in the full knowledge of
your forthcoming mistake. This could be known as an anticipatory
mistake.*

Mr Hunter is not an anticipatory mistake. He's a full-blown error of judgement, the feeling in the middle of the night when you know you've done something seismic which can't be undone. Mr Hunter has given Mrs Hunter a big fat baby called Cecil, whom she adores, but now Cecil is almost three and cannot walk or talk and Mr Hunter has lost his job so Mrs Hunter has come back to work. Mr Hunter is supposed to look after Cecil but once Cecil was found crawling along the main road because Mr Hunter was at the pub and had forgotten all about him.

Mrs Hunter is what is known as a looker, or at least she used to be. She is supposed to look like Norma Shearer, all flaring face and dancing eyes, but lately her eyes look like they are sitting down, being too tired to waltz around the room. She is always sweet to Hebe and me when we come into the office, maybe because the time spent away from her Living Mistake revives her spirits, making the world momentarily kinder.

The other 'journalists' are Mr Duncan Road, aged twenty-two (known as Dusty for obvious reasons; eager, competitive), Mr Bill Bishop (veteran of the Great War, been writing his memoirs ever since; once told me that the men in the trenches sometimes shook a dead frozen hand in passing if one happened to be sticking out of the mud) and Miss Doreen Evans (genteel working lady who finds Mr Hunter alarming, and who may or may not admire the questing zeal of Mr Dusty Road).

The Blowhole Examiner has been in the Griffith family since 1863, being established by Mr John Griffith's grandfather

Joseph. Mr Joseph Griffith was a Scot from Dumfries who sailed to Australia thinking it might be something like India, with darkies and elephants and tigers. Disappointed by its olive green dullness and patronised by Sydney's English aristocracy, he travelled further down the coast, finding the largely unclaimed green and gentle hills around the Blowhole more to his taste. The favoured son of wealthy shipowners, Joseph had his father cable out some money (although legend has it that he sent out gold bars secured in a safe in some captain's quarters). Within six months Joseph Griffith secured premises, invested in good presses sent out from England, selected staff and printed his first copy of the Blowhole Examiner.

My father Percy Morley wasn't a communist when he became editor of the Blowhole Examiner but he has had many run-ins with Mr John Griffith since becoming one. Indeed, he has been sacked and reinstated once, over an editorial he wrote during the Depression analysing the failures of capitalism and urging workers everywhere to seize the moment and revolt. Because paper was scarce and expensive in the Depression (just like it will be in the war), my father was accused of wasting valuable resources to proselytise.

The only reason he is still in the job today is that they couldn't get anyone to do it. Dusty is too inexperienced, and Bill Bishop too old, and they would never give the job to a woman. They advertised Dad's job the week he was sacked but not one person applied. Poor old John Griffith tried to do it himself but he couldn't get any of the copy to fit the page layouts (nobody in the office is any good at layouts except Dad) and the paper was late and lost a lot of money. Anyway, Dad had so much support from the local townspeople (there was even a rally for him in the town hall) that Mr Griffith eventually gave in and reinstated him.

'I suppose you are entitled to your views, Percy,' he said. 'Never let it be said that I am a proprietor who interfered with the freedom of the press.'

'Well said, sir,' said my father. 'I always thought you were a bonzer bloke. You will go down in history as a man of thoughtful and independent views.'

Mr Griffith was pleased to be seen this way, being otherwise inoffensive and ineffectual. The Griffith family is the richest in town, rivalled only by the landed Hewitt-Piggots, who own half the countryside around the place. They are graziers, whose sons are educated in England and whose daughters go to London with their mother for the season.

The Hewitt-Piggot land goes right down to the sea, to the cliffs and bays and sandy scalloped edges of the Pacific, to the place where we live all our days. Our edge of the country falls away down the hill from the steel town further up the road: if you stand on the very top of the cliff you can see the blue of the Pacific with its cuff of frilly waves, the green swaying hills, once thickly forested with Red Cedar. The sand is white in the Blowhole, there is the East Beach and the Main Beach and Booby's Beach and of course the angry spume of the blowhole. The Aboriginals around here call it the place where the sea speaks, although I think the sea speaks everywhere. The sea speaks and is prone to moods, sometimes it shouts, hurling its thunder into my ears, filling every part of me with its rage. It hurls me about then, throwing me down, so hard my shoulder scrapes the sand. When I emerge sand is coating my scalp— it is in my hair, my eyelashes, my crack—and the skin on my shoulder is scraped and bleeding as if I have skinned it on cement.

Look! The line of the sea's horizon is curly where the water leaps and falls. A frill of lace lies about the surface of the sand after a wave breaks. A girl leaps up from a wave, tossing her head back, sending a whip of silver water like mercury flashing through the air. 'Over!' scream the girls, jumping high into the air. 'Under!' scream the boys, going under into currents and salty blindness, the dishevelment of sand. Dig your toes into the sand and let the sea pull you, drag you with its great net across the sea floor. Sink your shoulders beneath the green glistening water so that your eyes are level with the surface of the curly sea and you are part of the whole, a creature of salt, a silver flash of girl upon the sea.

This is what the sea is capable of: it can grab me like a fist and drag me down, shaking my life out. It grabbed me once while I was fishing on the rocks; the hand of the sea rose up and claimed me. I was standing and then I was under, froth and gasp and sand, the wash and blur of green airless existence. From somewhere my father saved me, fist against fist, knuckle and bone. My father heaved me up, gashed and bleeding on the rocks, and all the while the hand of the sea pounded against our backs, our legs, still trying. This is what the sea is capable of: it provides me with a sandy rug, a safe place to rest my feet and in a split second it whips the rug out. The rug is gone, the floor, the sand: I am drowning in the winning fist of the sea. Where is land, safety, the sandy bucket which once held me up? Tricked you!

Sometimes the sea speaks quietly, turning its back, and then I have to woo it to me. I try to coax the lap of its salty tongue, in my ears, my mouth, my nose; I dive down, filling myself up, willing it to open wide its arms. Deep down inside it, I find the sea alive and pulsing, always moving, always speaking, a rolling carpet of tongues, talking, talking. Listen! Hear the slap of sea words, a liquid vocabulary, speaking low, murmuring fluently.

My name is Cressida Morley and when I am fifteen and talking to boys I will have a lot of difficulty paying attention to whatever it is they are saying.

All the time their lips are moving I will be wondering about that curled stalk in their pants and what it is doing at that very moment. I have only recently held one in my palm and I was immediately struck by the strangeness of it, the way it felt in my hand, unfurling, surprisingly weighty. And then it suddenly changed, and was seemingly constructed of bone.

I like the way Gavin Hunt presses the length of it up against me, so large and long it reaches my bellybutton. A quivering bow. A slender branch. A telegraph pole built for me! I like the way it presses up against my secret lips, the fragrant warmth it creates in the privacy of my pants.

My best friend is Pamela Crockett, whose mother is half Aboriginal. Pam lives out at the Aboriginal housing estate with her seven brothers and sisters. Pam's dad was a blow-in from Sydney, a sailor or a forester, anyway, some Irish fellow who got her mum pregnant and then shot through. There are a lot of half-Irish, half-Aboriginal people on the estate. Pam reckons the Irish are very similar to the Aboriginals and that's why they get on—they both love myths and stories, music and drinking. All Pam's brothers and sisters have different fathers, except for the first three, Clarrie and Arthur and George, whose dad was Mr Ryan, who was Irish too but died young of drink. Pam's mum drinks too, till her blue eyes turn marbled and opaque, otherworldly like a woman of visions.

Pam is very pretty, with large round blue eyes like her mum, heavily lashed, and malt-coloured skin. She gets a lot of stick from the other kids (especially Stephen Asmus who calls her Chockie Bickie or Vegemite Features or the Boong). Mum doesn't like me going out to see her at home, believing all Aboriginals are drunks and/or have loose morals (actually I have seen a lot of drunk people out there but I would never tell her, and Pam's sister Jenny is only fourteen and she's pregnant).

Anyway, Pam and I spend hours talking about penises, both of us crammed into the dark of the cupboard at the back

46

of the classroom, hidden by a curtain. The room is never locked and we go there every lunchtime, hidden, alone. She calls me Ressidacay and I call her Ampay or just plain Amp (we speak igpay atinlay—Pig Latin—and it's the first part of our names in igpay atinlay).

Amp likes them too, penises I mean, their ever-changing properties, their scientific mastery over matter. 'Roger's is very fat,' she tells me, 'ittlelay utbay ickthay.'

Amp is going with Roger Price, the school captain. This has given her a certain cachet among the other kids, and even Stephen Asmus has to watch his mouth around Roger. It seems to me that if you are pretty, people are more likely to forgive you for being Aboriginal—Amp says it is a well-known fact that the light-skinned, prettier kids from the settlement are the first to be picked for fostering.

Roger Price shaves and already looks like a man; Amp says his pubic hair is thick as sheep's wool.

'He likes it when I kiss his chest,' Amp says, which we both consider daring. To touch a live penis, as both of us recently have, is so wildly implausible, so dangerous, so against every law, that it is barely within the realm of imagination. Girls simply do not do such things; as far as we know, besides Amp's sister Jenny, we are the only girls in the school to have seen one. It is boys who own the kingdom of sex, who are free to roam its furthest boundaries. Girls are barred from its glorious gates and any girl who dares to venture inside will come to a Bad End, like Jenny Crockett. Jenny is going to a single mother's home in the country, but only because the welfare are making her.

So far for us, though, there is no anticipatory mistake in sight and Amp and I suffer our sins gladly: we know the might of watching a previously powerless finger reduce nascent men to blood and water. We feel the exhilarating charge of our hands, our lips, our tongues; we understand ourselves to be sources of influence. We love, too, the heat of our own skins, the heavy, swollen feel of our secret lips, the sweet trance of kissing on and on.

While Amp is talking in the half-black of the cupboard, her foot is sliding slowly towards me; we are facing each other, backs to either side of the cupboard wall, our knees drawn up hard. I can feel Amp's foot creeping, inching, falling, along the floor, coming towards me. Can't Amp keep her knees up? Is the floor slippery? Does she even know? Does she realise her foot in its gym shoe is creeping towards the dark of my legs, towards my bottom, my secret lips, that her shoe is headed directly for my most private centre?

Heartbeat like a bat; I cannot move; Amp's shoe makes a squeaking sound on the wood. Flooded with blood, desire, refusal, panic: both want the meeting and do not.

Steps coming; Miss Petersen opens the curtains, we are discovered.

'What are you girls doing?'

But we are her favourite students, her girls full of promise, her angelhearts of paint and words.

'Come on, out. You know you're not supposed to be in here. Quick, before someone else finds you. Shoo!'

And we are out the door, into the light; the cupboard, the foot, the slide gone.

We do not speak of it but at night I think about that slow creep towards my centre and I know this: I am christened sex, I am a miracle of light and desire, the world is a tender, soft place of boys and girls, and I am home.

I have taken to this flushed, blood-filled thriving place as if I was born to it, which I am, I am.

Not long after, I am getting ready for school, folding up a clean handkerchief to put in my pocket, when my father comes into the kitchen. I have written a love letter to Gavin Hunt and I suddenly see it there on the bench, folded up, next to my lunch, plain for everyone to see.

He will not pick it up. He will not pick it up.

But he does. He picks it up while I am still standing there folding my handkerchief.

There is a loud silence while he reads my words. A swollen, ringing silence in which I hear the ticking of the clock, the sound of the sea, or the hosing sound of my own blood.

I know every word in the note because I have re-written it seventeen times. I used special black ink, my finest arts, the throb, throb, throb of my blood.

DON'T SHOW THIS TO ANYONE!

Dear Gavin,

I'm sorry about saying that I didn't care if you went out with Shirley Mainwaring. I do care, but sometimes I say the opposite of what I really feel. I don't know why I do it and now you'll probably cut me because of it. I love you, Gavin Hunt. I love the way you've got pointy eye teeth and amazing brown eyes and I especially love the way that P thing in your pants springs to attention as if I was its captain. Please don't go out with Shirley Mainwaring, pretty please with sugar on top? Don't go out with Shirley Mainwaring, marry me! (Joke) Can you speak igpay atinlay (Pig Latin)—or is it only girls? Ampay (Pam) and I speak it all the time—I'll teach you if you like. (It's words with the first letter taken off and put at the end—with 'ay' added on. Some words don't change, they just have 'ay' tacked on, like 'anday' for 'and' and 'ayay' for 'a'.)

Iay ovelay ouyay (easyay isntay itay?).

Ovelay, Ressidacay

XXXXXXXX OOOOOOOOO

EMEMBERAY—ONTDAY HOWSAY HISTAY OTAY ANYONEAY!

*For a long time now my father has not touched me, not in caresses, not in hugs, not with his hands. When I grew breasts and hair and my beautiful face I became sulphurous to him,* something destructive and dangerous. It was as though I had sprouted fangs and a tail; he flinched when I touched him, as if burned. His temper has grown even worse around me; he cannot seem to bear looking into my eyes.

'Get to your room,' he says now in a low, mean voice. 'Now!'

I walk fast, I have to walk right past him, and when I do I instinctively raise my arm in self-protection.

'Dorothy!' he shouts to my mother as I pass. 'Dorothy! Bring me the strap!'

I am going to get strapped! I am going to be belted with his long black leather belt. I am fifteen years old, brim full of sex and beauty, and I am going down at the hands of my father.

I am in my room, waiting for him to open the door, my fifteen-year-old heart thrashing in its bony cave.

As he opens the door and comes towards me I vow that I will not cry.

I will escape.

I will be free.

I will spread my bounty far and wide.

Watch: I will arise.

*Sydney, 1941*

You are not going to believe this—SNOW WHITE AND THE SEVEN DWARVES HAVE MOVED IN NEXT DOOR!! I couldn't believe my eyes when I came home—I literally stopped in my tracks and my jaw must have been nearly hanging to the floor because the sight on the landing outside my room was unbelievable—dwarves or midgets, very small men all different ages, dozens of them, swarming all over the corridor, and this woman with a basket over her arm, opening the door to the big flat opposite mine.

'You'll catch flies like that,' said this tall woman in a long red skirt and a tiny apron and black hair done up like Snow White. I shut my mouth.

'Hello, young lady,' came a voice from the floor and I looked down to see the sweetest old man's face on a body the size of a six-year-old. 'Jack Delaney, otherwise known as Sleepy,' he said, extending his hand.

I put down my shopping (bread, the newspaper for the job ads) and shook his hand. 'How do you do,' he said. 'We are your new neighbours and we promise to be models of propriety.'

'If you can keep them away from the drink,' said Snow White, opening the door. Several of the dwarves rushed inside; Sleepy stood to one side and gave a gracious bow. 'Drunken dwarves are not a pretty sight. I'm Beryl Markham, sweetheart, of Beryl And Her Marvellous Midgets.'

'Oh, I thought you were Snow White and the Seven Dwarves,' I said, following Sleepy and Beryl inside.

'We did a special show for some boys out at Ingleburn,' she said. 'Care for a cuppa? This wig is hot as Hades and I'm dying for a wee.'

She disappeared before I could answer. 'Let me take those,' said Jack, taking the bags I was still holding.

I have always coveted the big flat—three bedrooms, a lovely black and white kitchen, but the best thing is the double bay windows at the front overlooking Rushcutters Bay. There was a young married couple here before and I only saw the view once—then I stood for a long time looking at the loop of the bay with its working boats, the dark mysterious green of the Moreton Bay figs in the park, and the palm trees dotted here and there. I thought it must be a bit like France.

'Well, hello gorgeous,' said a voice from behind me and I turned around. Standing there was a dwarf so handsome that if he had been six foot tall he would have been a movie star. He looked like Alan Ladd, all dark eyes and eyebrows and white flashing teeth. He had the most beautiful mouth. (What exactly is the difference between a dwarf and a midget anyway?)

'Er, hello, who are you? I mean, how do you do?' I said, flailing hopelessly, because I was really thrown—he was so good-looking it broke my heart. I don't mean it was more sad he was a dwarf because he was good-looking, more than the others I mean, just that his good looks somehow made me see straight away his humanity. I *saw* that he was just like me, immediately. I saw that he was just like me, only smaller.

'Ray Loosley,' he said. 'And you are?'

'Oh, I'm sorry. Kathy Elgin,' I said, shaking his hand.

Beryl Markham came back into the room, revealed as a bottle blonde of statuesque proportions. 'Ah, that's better. There was so much wee inside the old bladder I could have put out the Great Fire of London. Now, tea? Crumpets? What did you say your name was?'

'This is Kathy, love,' said Ray, walking over to Beryl and smacking her lightly on the bottom. 'She's going to give you a run for your money—she's stealing my heart as we speak.'

I blushed—were they lovers? My head was immediately filled with impossible scenes. She was SO tall!

'Now, now, Miss Kathy, don't you worry, I won't pounce on you just yet.' I smiled at him—he really was very good-looking— and sat down at the table in the chair that had been offered.

'Where do you do your shows?' I asked the old dwarf Jack, who had pulled up a chair to sit next to me.

'We do the Tivoli circuit mainly,' he said, 'but with the war we are doing shows far and wide. War increases the appetite for lots of things.'

There seemed to be people all over the place. 'Do you all live here?'

'Three bedrooms are all we need,' Jack said.

'And a spare couch for dalliances,' added Ray, offering me a cigarette. 'We've always lived around the Cross. The last place we stayed three years.'

'Till that old crow tried to make a wartime profit,' said someone else, who bowed his head at me and said, 'Clem Hogan, aka Grumpy.'

'I'll say. You can't speak to him before eleven,' said someone else, and then they were all there, around the table, and Beryl came in with the crumpets and the tea. 'A woman's work, etcetera,' she said. 'I don't know why I do it.'

'It's because you love us,' said Ray. 'Milk, sugar?'

They were all just ordinary men, some came from the country, one from a town just near us at Kurrajong Bay; most of them had gone into circuses at a young age. They were all fiercely patriotic and believed themselves to be doing war work, not fighting or giving their blood, but helping to keep spirits alive. After a while I even forgot that they were dwarves, or rather the knowledge of it moved right to the back of my mind— oh, it was SO interesting! Some of them had parents who had adopted them out, or else shunted them off to family somewhere else; others were kept at home but treated badly. Ray's mum, though, had loved him from the first and told him that everybody was the same inside. She had taught him to be proud.

'And look at me now. The star of a circus show, playing Happy,' he said, his mouth twisted.

'Now, now, chin up,' said Beryl, 'there are men out there who are dying.'

'All six feet of them,' he said.


I could hardly sleep when I finally got back to my room. Beryl had cooked up a huge pan of something called spaghetti bolognaise which an Italian friend taught her to cook. He was a magician, from Milan, and now she knows all about Italian food. It was really delicious and I had two glasses of red Italian wine, called chianti, which was *divine*! I thought: if they could see me now! Katherine Elgin, resident of Kings Cross, sitting around a table with seven dwarves and a peroxide blonde. I am fascinated by Miss Beryl Markham, absolutely fascinated— what kind of woman ends up spending her life cooking and cleaning for all those men, even if they are small? Oh, I can't wait to find out absolutely everything about her!!!

# Quotations

(FROM ELGIN'S JOURNAL, GREECE, 1961)

From Emerson's journals, 1864: '*Shakespeare's fault that the world appears so empty. He has educated you with his painted world, and this real one seems a huckster's shop.*'

Montaigne, *Essays:* 'Women when they marry buy a cat in the bag.'

## Sydney, 1969

Vanishings—light, colour, movement, growth—all gone. It takes all morning to rise from my dreamless bed, to dress myself and make a cup of tea. Sleeping pills don't bring sleep but stupor, a drugged and blind grope that lasts all day. David seems far away, a vague presence on the edge of my consciousness, and I no longer have the energy to fight him. The only thing I have the ability to long for any more, to actively desire in fact, is that moment of release into drunkenness. I want that all right, I *need* that—release, oblivion—I want loosed from me all pain, all anxiety, all cares. Without that liquid departure I remember I am trapped, and I see that David remembers he is trapped too—for I could never leave him and I know he will never leave me. Neither of us has the energy necessary for it.

The girls come and go—all bud and constant motion—and I know that I must love them but the feeling is a long way off, as if it belonged to somebody else. Everything requires so much energy, even love, and every action takes such energy that mostly I don't attempt anything at all. Sometimes whole days pass and I realise when David knocks on my door, asking about dinner, that I have been sitting here at my desk by the window for hours, staring into nothing. Yet I am obsessed by time, by the carrying away of life in each tick of the clock— I feel an exaggerated sense of the fleetingness of things but I cannot seem to perfectly express the anguish I feel about this in words.

The *deadness* of lost moments, the *lostness* of places and meals and people past—the inevitable death of things causes me such pain that I can hardly bear to look any more at a blooming rose, a child, a photograph, the bursting faces of the girls. The turning of the seasons are unbearable to me, I smell death even in the freshest morning. Summer is ending.

Yesterday I tried to write this journal for the first time in weeks but it seemed too difficult, the act of putting words on the page seemed imprecise, even meaningless. As for *The Broken Book*, I haven't touched it for at least six months, longer; when I last looked, the mock melodrama idea underpinning the whole thing struck me as silly. The deliberately heightened language seemed a mistake but I no longer have the energy to fix it. The column alone takes a full three days to write—I couldn't face it this week and begged off, blaming a stomach bug. I am having to concentrate hard even to write this, like a child who is beginning to imagine the scope of language. I can only attempt these few words at all this morning because for some reason hidden from myself I can tell that I am alive today. As I find myself alive I find myself writing, since writing is a bodily habit, perpetual as breath. One day soon I may forget to breathe.

The house is a mess (Anna came in last night, took one look and repeated our old joke, 'Call yourself a mother?' I attempted a smile). I cannot even begin to think about housework, and going on an errand to the shops takes forever— I may as well be planning a six month trip, it takes me so long to get ready and leave the house. Time itself has begun to seem strange, rushing or else queerly formless, so that I can spend a whole morning sitting at the kitchen table, staring out the back window into the seamless sky, believing only ten minutes have passed. While I am sitting there my mind seems curiously empty—I notice there are birds in the air, the dry wave of silver eucalyptus leaves, that the sky is still in its place. I suppose I notice the particular heat and dry-leaf look of Australia—and something else, something empty, forlorn. This country will always seem uninhabited to me in the same way that Greece always seemed peopled. Coming back, so poor and so broken, will always have the stink of defeat. Everything is behind me now, the things I have seen I can see no more.

Reading Wordsworth, when I can concentrate long enough on the words. '*Whither is fled the visionary gleam? Where is it now, the glory and the dream?*' But can the meanest flower offer solace to these thoughts too deep for tears?

I used to believe there was a pattern to life, or at least you could see in retrospect where a particular life had twisted itself into the wrong shape, buckled by rogue bad luck. I used to think my moment came when a handsome young man who smelled like Sunlight Soap burst like a firework inside me, turning me incandescent. Now I don't think there is any pattern, any shape whatsoever. All is randomness, chance.

When I was young and invincible like Anna and Elizabeth and everything was still before me, I loved knowing I could inspire fire and water. I loved making love without a French letter, that milky tattoo of desire running down my leg whenever I stood up. If I didn't catch it with a handkerchief it gently slid all the way down to the arch of my foot.

Flaubert's letter about the death of his great friend Alfred Le Poittevin—how surprisingly soon after death the waters of the body seek release. Life flowing out of the ears, the anus; the sheets wet.

My watery life of desire, my life of toil—the past, vanishings. The glorious hour, spent.

I am too tired to invent myself any more.

My heart has gone from the festival.

# Sydney, 1941

I finally got the chance to have a long chat with Beryl. She had sent all the dwarves off, every one of them, to do a variety of chores: some to get groceries, some to get beer, Ray had to go all the way to Kogarah to see the woman who is doing their new costumes.

'I have to get them out of my hair at least once a week,' she said, pouring me a shandy, 'preferably twice.' (I still cannot drink a glass of beer without the sweet relief of lemonade—the smell of beer always reminds me of that man on the beach.) Beryl drank her beer as if it was water, then poured herself another. She wasn't wearing a brassiere, or a girdle, and she sort of flowed out of herself, in a pretty silk nightgown, her dyed blond hair loosely caught up in a net. She was sprawled on the sofa, with a shaft of afternoon sun on her cheek: if I was a painter I would have liked to have painted her.

'Now, tell me all about yourself,' she said. 'Are you going to marry the first boy who comes along?'

I felt myself sitting too primly in my chair: I kicked my shoes off and curled up my stockinged legs beneath me. She offered a cigarette and I took one.

'Oh, no. I want to see the world,' I said. I didn't want to tell her that I planned to become a writer, the best writer I could be.

'And then you'll settle down. After you have walked up a mountain and sailed down the Nile.'

She made it sound stupid and I blushed. I don't like to be misunderstood: I have this dreadful need to explain myself, so that no one gets the story wrong. I suppose you might say I have an obsessive need for control, which is maybe one reason why I am planning on being a writer.

Suddenly my impulse was to tell her everything, to explain exactly who I was. I wanted to sound intelligent, and noble, a girl full of passion and high intentions.

'No, I want to live the fullest life possible,' I said. 'I never want to settle down.'

She smiled at me (she has dimples on either side of her mouth when she smiles; she is pretty in the manner of a young girl). 'How sweet,' she said, ashing her cigarette, 'but life won't be easy. The world does not enjoy people who don't play by the rules.'

I wondered if she was speaking about herself. I was dying to know how she became who she is.

'By thirty you will have changed your mind,' she said. 'Most people choose a life of certainty, of financial security. By forty the eggs are well and truly sorted from the bacon.'

'Oh, I don't want financial security,' I said. 'I don't want safety. I want to have experiences and joys and—oh, everything! I want to die knowing that I have reached the very limits of myself, that there is nothing left undone.' I sat forward in my chair, desperate to reach her, desperate to talk soul to soul.

'Aren't you a little firecracker,' she said but it wasn't unkind. I smiled at her and she smiled back: I felt she understood what I meant.

'I hope the world gives you everything you wish for,' she said. 'Who knows? It might.'

'Has it given you everything you wished for?' I asked, supposing that I had won the right to know.

'Very few people get everything they want,' she replied. She did not look unhappy. 'Personally, I reckon you can get one thing, or maybe two, but never the lot. Love, maybe. Money, yes. Doing something you love, no. I've only met one couple in my life who had everything—they owned a circus in Adelaide, happy as two pigs in mud, rich too, and just as in love with each other as the day they met.'

'So, it *can* happen,' I said.

'Yes, and then the wife, Doris was her name, got this horrible disease, something in her nerves. First she got dizzy spells and then her legs started to go. Herb, that was the husband, spent a fortune on quacks trying to find a cure. When you're older you'll understand that there is no cure.'

'I don't understand. No cure for what?'

She took a huge drag of her cigarette. 'For life,' she said.

'There's nothing for it but to take your little basket—the one with everything in it—the good, the bad and the in-between. You have to take the basket that you're given. There's no more and no less.'

I didn't want to believe her. Sitting there with my huge hope I didn't wish to believe that life will not grant me everything. I am ambitious for life in a way she will never know: my waiting basket is hungry for the lot.

'Don't look so smug,' Beryl said. 'Life'll wipe that smile off your face before long.'

She sat up and put her hand over mine. 'You know, I fell in love with dancing when I was a little girl looking at pictures of Irene and Vernon Castle. I used to think, "One day I'm going to do that." And I grew up and learned the foxtrot and the tango and the charleston—I became New South Wales's champion lady dancer. When Fred and Ginger came along I thought, "I could do that." Actually, I secretly thought, "I could do better!"'

She had a dancer's body: lithe but strong, as though used to the rigors of the barre. How interesting, I thought, Beryl doing the tango with some chap in a suit, her dress frothier than a wave.

'And you know what? Life showed me that I was never going to be chosen. I was good but I was never going to be great. There was this unbreachable gap between who I thought I was going to be and who I actually was.' Still she refused to look sad.

'It's in that gap that you grow up,' she said, 'in that gap you find maturity, a place to square yourself with the world.'

'Oh, I don't want to live in that gap,' I said, my feelings rushing out of me. 'I want to be free. Always.'

'Do you, little one,' she said, 'good for you.' She saluted me with her glass. 'Here's to freedom.'

I saw that she didn't understand. 'Have you read *Moby Dick?*' She shook her head and I sat even further forward in my chair, '"Better is it to perish in howling infinite, than be ingloriously dashed upon the lee, even if that were safety."'

She looked puzzled. 'I'm going to be a writer,' I announced, conscious that the expression on my face was one of pride.

'Ah, I see,' she said, offering up the beer bottle. 'I'm not much of a reader myself.'

I felt a kind of lurch: I am mad for books, just mad for them, and I saw that for some people a book might be just another object, like a shoe, a loaf of bread, a cup. The universe of a book might not be visible to them, for a book's universe of words does not exist without the participation of eyes.

'Oh, I'll lend you some wonderful books,' I said, jumping up, ready to dash to my room. 'I'll *make* you a reader!'

She stood up and sat on the edge of my chair. 'That's very kind of you, Kathy, but perhaps some other time—the boys will be back any minute. Would you like to stay for dinner?'

I said I would, even though Atpay was coming later (she's joining the Australian Women's Army Service next week). Following her into the kitchen I suddenly felt embarrassed, as if I had revealed too much of myself—as if what I had revealed was too ambitious and not very nice. I felt a sharp shame, for in Australia no one likes anyone with tickets on themselves.

'Beryl, I don't think I'm a genius or anything,' I said quickly. 'I don't have tickets on myself.'

She put the empty beer bottle down by the sink. 'I know you don't, love. It's good to love something as much as you do. Don't apologise for it.'

But I still felt sort of dirty, as if I had shown unbecoming greediness or pride. In Australia there is no greater sin than being a show-off, in thinking you are better than anyone else. I remembered Betty Gordon at school teasing me for loving myself, as if loving yourself was morally wrong.

'I don't love myself or anything,' I went on.

Beryl shut the door of the fridge and crossed the room to give me a quick hug. 'Kathy, you'd be better off loving yourself a bit more,' she said.

I wonder what she meant.

It turns out that Beryl grew up in Rose Bay and went to that fancy Catholic girls school on the hill overlooking Sydney Harbour. She's just turned thirty-five and her dad was a bank manager who lost everything in the Depression. Apparently her mum was a bit of a society queen—always trying to marry Beryl off to various suitable beaus. She even had a coming-out party and was presented to the Governor at a ball at Government

House. I tried to move the conversation in the direction of men in general, the dwarves, and whether her mother knows—I'm still fascinated by that part—but the only thing she said in passing was that she had only ever had one boyfriend in her life whom she adored but who was also capable of charming the pants off her mother. 'And she didn't want me to marry *him*,' she said.

Beryl hardly ever sees her parents—they think she fell in with the wrong crowd when she took up professional dancing—I wonder what they think of her now!!


I was drunk by the time Atpay got here. The dwarves came home and we drank more and more beer, and then Ray opened a bottle of chianti. They were telling funny stories of their days around the traps. (On one trip to Singapore before the war Ray got attacked by monkeys. 'Just imagine,' Ray said, 'back home everybody would be saying, "Oh, poor Ray's been killed!" And then they'd say, "Yeah, but did you hear how? He was eaten by monkeys!"') They were a funny lot, and I drank and smoked till wine and nicotine roared through my blood like power—the windows were open and the world rushed in, the world of possibility, of hope, of the immense pleasures of the unforeseen. The streets below were full of soldiers, the sound of a band playing somewhere far off, the press of existence.

At some point Ray leaned across the table and kissed Beryl full on the lips; I saw her trace with one finger the lines of his beautiful mouth. Happiness rushed in on the silky air, on the fresh smells from the harbour. I felt a surge of rapture.

'Oh, this is bliss,' I said, turning up my face to the open window and closing my eyes.

'Kathy, you have a talent for happiness,' Beryl said, 'you're blessed.'


I don't think Atpay was pleased that I was blessed, although she usually likes a beer far better than me.

'Darling Atpay! My oldest, bestest friend in the world!' I rushed up and covered her with kisses when I finally opened the door of Beryl's flat and found Atpay knocking fruitlessly at my front door.

'I've been knocking for twenty bloody minutes,' she said. 'I thought you said Flat 2.'

The dwarves spilled out behind me. 'Come and meet my friends!' I said, pulling her by the hand towards them. 'Everyone, this is darling Atpay, my darlingest friend in the whole world!'

She snatched her hand back crossly.

'But I love you, dearest Atpay,' I said, stepping on her shoes by mistake.

'You'd love Adolf Hitler if he was here,' she replied. 'Have you had anything to eat?'

'A cherry,' I said, leaning against the wall, 'a cherry with a fringe on top.'

'Where are your keys?' she asked, taking off her coat and glaring at me. 'Don't move until I come back.'

I leaned against the swaying wall, dazed with life, filled with love for Atpay, for the dwarves, for Beryl, for the universe. Then I saw that Atpay was back and that she was opening the door; I saw Beryl saying something to Atpay and Atpay looking annoyed. I waved to the dwarves as I fell in the door.

'Sit down while I get you something to eat,' Atpay said but it was too late: my stomach was coming up, rushing fast, hurling its contents even as I ran.

'Bloody hell,' I heard her say as I reached the washbasin, my stomach's contents splashing up the newish wallpaper.

'I'll never make an alcoholic!' I yelled to her before I was sick again.

'Shut up and be sick,' she replied.

Dear Atpay shared the bed with me while I got up to be sick several times that night, fetching water and endless Bex powders for me. In the morning she made me a piece of dry toast and went out to buy oranges which she squeezed for juice.

While I was drinking she gave me a lecture on the badness of the dwarves, on the evil of Snow White. 'If you ask me, that Beryl's a piece,' Atpay said. 'Why do you find those sorts more interesting than anyone else?'

'But they are!' I said. 'You should hear their life stories!'

'Oh, Athykay, *everyone's* life story is interesting!'

While I know this to be true, it doesn't mean that I wish to spend my time with just *anyone*.

'Of course I know that everyone has a story,' I said, 'but I prefer interesting people. I always want to find out everything about them.'

She snorted with contempt. 'Do I qualify as an "interesting person"?' I nodded vigorously.

'Why? Because I'm Aboriginal?'

I blushed. 'Ah ha!' she said. 'I knew it!'

'No! It's not only that—but it *is* interesting, you being Aboriginal! It meant I had something to learn.'

She smiled and shook her head. 'Athykay, you're an idiot.' I grinned at her. 'But a nice idiot.'

It will be great having Atpay around for a while.

*Letter*

(UNDATED, PROBABLY PERIOD 1953–54, LONDON;
WRITTEN BY ELGIN'S ELDEST DAUGHTER ANNA B. 1947)

To Mummy hello
To Mummy I love you thank you for the present and well
be coming back on 21st July and I miss you Mummy Did
you have a happy holiday because I hope you did soon Ille
be going to Kent and Ille like it there but Ille still miss you
there to but of course I wont miss you a lot
Love Anna

# The Broken Book

*My name is Cressida Morley and when I am sixteen years old Mr Hunter, otherwise known as Mrs Hunter's Living Mistake, will try to rape me on Booby's Beach on a sunny morning in December. I am supposed to be meeting my best friend Ampay Rockettcay but she is late: in fact she is nowhere to be seen. 'Boongs are notoriously unreliable when it comes to time,' Mr Hunter will say after we have been sitting together on my beach towel for ten minutes staring out to sea. I will be distinctly uncomfortable with the Living Mistake sitting so close to me, so close that I can feel the heat of his thigh. He will smell of beer, even though it is only nine o'clock in the morning.*

*'Please don't call them boongs, Mr Hunter,' I will say politely, 'they are Aboriginals. Actually, they are just people.'*

*'Dirty people in need of a good scrub,' he will say, 'and a good douse of kero for the head lice.'*

*'I got lice last year at school,' I will say.*

'Probably because the lice found you beautiful,' the Living Mistake will tell me.

I will look up the beach, desperate now, for Amp, for the saving sight of any human face. My sixteen-year-old heart will beat in my chest and the air in my lungs will appear to be coming too fast so that I am conscious the force of my breath is causing my breasts to rise and swell like a tide.

I will notice that the Living Mistake's eyes are on my breasts, that their rise and fall is hypnotic to his eyes. I will see his hand lift to land on my upper leg, where it stays only because I am unsure whether I have the right to push it off. I have been trained to be a nice girl, not to be rude, and I am embarrassed because I don't know what to do next. Surely someone will come along, surely someone will come to see the waves or the sun, even though it is only nine o'clock in the morning?

But The Living Mistake's big red hand is travelling up my skirt where it comes to rest near my outer thigh, on the fraying elastic of my underpants. I am on the rag. I have a thick washer pinned to either side of my pants with a large safety pin: a girl's nappy. What if his hands find out? What if blood leaks out all over him, a shaming flood? I quickly bring my legs together, straight out in front of me, so that the Living Mistake is forced to retrieve his hand.

'Cress, darling, you are a very beautiful young woman,' he says. 'I have fallen in love with you.'

I turn my head away from him, looking back up the beach,

my mouth dry. Am I allowed to get up? To go home? To run away? Oh, Ampay, where are you now, why can't you save me?

While my head is turned the Living Mistake throws me back onto the sand, where he lands on top of me, his thick tongue lapping at my mouth. I can feel his penis, ugh, against my leg, hot and hard like a rock in the sun. I am struggling to sit up but there is nothing but the smell of beer and the press of my bones into the sand, the universe of him blocking out the passage of air. I am trying to wipe my mouth, the snail's trail of his saliva is all over my face, I think the washer between my legs is preventing him from getting his freed cock inside. I can see it! Springing up, waving, an ugly mean thing without eyes. He will climb off me to get the thing out and I am out and free, standing up, pulling at my dress and my face.

'We shall have to try again when Miss Curse has gone away,' the Living Mistake will say, sitting up and beginning to brush off the sand.

He knows I've got the curse! The Living Mistake knows I am on the rag! I will blush hard, my head will feel hot and swollen, so that only embarrassment will force me from the beach. I will snatch up my towel and my new beach bag that Hebe gave me for my birthday and tears of shame will spill out of my eyes.

I will rush up the beach where I will run into Amp and immediately burst into wails.

'The Living Mistake knows I've got the curse!' I will cry and this is the one fact I will cling to, the saving shape of my ruin, the one idea my sixteen-year-old mind will safely hold. 'Mr Hunter knows I've got the curse,' I will say again and again before I begin to sob, before Amp cradles me in the dark sling of her arms.

## The Island, Greece, 1961

All day I have been sitting in our little walled garden, remembering. I have been doing a certain amount of counting, so to speak, some adding up. On the creaky blue table in front of me are my notebook and pen, a scattering of lemon blossoms, an old journal with a broken spine. Above my head the Greek sky, lemon trees, bitter oleander, two plum trees. Sounds reach me: the knock of donkeys' hooves, the voices of the boys leading them up and down the lanes, Soula's nervous chickens, the cries of children from the school on the hill. It is not yet hot enough to force me indoors—within weeks the sun will batter us senseless, but for the moment the air is sparklingly fresh and everything appears newly rinsed. The lemon trees smell wonderful and every now and then I stand up from the table and bend towards them. I am trying to fix my eye upon the particular: upon the white centre of the lemon blossom, upon the tiny, trembling puffs of pollen, upon the unfurling of the most tender new leaf. I am trying to remember my way into the past, into the particular, into a new book to be exact—at the same time I am trying not to flail in panic. Are we to go on like this forever, each successive book bringing diminishing advances and ever smaller returns? Am I to spend the rest of my days worrying about whether we can afford new coats for winter because our old ones are worn out? I am so ground down by fears about money, about the future, about how much my unwritten book will bring us. Surely we cannot go on being poor forever. Can we?

As I sit here I am forcibly reminding myself that my belly is full and that our poverty is relative. We are warm, sheltered, we have blankets for our beds, sunlight. We have more than enough to survive on a spring day like today without worrying about new coats for winter. Would I swap this day for a staff flat, a regular wage, our old safe life back in London? I remember myself standing for forty-five minutes in the blistering cold one spring morning on an ugly street in Highgate, waiting for a bus that never came, when suddenly snow began to fall. The man standing next to me turned up his face and announced in an impeccable public school voice, 'God, how I loathe this wretched country.' I laughed, uproariously and inappropriately, and he asked me out for a drink (I declined). I don't think such a man would ask me out today.

I sit now in my worn artistic shabbiness, my hair badly in need of a cut, trying to count my blessings. It is a perfect day for remembering, a shimmering day just like those from my childhood by the sea. A letter from my mother tells me my father is doing far better than expected and is even starting to speak again. I cannot imagine my father without words.

I have not seen my father since that morning ten years ago when our ship sailed for London from Circular Quay: I can still see him standing next to my frantic mother, refusing to wave. I have been trying to imagine him old and faded, but I find I cannot. It is hard to picture the powerful figures from our childhood as vulnerable, no matter how old we get. In my heart I will always be fifteen with my father.

Above my head, up on the roof, my husband is working in his studio, writing his novel which he hopes will bring us salvation. We are a house of memory here, every door opens on the past, every corner cherishes a lost moment. For months now I have been helping David to remember—after the girls are in bed we sit together on the roof, drinking ouzo, while I talk about Australian food we used to eat when I was growing up or long-forgotten expressions. (I remember the things my father used to say, such as calling children 'nippers' or women he thought unattractive 'old boilers' or young men 'two-bob lairs'. Dad used to say 'give it a burl' when he meant give something a try and 'blimey bloody Charlie' when he was cross, which was most of the time.) I remember the clothes we wore, the songs we sang, and all this remembering is going into David's new book. His novel is packed with lost remembered life, humming and sure as a pulse—it's about his youth and Australia and our early life together, about the sad, lingering effects of war—if it works he's planning on turning it into a trilogy.

Last night, sitting in the moonlight up on the roof drinking and talking and remembering, I knew again we had done the right thing in coming here, and—despite everything—David felt as close as my own skin. 'Darling, you're a witch,' he said at one point. 'How is it that you can remember everything?' He asked if I minded him using the name Cressida Morley for his main female character and I said he was welcome to it. 'It's a beautiful name. Euphonious,' he said. When he is happy David is the best of men—when his work is going well he is pleased with everything and consequently pleased with me. Increasingly I find myself doing all I can to provide the conditions in which his happiness might flourish.

These days I rarely tell him bad news or speak of sadness. I have never told him, for example, that for a long time the only thing my remarkable memory seemed to recall was pain. I used to think that painful memories were more deeply seared into our cells than happy ones. But as I've grown older I've come to believe there is no such thing as a 'fixed' memory, painful or happy—that is, an actual event recalled exactly as it happened—but only the act of remembering.

Here we are now, remembering, on this shimmering Greek day—David up there remembering his version of our story, and me down in the garden counting mine. *'As two spent swimmers, that do cling together / And choke their art . . .'* But must we both drown because we share the same story? Surely there was some point when our stories diverged, when each of us struck off in a secret, unknown direction? In the house of marriage, whole rooms are closed off, windows grow darkened, there is a small place where husband and wife must always sit separate and alone. David is sitting there now, and as a writer as well as a wife I must respect his right to sit in that place and make of our story what he can. Will I cry foul, claiming privacy for all my spent tears?

Both of us made the story.

Each of us must make of it what we can.

I've read enough of his book to know that I appear in the guise of an earthly mermaid, dining on the bones of breathless men. David said to me, on our first night together, 'You arose as if from the sea.' If he remembers me as if arising from the sea, what do I remember? What are the things I must count?

In fixing my eye upon the particular I will begin by recalling my strange and fatal first interview with David. ('*By our first strange and fatal interview/By all desires which thereof did ensue/By our long starving hopes . . .*') The date was May 14, 1946—I was twenty-two and demobbed for six months, working at the *Herald* for four—we met in the foyer of the Fairfax building in the city. I knew who he was, his fame preceded him, and I recognised him immediately. He was on his way into the building with the editor Vince Atherton and I was on my way out to cover one of the Lady Mayoress's sticky garden parties for Women's News.

When we looked at each other it was a bodily shock: erotic, charged. I felt my lips twist up in that way they used to when I was young and embarrassed, so that people thought I was smirking.

'David, I don't think you've met our new star? Katherine, this is our paper's oldest star, David Murray.'

'Katherine Elgin,' I said. 'It's an honour to meet you.'

Our skins touched; our palms. Everything we needed to know was in our skin.

'You make me sound like I'm about to burn out, Vince,' he said, turning to me and smiling, 'an old, burned-out star and a shiny new one. Is there enough room in the sky for both of us?'

Standing there, holding his hand for too long, everything in me opened, everything previously locked up. He seemed to me full of something I wanted, the possessor of some idea of life that was bitter and hard won. He was instinctively graceful, even standing motionless his body had natural elegance, an air of sensuality. He was not beautiful, not handsome; his face was jagged, heavily lined, the bluish skin of his eyelids already collapsing over his intelligent eyes. He was fully present in a way I had never before witnessed in anyone, every part of him was alive and searching; he was all discernment, all appraisal, all perceptive open eye. Some suffering in him was known to me, his inner life was recognisable in the alert lucidity of his face.

What exactly did I know of him? What did his skin tell me that his words could not—that he would cast me as his muse, that he would marry me, marry me?

'We must have a drink,' he said as Vince Atherton led him away. 'Soon.'

'Five-thirty at the Australia Hotel,' I said as I turned towards the door.

'Tonight,' he said, over his shoulder, and I nodded.

David told me later that Vince Atherton had warned him I would burn his fingers. 'And that's not counting what she'll do to your heart, mate.'

Back then I planned on burning up, on leaving nothing but the whitest ash.

I was so young.


When David came into the bar I had already been there for half an hour and downed three shandies. 'Murray! Murray, over here!' half-a-dozen people shouted as he came in and he was immediately surrounded. The famous war correspondent himself! The poet of war, of suffering. He cast a look at me, of raised eyebrows and helplessness, insisting he was only staying for a quick beer. 'I have more important business to attend to,' he said, nodding in my direction. 'I'm not wasting time with you lot.' I lowered my twenty-two-year-old marine eyes and blushed.

Several men turned and the hooting and whistling began. 'Not our Kathy,' the Count said, 'she's mine!' The Count was called the Count because of his presumed likeness to Count Dracula—with his slick black Brylcreemed hair, styled straight back from his forehead, and his adoption of a silk lined black coat, he was creepily handsome; no female copy girl or cadet journalist was safe from his vampire hands.

'She's already said no to me,' said the Count, 'she can't possibly say yes to you!'

Actually I had never said no—I tried never to be alone with him and therefore never had the chance—he kept up a running commentary on me whenever I happened to venture into the newsroom from the sanctity of Women's News. 'Boys, this is what I would like to do with Miss Elgin. I'd dress her in satin and place her fully dressed in the bath so that her dress was very, very wet.' He knew I would laugh and pretend to be a nice jolly girl who could take a joke, he knew I would refuse to run crying from the room like Anne Jones, telling tales to Miss Mattingley.

(Miss Patience Mattingley, Women's News editor, spinster, large men's hands, smoked, incongruously wore fine lace gloves. Rarely smiled, kind to girls, fiancé killed at the Somme—there were lots of women like this when I was growing up, women without men—strangely sexless. Heard years later that she had been having a long-standing affair with the married editor Vince Atherton—which just goes to show how impossible it is for the young to believe the old have sex. She was like an old, shaggy animal—large yellowing teeth, faded hair. Skin yellow from cigarettes. Hoarse voice; kind. Did not believe she possessed sex parts.)

Evelyn Simpson, assistant political correspondent (Canberra) had succumbed and gone out with the Count. It is true that he was vaguely glamorous in a matinee-idol kind of way—very well turned out, shoes highly polished, suits well cut, cuffs clean. Police reporter, which meant that he sat in the little lino-floored room just off the newsroom with the police radio blaring out at all times. Evelyn Simpson said he took her to the Chevron (expensive champagne, oysters, steak) then on to a nightclub in Kings Cross, where he knew everyone and was very charming. He was forty-five at least, three wives down; he made me feel naked when he looked at me.

He was looking at me then, but out of the corner of one eye I saw David walking towards me, striding really, coming straight at me, pulling me up from my chair hard by the wrist. 'Ouch,' I said and he swung me around and sat me on his lap. I smelled him—cigarettes, alcohol, with something compelling and fragrant underneath—can someone's whole life be decided by such an animal instinct? He smelled familiar, good; faintly sweet, like a loved child.

'That'd be right,' the Count said with a sneer, 'trust Murray to get all the best ones.'

And David Murray did get the best ones. He got the choicest, most succulent part of me, my youth, my freshest hopes. When we embraced on the bed at a cheap hotel in Kings Cross that same night, he got the best part of my tender skin, my mermaid's eyes, my stubborn unbroken belief in love. He got my unsimple heart, my long starving hopes: he opened the cave of my chest and I believed all the yearning and pain inside flew up and away. We rolled together and our eyes swam with common tears; when he shuddered inside me I felt the pulse of him in my deepest self, as if he had reached some private core. I lay on the sheets and he traced every part of me, the jutting bone of my hip, the flare of my ribs. He found the scar on my leg from the day my father and I had been swept out to sea only to be smashed upon the rocks of land and safety. He found the secret part of me, the tender carving down my centre, a lingering smudged brown line that was the only bodily evidence left of my most terrible dream. His whole self seemed transparent to me so that I found I could tell him everything, believing that his chest and arms and skin were ready for burdens. I thought my sad waiting was over, that he had come to tell me some central truth for which I had been waiting.

In the night I built him with tongues and teeth; I made him with my own bare hands.

In the night he told me he was still married, but only technically. 'It was over before the war started,' he said. He told me that on the plain stone floor of the newspaper building I arose before him as if from the sea. He said, 'You are the most beautiful woman I have ever seen in my life.'

Then he took my head in his long brown fingers. 'Katherine Anne Elgin, you are my born wife,' he said, cradling my dreams, kissing my eyelids.

I knew that I was. The moon had married us.

⟨⟩

I remember sitting on the bus the next morning going back to my room in the boarding house at Bondi Junction.

I remember thinking that the world had been cleaved into Before and After. I looked around in amazement at the people sitting dead in their seats. Didn't they realise there was a whole new land on the other side of the curtain? Didn't they know that love revealed this other land, allowing you to step outside your own life and see the transparent workings of time and being? I wanted to tell them that life was a gleaming, single moment, translucent, already fleeing, that we were all sitting together in time on a bus, sharing our heartbeats and our breaths. *Tell me everything about yourselves!* I wanted to cry. *Tell me if your life is sad, if your tongue cannot speak its sadness. Tell me your hesitations, your doubts, your yearnings. Tell me how it is that you live.*

When I got back to my room I immediately rushed to my notebook. I have it still, open now before me on the blue table, its spine broken, its pages coming loose. I can see with my own eyes the wretched poem and the spilling words I wrote:

*Knuckle, lip, ankle, flesh:*
*If I were a man I'd be him.*
*Our kin of bones*
*Our seamless skin:*
*Body of my body*
*Flesh of my flesh.*
*Our bony harmony, our common tears:*
*A single tongue, unleashed.*

*His orgasm—soft and unfrozen—the sweetest, most silent orgasm I have ever known, a gentle sigh; if you breathed too loudly you'd miss it. As though everything has stopped: time, the movement of the earth, everything but the gentle throb in my dark centre. I am lost in the smell of him, the sugared oiliness of his skin, the surprising plump softness of his mouth.*

*Thank you, God, for the feel of my bare feet on the cold lino, for the balance of construction, the way my body of nerves and blood is held up. Thank you for the wonder of movement, for the settling of my shoulders, the swing of my arms, the bliss of animated life. Thank you for the breath of in and out, the hidden bloom of lung. Thank you for the sight of sky, of sun, for the sight of his wounded face.*

Who is the deceiver in this picture, who is the deceived? Didn't I build an image of my husband with my own bare hands? Certainly I wished to believe that he was handing me the head of poetic life. I was a girl who relished the bursting of her skin, who could not resist the idea of a man delivering a new world.

Sitting here almost fifteen years later in the late afternoon sun I don't know whether to feel sorry, or embarrassed, for that starving girl of twenty-two. I have since learned, of course, that no man delivers anyone the head of poetic life, let alone life itself. I have since learned that men who see girls as if arising from the sea might later come to view them as fatal sirens, bent on shipwreck.

Mrs Muse, Mrs Muse, what have you come to, sitting dry in your garden? A permanent stranger in a strange land, a time-wasting, poor excuse for a mother. Get up, Kate, the girls will soon be home; take your remembering fingertips and pick up the paring knife. *Domates*, *patates*, *psomi*, hungry schoolgirls, the disapproving frown of Soula, your plump hawk-eyed neighbour, that superlative housewife far better organised than yourself. Dinner! Here's a particular truth for you, love: an unfed husband is more solidly of the moment than a thousand fugitive words.

*Sydney, 1941*

## Sunday

Haven't written anything for a whole month—so much has been happening—where to start? Four Fridays ago I went with Atpay down to Victoria Barracks—it was all so exciting and full of daring and adventure that I almost joined up on the spot. Oh, the *intent* of it, the sense of mission, the clearness of the boundaries, whole lives bundled up and labelled. When I came back from saying goodbye, life in the flat seemed suddenly purposeless, with no edges or direction, and I decided I *would* join up. I was gathering up a few things—my birth certificate, bank books—when Ray knocked at the door, asking if I wanted to go for a drink. He was in a really bad way—he looked like he'd been crying.

Anyway, I thought I'd better go with him. I didn't tell him about my plans—I just immediately picked up my purse. When we were downstairs in the street we attracted the usual stares—

I asked him how he stood it. 'It's like the sun in the sky, Kathy,' he said, 'the stares are just there.' At the club the tables were all taken and there were only stools at the bar; he made a wisecrack as I helped him onto a stool. 'Thank you, Mummy,' he said but I could tell he was embarrassed. I think Ray has designs on me and I haven't yet worked out what I am going to say if he tries to get me into bed. This time, though, he only wanted someone to talk to—he's been trying to get into the entertainment unit but none of the other blokes want to join him, and Beryl is dead against it—she thinks they're doing all right as they are. 'And there's no vacancies for a lone dwarf at the moment,' he said. We sat there for a long time and I listened while he went on about his fears for the future, how he saw himself at seventy-five, still playing Rumpelstiltskin. He started doing this impression of the evil Rumpelstiltskin dancing around the fire, joyous in the knowledge that the beautiful girl would never guess his name. I couldn't help smiling, and then he started laying it on thick, cackling and rubbing his hands, gloating with menace. After a while we were drunk and laughing.

Anyway, going out with Ray for a drink is not the point of this—or perhaps it is!!— perhaps it was fate that made Ray knock on the door and stop me from joining up. For the very next day I met the most wonderful man!! Thank God I didn't join up—now I know there is always a reason for everything!! I met him—his name is Kenneth Howard—when he came into the Saturday matinee session with his sister and a group of friends. He'd joined up a couple of months previously and he's been training somewhere in the country; it was his first leave. Anyway, he came in, sauntered in really, half drunk, his uniform unbuttoned, his hat falling off.

I showed them to their seats but they were laughing and shouting so much everyone was going 'Sssh!!' and 'Knock it off, will ya!'

The lights were down but I hadn't shut the door yet when I saw the silhouette of Mrs Benn, the manageress, standing in the entrance. 'Those young people are making too much racket, Miss Elgin,' she said when I reached her. 'Please ask them to be quiet or they will have to leave.'

'Do I have to?' I said but she closed her lips in an unforgiving line and walked away.

I made my way back down the darkened room, my torch parting the black at my feet. 'Excuse me,' I whispered and Ken was right there, sitting next to the aisle, and straightaway he said, 'Whatever you want, the answer is yes.' Everybody clapped and hooted.

It was hopeless, hopeless—the audience hissing, the film already starting, the entrance door opening again to reveal the stout form of Mrs Benn. 'Oh, please! I'm going to lose my job!' I said, beginning to cry.

And Kenneth Howard took pity on me and quietened them down, with an authority and firmness that I clearly do not possess. 'You can thank me by having dinner with me, beautiful,' he said. 'I'll see you outside later.'

Ken is only twenty-four but he looks and seems much older. He's got a natural authority about him, he's very self-possessed and confident—actually Beryl met him briefly last week and said she could see why I liked his 'casual arrogance'. 'He's the cocky type, Kath, and I mean that in more ways than one,' she said. Blood pulsed behind my face.

'I can tell you're going to fall for dashing, dismissive types who will give you a hard time.'

'Ken's not dismissive!' I said. 'He's attentive and loving and . . . kind!'

She gave a tight smile. 'Aren't they all,' she said, 'in the beginning.'

For the first time I thought that Beryl might be jealous of me because of Ray—I'm still not sure whether they are a couple. What is she doing living with all those dwarves anyway?

This is what Kenneth Howard looks like: he has a permanent shadow around his eyes, which are very dark brown (almost black) and deep-set. He looks like what I imagine an Egyptian to look like—his hair is very, very black too—like his eyebrows—but silky like a baby's. He has burned, olivey skin and he is tall and very broad-shouldered. He has a large hairless chest where I sometimes lie as if shipwrecked, the wash of his blood sounding in my ears.

He's lived all his life in the same block of flats in Rose Bay (his mum and dad and sister still live there), where his parents own a grocery shop. His dad wants him to take it over, but Ken says he doesn't want to end up like his father. 'Working his guts out seven days a week for a pittance. No chance to dream.' Ken wants to be a painter—he's shown me some of his stuff, some pencil drawings and charcoals, and I think he is very, very good. He showed me some portraits (which I preferred, but didn't tell him), but what he likes best is drawing machines and various technological stuff—he believes the world is going to get more and more taken over by machinery and artificial intelligence, robots!! He's had a couple of meetings with some government art committee trying to get taken on as an official war artist but the negotiations are still going on. ('Artists and governments don't speak a common language,' he said. 'The bloody war will be over by the time they make up their minds.') In the meantime he is doing ordinary army training—with the camouflage unit.

What else? What else? Well, his friends are mostly other painters (he was going to the Julian Ashton School before he joined up) but he knows some writers, too, even poets! I met them all with him just last night, this big group of people at a pub in the Rocks—some of them are at the University of Sydney—girls, really clever girls who can speak as wittily as the men. They were talking about politics and books and whether art played a moral part in the overall scheme of things; one conversation seemed to be about the question of whether one could be moved by bad art.

'This is Kathy, the flower of my heart,' Ken said when he introduced me into this conversation—several of the men smiled but only one of the girls. She was the little red-haired one who swears like a trooper—Val is her name—and she sort of looked after me when Ken disappeared into the crowd. Oh, I couldn't speak, I couldn't think of one single clever thing to say! They were so brilliant and funny and confident—I was listening very carefully to how they spoke, hoping to pick up some clues. One thing I noticed was that they kept saying 'in the sense of' when they were talking. It sounded wonderful.

When I was coming back from the toilet I stepped outside— to gather my wits and my courage really, before going back in. I was sitting on the step leading to the footpath when this man came out, all open shirt and kerchief at the throat, supercilious, haughty. I had spotted him before and immediately steered a course away from him. He sat down beside me!!

'The company too dull for you, my dear?' he said, in this arch voice as he sat down.

'Oh, no,' I said at once, immediately knowing I was going to gush, 'oh, no, everyone is really wonderful! I've never met so many interesting people—all together in one room! I just thought I'd get some air, you know how smoky it is in there, how crowded. My name's Kathy Elgin, how do you do?' I stuck out my hand.

He peered at my hand for a moment and then disdainfully gave it a small, wet shake. He did not offer his own name. 'Miss Kathy Elgin,' he said, 'do tell me all about yourself. I am quite sure you will.'

My tongue was glued up: I couldn't think of a single thing to say. I laughed in this really pathetic way, *ha, ha*, pretending that one of us had made the most wonderful joke. I sat there with this rigor mortis grin, a stupid girl devoid of brilliant words.

Then Val came up, with two beers and she handed one to me. 'Is he poisoning you?' she said. 'Bitter John, be a good boy would you and bugger off.'

He gave an elaborate sigh. 'I'll leave you to get on with the sapphic seduction,' he said, rising gracefully.

My blood lurched: I had never met a lesbian!

'It's all right, sweetheart,' she said, giving me a pat on the knee, 'you're not my type.'

I laughed at that too, *ha ha*, my face aching with effort. Why was she sitting so close to me?

'Bitter John is called Bitter John for obvious reasons,' she said. 'He cannot stand to see hope personified. Now tell me, where did you meet young Ken?'

I told her everything, about Ken and me and wanting to write and my father and my best friend Atpay who had just joined up and my sister Ros. I went on and on and she listened kindly, filling me in on her own background as we went (Methodist Ladies' College, Melbourne; daughter of two doctors; started off doing med but realised she was only doing it for her parents; now doing arts at Sydney). Val speaks out of the side of her mouth, like Mae West or someone, delivering lines as if they were scripted. We talked a lot about books we were reading— she said I should read someone called Nelson Algren—and then we spoke about the business of being an artist, how one might best learn to write. She didn't patronise me or speak down to me once—she did me the honour of taking my intentions seriously.

'Art is about discipline,' I remember she said. 'How good you will be sometimes depends on how firmly you bend to your task.'

She was fascinating but after a while I knew I wasn't listening properly, that my inner ear was straining to hear the sound of Ken Howard's voice. I wanted to hear his voice making people laugh, to see him standing in the very centre of a pool of attention, knowing that I was his girl. I wanted everyone in the room, every girl who was cleverer than me, or more beautiful than me, every girl who was in every other way my superior, I wanted all these girls with brilliant minds to know that Kenneth Howard had personally chosen *me*, Katherine Anne Elgin.

Oh, he is *gorgeous*! He has the softest skin imaginable, and when he is lying next to me he nestles in so close it is as if he was suckling. I don't know how a big, grown man can seem so boneless, so velvety and plush—it is like holding a bunch of feathery blossoms in my arms. When we lie together I am in ecstasy—he smells sweet and good, like Sunlight Soap and innocence—I could dive into him as if leaping into a cloud.

And I'll tell you something strange—the film that Ken and his sister and friends came to see was *How Green Was My Valley* (Ken said he was indulging his little sister and that he didn't want to see it particularly). It's got that scene where all the old men of the village are screaming at the poor defenceless unmarried mother that she will be 'cast out into the outer darkness till she has learned her lesson'. She cradles her baby, like a stranded Tess, huddled pitifully. But what is the lesson she is supposed to learn? Not to love with her body? Or not to get pregnant? What about the Bible's 'With my body I thee worship', or is that just about bodies that are married? MY BODY DOESN'T KNOW IT'S NOT MARRIED! MY BODY WANTS TO WORSHIP KEN HOWARD'S BODY! Ken Howard has single-handedly made me forget all about that awful, awful man at the beach and his ugly face and his ugly evil hands and his ugly stinking foul breath—Ken Howard has saved me. His penis is LOVELY—long and slender, gracefully shaped like a kind of bow (I must write to Atpay that I have found the most beautiful penis in the world)—he has come SO close to putting it inside me. I've only known him a month—and I only ever see him in short snatches when he comes into town to talk to the bigwigs about being made an official war artist—but I already feel as if I have known him forever.

Anyway, we always stop before it's too late—he's going to buy a packet of French letters. I dare not ask him whether he has done it before because I don't want to know if he has. I cannot bear to think of him with anyone else; I cannot bear the thought of that lovely penis rising elsewhere in homage. Surely it can only fly up because of me? Surely it is not possible that he could feel the same things for anyone else? Everything between us feels so precious, so fresh, so unique, I cannot imagine feeling in a million years the same way about someone else. It *must* be the same for him.

I am a trembling, waiting thing, a creature of longing, of yearning. I am gathered up into one still, waiting point— a poised moment—a caught breath.

## Friday

Beryl and the dwarves have been giving me gyp over Ken. 'Here she is, the soldier's fair maiden,' said Beryl this morning when I ran into her on the landing after walking Ken downstairs.

'He's finished his leave,' I said with as much dignity as I could, since I was clad only in my dressing gown, my feet bare. She was dressed up as Snow White again and the dwarves all started coming out as I opened my door.

'Kathy, *au naturel!*' said Ray, his hand over his heart, his beautiful eyes turned heavenward.

'I think the word is *dishabille*,' said Beryl, smirking.

'Your Ken's a bit of a ladies' man, love. He's obviously got his ball in your pocket,' said Bernie, the rudest dwarf.

'Be a gentleman please, Bernard, if that is possible,' said Ray, giving Bernie a dirty look.

'What's his secret war mission, Kath? Screwing for Australia?'

Ray walked swiftly over to Bernie and gave him a sharp clout to the ear. 'Mind your mouth,' he said.

Bernie immediately put up his fists but in the same instant Beryl crossed the corridor and wrenched them apart. Bernie was trying to kick Ray in the shins, shouting, 'Fuck off, Beryl! Let me 'ave 'im!'

She stood between them, a colossus in skirts, holding them apart with bare hands. 'Boys! Boys!' she said, giving their shoulders a rough shake.

'Ray! Come on now,' she shouted as they continued to lunge for each other. 'Bernie! Behave yourselves.' Suddenly she let her hands fall to her sides; Bernie and Ray, unexpectedly released from her firm fingers, lurched forward. Their heads knocked.

'Jesus Christ, your nut's made of cement!' Bernie slumped to the floor, rubbing his forehead.

'At least it's got something in it,' Ray said, smiling at me. My dressing gown had come apart, right down the middle, and my curled mound of pubic hair was revealed, a dark nosegay in a sliver of light.

I quickly covered myself up and rushed through the door.

'Lovely. Just lovely,' Snow White said as I closed the door.

# The Broken Book

*Ymay amenay siay Ressidacay Orleymay anday Iay atehay
Istermay Unterhay. Istermay Unterhay illway ebay evengedray.
Otnay odaytay, utbay neoay ayday.*

Ampay has promised to help me. We don't know what we
will do yet, but we reckon we will know what to do when the
time comes. I tried to tell Mum when I got home but I could
tell she was thinking it was my fault. 'What are you saying,
Cressida? Calm down! Please! Now, where did you see Mr
Hunter?'

'On the beach. He was sitting next to me.'

'He's allowed to sit next to you, isn't he? What do you mean
exactly?'

My name is Cressida Morley and when I am sixteen my
words won't come out properly. I have a whole army of words
in my mouth, a populous country, but none of them will march
out to order. I am a dreaming head, a teeming multitude, a
continent of unuttered letters.

'Mum, he touched me!'

Her face is shutting its doors! Her eyes are covered up against the coming storm. I am her worst dream, a grown-up girl of soft bosoms and hidden crevices, a girl of dangerous currents and oozing scent. I am all closet invitation, warm breath, a clearing house for every man's worst intention. 'I've got the curse,' I will say, 'I've got the curse and Mr Hunter knows.'

'Oh, Cressida, how on earth would Mr Hunter know you've got your period?'

'He was . . . ' My words are balking! They won't reach the air, they won't emerge into the light. My words are stuffed inside me, inside my head which is my world; I cannot get the world of myself into the air of the earth.

'You weren't flaunting yourself about the place so he could see your underpants, were you? I've told you about sitting and standing up properly.'

'Mum! He tried to kiss me!'

'A lot of men will try to kiss you. You have to learn to put a higher value on yourself.'

I will not cry. I will turn and make for my room and my mother will grab my hand. 'Cress,' she will say, her face cracked, 'you are a very pretty girl and men will try and take advantage of you. It's going to be up to you to win their respect. You have to show them that you respect yourself first of all.'

I don't know what this means: respect myself. What am I supposed to respect: my perfect toes? Am I supposed to carry my body as if it is a prize to be won, a jewel destined only to be bestowed upon the highest bidder? Would respecting myself more have stopped the fatal trajectory of Mr Hunter's penis, faultlessly aimed at my choicest prize?

I am a pretty girl with a rosy site, at which all the penises of the world are aimed.

Now I understand. I understand both that I need to be vigilant and that I have discovered the biggest secret which I did not know I possessed.

Istermay Unterhay: atchway outay!

Iay amay ayay irlgay ithway ayay eryvay angerousday ecretsay!


The same summer that Mr Hunter tries to rape me I will play a lot of secret tennis. Secret attempted rapes! Secret tennis! That summer I will be one big secret, setting the template for the rest of my life, that upcoming life which will mostly be lived inside my head because the words inside it will continue to fail to come marching out.

I will not buy my own tennis racket but I will borrow a lovely new one, the wood still golden, from my friend Dorothy (Dot) Barker, who has a handsome brother called Gordon who will grow up to die in the war. I will borrow, too, a white tennis outfit from my friend Dot and play doubles with her and Gordon and his friend Harry. Sometimes Ampay comes along, but only to watch, because she says she has never played tennis and is now too old to learn. 'But Ressidacay's a natural,' she says and I cast her a filthy look for using my nickname in public. 'The only sport Aboriginals like is boxing and only boys can do that,' she adds. Ampay often makes remarks about Aboriginals, which are sort of like jokes, but when she does Harry and Gordon look embarrassed. They have never known an Aboriginal so intimately before. 'What did you call her?' Gordon asks, ignoring Amp's remark about boxing. The oybays tease me for the rest of the day.

Oh, the sun on the lawn! Grass courts at the back of the Barkers' wonderful house! The power of my arms and legs, the cushioned swell of my calves! You would not know to look at me that I am indulging in a forbidden act, the playing of organised games: I am the family revolutionary, the player of sport, the asp in the sports-loathing bosom. I am playing a match, winning or losing, I am partaking of sporting civilities and rules. If my father finds out, will he cast me out? Will he feed me to the lions or bruise me with stones?

I leave the house furtively whenever I go to play, for I have not yet completely lost the childish impression that my father can see right through me. Somewhere inside myself I still believe he can read my thoughts, see into my soul as if I were the clearest glass. Somewhere inside myself I believe he knows if I am telling a lie; in fact, I am still not entirely sure that I have the right to a private existence. I believe he made me, that I am a kind of perpetual limb grown from the trunk of his tree, and that I will never exist independently of him. I am born of my father and my mother and I do not yet know whether I exist as anything other than genetic DNA, like spit from their mouths, a mutant offshoot whose finished shape is already predetermined.

Look at me: I might as well be the kind of girl who visits the Chinese opium den which still exists on the outskirts of town (public distaste will force its closure sooner rather than later, but for the minute it is the worst place of vice imaginable, where it is rumoured young girls are lured and lost). I could be the girl who too easily gave up her jewel, a girl who has already opened the floodgates to that most secretive of channels.

But instead I am the kind of girl who is playing secret tennis. I am hidden by the hedge which runs down the back of the wire fence bordering the grass courts, where no one can see me indulging my secret vice. Oh, my brown arm swinging the racket! The thwack of the ball! The hypnotic play of tennis balls pushing through the air!

Oh, Ressidacay: tennis. Whatever next? The full-blown crime of hockey?

That same summer when I am sixteen my father will lead a campaign against the Blowhole County Council. His paper, the Blowhole Examiner, will run a series of articles and leaders arguing that public money should not be spent on yet another sporting venue, the proposed Kevin Beatty Oval.

Now is not the time to be spending public money on sport. Events in Europe should make us mindful of the very real possibility of another war. But even leaving aside the large issue of an impending war, we might ask ourselves this: do we really need another sporting venue? Our community already supports a large number of sporting organisations, and there are numerous ovals, cricket grounds, tennis courts and football fields in and around our town already. If we have to spend public funds at all at this time, why couldn't the money go towards the establishment of a community orchestra? Our own dance company? Enlarging our already beautiful library? This newspaper gives over a dispropor-tionate amount of space every week to the listing of sporting results and it is time to ask ourselves why.

*'Because human beings love sport, Perce,' Dusty Road will tell him when he reads this editorial. 'They don't want to sit around in poncy suits getting bored listening to music they don't like.'*

*'Nonsense, Dusty,' my father will snort, 'which comes first, the chicken or the egg? You have to live with things in order to love them. The French have this expression,* la bain de culture, *which roughly means the culture in which you live. What is it that surrounds you? The latest league results?'*

*'People will always love games with clear winners and losers. The Frogs will never fill a football stadium with art lovers. Even in bloody Paris.'*

*'You're a nong, Dusty—you don't know what you're talking about. When Victor Hugo died, you couldn't move for ordinary Parisians trying to join the funeral. Workers, washerwomen—*

the whole of Paris came out to mourn, thousands of 'em. Can you imagine Australians giving a stuff about Banjo Paterson? Look at the way they treated poor old Henry Lawson.'

'He was a pisshead.'

'Very profound, Dusty. Thank you.'

But Dusty knew that Dad wasn't going to win. Dad had already had to back down from his stance against the sports results: he had tried to cut them by half but Mr John Griffith had made him put them all back in. 'It's what people want, Percy. You can't always swim against the tide.'

Dusty gave him a pat on the back when he came out of that sombre meeting. 'Mate, you're in the wrong country. If you want culture you'd better move to bloody Paris.'

At which point Miss Doreen Evans, long suspected of having plans upon Mr Dusty Road's person, let out an unladylike guffaw.

'What are you laughing at, you old boiler?' Dad said, walking out.

Miss Evans complained to Mr Griffith, Dad made his apologies, and by the time Dusty put his lead story in that week, Dad did not change a word. It read: 'There were cheers, tears and of course beers last Saturday as the Blowhole's premier rugby league team won against some quality opposition, the Wollongong Bears.'

He came home, locked himself in the front room and read Shakespeare.

# Katherine Elgin's World

(NEWSPAPER COLUMN, 1969)

'In OUR age,' said Auden, 'the mere making of a work of art is itself a political act.

'So long as artists exist, making what they please and think they ought to make, even if it's not terribly good, even if it only appeals to a handful of people, they remind the management of something managers need to be reminded of, namely, that the managed are people with faces, not anonymous numbers, that *Homo Labourens* is also *Homo Ludens*.'

I was thinking of Auden and his Homo Ludens the other morning as I listened to yet another public figure on the radio getting cross about Christo's plan to transform a slice of Australia's coastline into a work of art.

In case you haven't heard, Christo plans to wrap up like a present one and a half miles of shoreline near Little Bay, north-east of Captain Cook's landing site in Botany Bay.

By concealing the cliffs and rocks and stones he hopes paradoxically to reveal it. *Wrapped Coast* will be on display for some ten weeks before it is returned to its natural state.

'Puerile,' announced one public figure on the radio show I was listening to. 'Absolutely ridiculous,' said another, 'in fact, the most stupid idea I have ever heard of. This is exactly the kind of thing which gives modern art a bad name.'

'But it's a wonderful concept,' argued my second daughter, who wants to be a poet and who naturally believes in the idea of artistic transformation: 'Christo's creating a living work of art.'

All these divided opinions got me thinking. What is art for? Aren't there more important, more constructive, things to be doing right now, such as protesting about our sons going off to war in Vietnam? What is the point of any art—good or bad—in times such as these?

Specifically, what is the point of employing one hundred and ten labourers and fifteen professional rock climbers to haul one million square feet of fabric and thirty-five miles of rope to cover up naturally beautiful cliffs?

All week I've been thinking about the meaning of art, its use in our lives, and yesterday I ferreted out a poem I used to love when I was a girl growing up near some cliffs similar to those that attracted Christo. I used to quote the poem to myself as I swam in the sea beneath the cliffs, dreaming myself into existence.

The poem was Elizabeth Barrett Browning's *Aurora Leigh*:

> ... *What is art,*
> *But life upon the larger scale, the higher,*
> *When, graduating up in a spiral line*
> *Of still expanding and ascending gyres,*
> *It pushes toward the intense significance*
> *Of all things, hungry for the Infinite?*
> *Art's life ...*

By yesterday afternoon I had worked myself up into such a state that I decided to have a look at Christo's project for myself. I took a bus from the city down Anzac Parade, a trip I haven't made for a long, long time.

I passed the University of New South Wales (where my elder daughter studies the more reliable rules of mathematics rather than the lawlessness of poetry), then the old rifle range at Malabar where I was stationed briefly during the last war, and finally we came upon Long Bay Gaol. I wondered if the prisoners could see the drapery from their cells.

It feels pretty remote out that way, a million miles from Sydney Town, rather than ten or fifteen. As the bus drew close to Christo's project, you could see a lot of activity: it resembled nothing less than a building site, and conversation immediately started up.

'Whatever happened to real art,' said the woman sitting next to me. 'I mean proper paintings of people with faces.'

'If that's art I'm bloody Michelangelo,' said the bus driver, turning around to join in.

I was the only one who got off. As I walked towards the strange apparition I passed men in hard hats wearing special tools slung around their waists. 'Beautiful day,' said one.

I stopped and spoke to a young man having his smoko. 'What do you think of it then?' He turned and looked out over the vast, weirdly covered landscape.

'To be honest, I used to think Christo was a whacker,' he said, 'but now I think this is sort of like a dream.'

*Sort of like a dream.* You couldn't get a better definition of art than that: art is the place where we dream our lives, where we momentarily leave the heaviness of life behind.

'Human life is a sad show, undoubtedly,' wrote Flaubert, 'ugly, heavy and complex. Art has no other end, for people of feeling, than to conjure away the burden and the bitterness.'

I understood, looking at those disappearing cliffs, that in covering up such natural beauty Christo was asking us to see the grace within. By covering up the ordinary world in front of our eyes he was pushing us towards the intense significance of all things. He was reminding the management.

For what is art but an act of grace, a creation of some alternative world so that our own world is momentarily shot through with meaning? If we don't know why life itself exists, surely art is our last poetic gesture towards the mystery at the heart of us.

This is the reason art still exists through wars, through famine, through our deepest misery. It is the reason why I welcome with open arms my second daughter's potentially foolhardy vocation as a poet, even though she may well spend the rest of her life in poverty.

Art is not measurable in dollars and cents, or only in proper paintings of people with real faces. Art is an invisible commodity with the highest of invisible values.

'Surely the arm of this woman is too long?' said a woman to Matisse of one of his paintings.

And Matisse replied: 'It's not an arm, madam, it's a picture.'

To which I might paraphrase: 'It's not a wrapped coast, madam, it's an act of faith.'

Please, Mr Bus Driver, walk over from the bus depot one lunch hour and have a look. Each of us dreams, and sometimes it is not only the management that needs to be reminded that *Homo Ludens* translates as humanity engaged in joyful play. To dream, to play: art's life, found wherever life is found.

*Sydney, 1969*

## Midnight

Sitting here snivelling in dirty pyjamas, with a glass of whisky and a cigarette, David already slumped off to bed.

We have not slept together as man and wife for the last two years. Something in me is repulsive to him.

I wonder if there was some precise moment when he first began to hate me. Is hatred too strong a word? Sometimes I try to imagine his feelings towards me and I can only picture those magnified images of cancer cells, the way the rough and buckled nodules meet to form a malignant whole. Perhaps all our fights over the years, all those moments of bitterness and rage and disappointment and frustration finally joined up so there was no space left for goodwill, health, forgiveness.

One of the first rough and buckled moments came when he found himself shackled to a dependent wife and two unexpected children just when he had planned on leaving journalism and devoting himself to writing full-time. My eyes were suddenly wrenched from him to the children; he was bitter that we had barely a year together before I was pregnant. He was bitter, too, when he found out I planned to keep writing, that I was the kind of wife who cared more for the arrangement of a sentence than the arrangement of a nutritious family tea. He began to hate those moments when my mind was elsewhere, when all my focus and passion and will was on my work instead of him.

There were other buckled moments when I failed him, when I was not admiring enough or grateful enough or when I didn't listen when I should have. The worst moments came when he was jealous, when he accused me of being deliberately cruel, of breaking the bond of trust between us. I see now that when he found out about Jerry some part of him turned from me forever.

Sometimes if I haven't drunk too much I lie in bed and imagine David lying on the other side of the wall. I remember a long time ago he said he could not believe his luck in having won me. He used to say I was like a prize he did not deserve which any moment might be taken away. I wonder if he remembers.

This is the first time I have had my own bedroom since I was seventeen years old, living at home with Mum and Dad at Kurrajong Bay. I moved in when Lil moved out, taking everything with her but the bed. The bedroom of my virginal forty-six-year-old self contains my daughter's cast-off single bed, now draped with a rich, sienna-coloured cloth from Kathmandu, a present from the girls; a bowl of spring flowers from the garden in an old peanut butter jar on this desk by the window; a Byzantine cross I found by a derelict monastery in the hills of the island, and a favourite photograph Claudio once took of our house on the only visit he and Rosanna made to us there in 1956, when we were still happy.

1956. How long ago. How very far away.


Lil was here earlier tonight, with her boyfriend Paul, who is clearly in love with her. He wants to get married but Lil wants to 'live' first. I wonder if it is my fault that she appears to equate being married with not being able to live. She sees marriage as a form of closure, as an ending rather than a start. 'I want to get established first,' she said. 'I want to be published before I get married.' Paul was fervently nodding his head. 'That's cool,' he said. 'I'll wait.'

She looked at him. 'Actually, I don't know if I believe in marriage. Why should the Church or the State have anything to do with love?'

Paul appeared stricken. He is a freckled, hairy youth, intense, fond of quoting in impeccable French the more extreme maxims of his hero Baudelaire. Lil told me that he won her heart when he quoted Baudelaire in the context of the legions of cruel girls who had previously betrayed him: 'Ne cherchez plus mon coeur; les betes l'ont mange.'

'Oh, dear,' I said, 'make sure you don't eat what remains of his heart, darling.'

'Oh, Mum! He's passionate, that's all.'

Passion. How exhausting it is to be young.

When Paul left, Lil and I got into an unpleasant disagreement, which of course led to David and I arguing, which consequently leaves me sitting here at midnight snivelling in my pyjamas writing this. For someone who once liked to think of herself as happy I seem to have spent a lot of my life crying. I am only ever a step away from grief these days.

I'm trying to muster enthusiasm for Lil's poetry, I really am, but I also don't want her to live a life like mine. This all started because she wants to leave university, without finishing her degree, to step blindly into poetry's thin blue air. I told her she was being foolish, and she accused me of not supporting her decision to become a poet.

'I'm not saying you can't be a poet, Lil. Of course I'm not! I just think it would be sensible to have another way of earning money just in case.'

'You and Dad didn't! You gave up everything to write!'

'Dad and I were trained as journalists. We had money before we started out, and jobs we could go back to if we needed to,' I said.

'But things are different now,' she said. 'I can go on the dole.'

David came into the kitchen. 'How's my favourite girl? Still beautiful?' She rushed towards him and hugged him theatrically. 'Why is Mum so against me taking up poetry? You understand why I want to do it, don't you, Dad?'

He smiled down at her. I remembered that smile.

'A girl as beautiful as you should be allowed to do anything,' he said.

She broke away from him. 'That's got nothing to do with it. Shit! Doesn't anybody in this stupid family think straight?'

David looked angry. 'I was simply trying to compliment you, Elizabeth. It's a sign of the times that you take a compliment like that as an insult.'

'Yeah, yeah, when you were young women knew how to be women. Fuck, I've had enough. See ya.' And with that she grabbed her bag and stalked out.

David and I were left in the kitchen, staring at each other.

'What have you got against her becoming a poet exactly? You seem to have an abhorrence to the idea.'

'Of course I don't. I just think she should make an alternative career for herself first. If she tries to survive on poetry she will be living on air.'

He cackled. 'My, my. If your dear lady readers could hear you now. What a hypocrite you are, Katherine.'

'Oh, for God's sake. Shut up.'

'You know what I think? I think you're jealous. I think you can't stand the idea that Elizabeth is young and beautiful and talented—all the things that you are not. You can't even finish your novel. I think you can't stand the thought of Elizabeth making it where you have failed.'

Against my will, tears sprang up in my eyes. 'You know what I think, David?' I said. 'I think I don't want Lil to be a poet because I don't want her to need another life. I want her waking life to be enough.'

So here I sit in my stained pyjamas, fat and crying, alone in my middle-aged single bedroom writing an abridged version of my pathetic little life.

I can't see where the story is going. What is the end of the story? Cressida, what is the end?

# The Broken Book

DECLARATION OF WAR

*My name is Cressida Morley and it is my melancholy duty to inform you that I am at war. As a consequence of the persistence of the Living Mistake's attempts to illegally enter my body I have declared war on him and, as a result, my best friend Pamela Crockett is also at war.*

*I wish to declare that I am sixteen years old, sound of body and mind, and that I will do everything in my power to defend the rights of my body and soul from further attacks.*

*Signed,*
*Cressida Anne Morley*
*16 Bongaree Street*
*The Blowhole*
*New South Wales*
*Australia*

It is late afternoon and Ampay and I are standing around a young ghost gum in the paddock next to the house filled with drunken Aboriginals. 'Aren't we a bit old for this?' Amp will say, taking another contemplative drag of her cigarette as I finish carving my initials into the skin of the tree. We have carved a heart and the initials of our names so that now we are fixed upon the earth, part of the elements.

'Just think,' I will say, 'this tree will be here long after we have gone. Our names will be part of the tree as it grows into the sky.'

'And no one will be able to read it except the koalas,' Amp will reply.

'But we'll know they're there,' I say, 'no matter where we are in the world, or if one of us dies.'

Amp took another long suck of her cigarette. 'Well, I don't know about you but I'm planning on coming back and climbing the tree when I'm eighty.'

'It's hard to believe there's a war on.' I say. 'Germany seems a long way off.'

And we will lift up our heads looking for evidence in the peace of the sky. There is only the bluest lid, a few cockatoos, the empty sound of afternoon heat and crows.

Does anybody know if Germany actually exists?

'Give us a drag, Ampay,' I will say before we head off to join the Aboriginals to get drunk. Amp's mother's eyes are large and blue as the heavens and when she is very drunk a filmy wave of white washes across them as if she was blinded by

120

*glaucoma. She is a milky blind drunk then, with extraordinary otherworldly eyes, like a visiting alien. I love to watch those beautiful eyes slowly filming over.*

*Of course you know that the best form of warfare is guerrilla warfare: it's defeated the French, the English, various Americans; it's slaughtered many a well-trained traditional army. Sneak attacks. Constant movement. The disconcerting element of surprise! Sneak up on Mr Hunter's Hillman and let the air out of his tyres; throw a brick through the window where he sleeps drunkenly in his chair after returning from the pub. (Comrade! Always make sure you know the whereabouts of young Cecil before you hurl.) Can you possibly sneak into the pub and put upright tacks on his favourite chair? Can you spit into his beer before he takes an unknowing first sip?*

*Soldier, be constantly vigilant: never venture onto the beach alone, always walk down streets in daylight. Surround yourself with boyfriends, girlfriends, your hateful sister Hebe, your secret army. Remember: forewarned is forearmed.*

*My father Percy Morley, editor of the* Blowhole Gazette, *informs me that Mrs Hunter, she of the Norma Shearer dancing eyes, is out of sorts after some hooligan threw yet another brick through her window. Presumably her dancing eyes are too tired to dance any more and instead are soaking their feet.*

'Bloody hoons,' my father says. 'They need a good kick up the bum.'

'Poor Theresa,' my mother comments, 'do they have any idea who's doing it? Three times seems more than coincidence.'

But I am saved from the giveaway of my guilty face by the appearance of my big sister Hebe. 'Guess what?' she announces and something in her boastful stance alerts me to danger.

Everyone looks at her, standing in the doorway with a haughty look on her face. My sister, the genius.

'Well? Spit it out!' My father is looking grumpy (as usual) for no other member of the human race is in the room except us. No smiles for the public, Dad? No Hail Fellow Well Met? What happened to your good-tempered self—leave it at work?

'Cressida has been playing tennis!' Hebe cries.

Everybody turns to look at me. I am sitting at the table doing my homework (The Fall of the Roman Empire) and I look up from my papers into my father's hot eye.

'So what?' I will say. I will feel my chin involuntarily rising as if in preparation for a mighty punch. The Fall of the Empire of Cressida.

To my surprise my father slowly walks towards me, carefully pulls out a chair and quietly sits down. 'Cressida, I am disappointed in you,' he begins. 'As a member of this family you know very well that every one of us has a duty to refuse to take part in organised games. It is our family's way of subverting the ruling sporting culture of Australia, our family's

122

*means of illustrating what is and what is not important. Do you understand?'*

*I nod cursorily at him in the hope that this might encourage him to wind up his little speech and go away.*

*'I know our family protest is unusual, even eccentric, but if our actions encourage just one person to stop and think about the implications of living in a sports-mad society we will have done a bloody good job.'*

*Do I have to listen to this bullshit? Do I have to remain in my chair while my father goes on and on? Do I have to listen to him expounding on the joys of physical expression in natural surroundings, running on beaches, frolicking in open seas; do I have to wait while he tells me again that I will be free to do whatever I like once I leave home?*

*'And while you live under this roof, Cressida, you will abide by the rules.'*

*For the first time it occurs to me that my father is mad. It dawns on me that his quaint, endearing little eccentricities might be evidence of some inner flaw of wiring and scaffolding. What holds him up? What scanty grid of nerves animates the strange and furious web of bizarre thoughts which form his personality?*

*I am thinking these things while I am looking at his head and consequently I do not answer the question he has asked me. I can only suppose he has asked me a question because the flow of his words has stopped.*

*'Well?'*

'Well what?'

'What is your answer? Do you promise to refrain from playing tennis?'

I am still looking at his head, trying to imagine the interior network of fibres and nerves. 'No, I do not promise,' I reply.

'In that case you will have to leave this house,' he says.

The fact that I start to laugh does not help. 'Cast into the street over a game of tennis!' My voice is high, slightly hysterical because I cannot stop laughing. I look at my mother, who is looking frightened, at Hebe, who looks upset.

'Happy now?' I say to Hebe between laughs. 'Is this what you wanted?'

'Oh, Percy, don't be stupid,' my mother is saying, 'you don't know what you're saying.'

'On the contrary, Dorothy, I know perfectly well what I'm saying. A family has to work as a unit, as a team, every member has to play by the rules.'

I am still laughing. 'Play by the rules!' I sputter and he ominously stands up.

'Go to your room! Now!' my father shouts, the network of nerves somewhere in his head radiating heat.

I go, but I am still laughing and even when I close the door I find that I cannot stop. Dad, don't you know there's a war on? Don't you know German planes are spreading across the unaware sky like a successful disease?

Thinking of the German sky causes me to stop laughing.

*I am sitting in my room, breathing heavily, imagining the dark freight of bombs.*

*My name is Cressida Morley and when I am sixteen my mother will talk my father out of throwing me out of the house. I am not sure how she does it exactly but I suspect it has something to do with me finishing my Leaving Certificate. I know she could not have appealed to my father's common sense (he has none) or his fear of public opinion (ditto), but she might have successfully appealed to his sense of narcissistic pride in the possibility of his second daughter's glossy future. For hasn't he always believed we are better than everyone else? Hasn't he prided himself on the flexibility of his own intellect, the breadth of his knowledge, feeling nothing but scorn for the poverty of thought that surrounds him? Am I not, first and foremost, the promising second daughter of Percy Morley? (Certainly never destined to be as brilliant as my father, nor indeed as clever as my older sister, but nonetheless I remain his second daughter.)*

*That's my guess, anyway, for when I sit down for breakfast the next morning the subject of my leaving home is never mentioned. In fact, nothing is mentioned. My father does not address one word to me during the entire meal: my father is not speaking to me.*

*Hooray!*

And so it goes: *my father does not speak to me for six whole months. If he needs to address a question to me he does so through the conduit of my mother or my sister. He never quite looks at me either, which is strange because I always thought he could see right through me anyway. Perhaps I really am a girl of glass, a see-through vessel, something so flimsy and insubstantial that I have become erased. Where are my edges, where is my tongue?*

*I know I must exist, though, because Ampay speaks to me, even saving me a seat on the bus. I know I must exist because Gavin Hunt continues to press his quivering bow against me, even though we broke up four months ago. This does not stop him from trying to put his hands down my pants when I go over to his house to see his sister Jeanette: we are in his bedroom looking for cigarettes when suddenly he closes the door. I let him pass his fingers over the hidden steel wire, let him part the sliver of lips nestling in the steel wool. Afterwards he will tell everyone that I let him finger me, even though he dropped me and is going out with Shirley Mainwaring.*

*Throughout it all, throughout the days, my father will keep refusing to look me in the eye or to address one single comment to my person.*

*What exactly is my crime? Independent existence? Am I the cruel branch about to take up the saw and let the trunk's sap weep?*

*I know myself to be an invisible girl about to blow far, far away. A branch, a leaf, a moment passing. A shiver of air. Away!*

*Now the brainbox is leaving school, as dux of course: Hebe Morley, the first Morley to go to university. As the new year dawns, off she goes, wreathed in glory, off to study arts among the dreaming spires. But this is the University of Sydney, Australia; Oxford writ small, replica Oxford, the colony's little echo. There she goes nonetheless, walking the quad, passing over the lawns and gardens planted with oaks and elms once carried as acorns and seeds in the bellies of wooden ships from that greener, wetter place. There goes Hebe, the family's star, the firstborn with the nimbus around her curly head. The intellectual, the first Morley to tread the academy's marbled floor. My sister the killer, the one who fed me to the prowling lions without once looking back.*

*We will all go up to Sydney to see her settled in her university hall residence, to see her take her place among the gods. My father will wear a formal hat and tie; my mother her only string of pearls. My father will appear strangely discomfited, ill at ease, even more blustery and jocular than usual. I guess this is because he is intimidated by the idea of all those hard thoughts being thought, by clever men and women tidying up loose arguments all around him. Will some brainbox look upon him and be able to tell that he is only a wanting head filled with idle facts, random thoughts? Will someone guess that Percy Morley's head contains a pile of disjointed facts: the line of ascension of British kings and queens; the causes of the Russian Revolution; the name of the small New South Wales town on the most easterly point of Australia? A fact is safe, a solitary true thing; extrapolation and reasoning are dangerously murky. Percy Morley, careful now!*

*Goodbye, Hebe. Goodbye my loved and hated elder sister who I have long believed to be better loved than myself. Goodbye to you and your winning ways, to the stories my mother tells about you being their ray of joy, a parcel of sunshine delivered to their undeserving door. How you make Mum laugh, how you cause Dad's chest to swell. What a silent sad sack of a child I am, compared to you.*

*Goodbye Hebe, holder of my secrets, fellow giggler, kind girl who pretended to bump into Mrs Hunter's Living Mistake in the newspaper office while carrying a hot mug of tea. I will love you forever, Hebe Mary Morley, sister and friend, first and most terrible foe.*

*My father will begin to talk to me by mistake one morning when the news comes over the radio that Italy has entered the war. 'Mussolini's a clown,' my father will say, and since no one else is in the room, this remark must be meant for me.*

*'I don't know much about him,' I will reply, careful not to look directly at my father. I will concentrate on buttering my toast.*

*'A bloody dangerous clown too,' he says by way of clarification.*

*It strikes me that this must be a very terrible thing to be: a clown, a fool, a person not entirely in charge of themselves or their emotions. Stupidity armed with a gun.*

*While I continue to eat my toast, my father goes on in this* vein: the long and noble history of the Italian left, Garibaldi et al, the valiant struggles of the Italian people. He is still talking when my mother comes into the room; she stops, looks at me and then at my father. Being well trained in Morley domestic politics she makes no comment but simply continues on her uneventful way to the sink.

My name is Cressida Morley and when I am seventeen I will fail to win the school English prize because I am not as clever as my sister Hebe. 'Cress, there will always be people cleverer than you and others who arc not as smart,' my mother will say, 'that's life.'

But where is the place I can polish myself, learn to carve myself into marble perfection from the dumb block of stone that I am? Where are my tools? I am seventeen years old and my life is something large and unbroken that must be hewn into a finer, more artful shape. I am the block that holds the waiting story.

I am Cressida Morley, the teeming stone which must learn to be both stone and tool. I am the unbroken girl who does not wish to make even the smallest of anticipatory mistakes.

And so it is that I finally come to leave home, to find a flat, to begin my real life. The war is on, the Japs are coming, I am certain that waiting out there is a man with my name written on him.

*Sydney, 1942*

*Saturday*

The Japanese have taken Singapore (an *entire* division of men has been lost—I can't bear to think of all the bereaved sisters and mothers and brothers and fathers newly left . . . ). Now Darwin's been bombed—and suddenly I feel very frightened. At night I lie in bed listening for Jap planes, worrying about Atpay and Ken and everyone else I know who is standing in their skin out there in the open.

I rang Mum when I heard about Darwin and I could hear Dad ranting in the background. 'What's he saying?' I asked but she covered the mouthpiece at her end. I could hear her muffled voice saying, 'Arthur! I can't hear!' (Actually, she does the same thing when he's on the phone—both of them talk loudly at the same time.) I heard a scuffle and then my father's voice boomed out, 'Listen, Sleepy, don't believe a word of it. It's all bloody government propaganda.'

'What,' I said, 'you mean Darwin hasn't been bombed?'

'Of course Darwin's been bloody bombed! Blimey bloody Charlie, Sleeps, don't be so literal-minded!'

I didn't say anything more because I could tell I was going to get an earful. He went on about government propaganda, the effect of war on the economy, the sheer impossibility of the survival of rational thought. 'The federal government's already assumed control of all the state budgets. Wars inevitably provide perfect conditions for capitalist governments.' I was only half listening: I knew that if I spoke it would only inflame him further. The drama of war suits him—he can froth and steam all he likes because everyone else is doing it too. The innocent people of Kurrajong Bay should be grateful that Arthur Elgin is not the editor. Imagine the editorials if he was in control! He's much safer where he is—chief sub of all he surveys, umpire of words. It suits him—spotting other people's mistakes and their incorrect use of the English language— allowing him to gloat about his own superior mind. As he went on and on about war and governments (he was saying something about Neville Chamberlain) I recalled how he used to test Rosalind and me about our general knowledge, just to prove how much cleverer he was than us. 'Girls!' he would start, 'name one British prime minister during the Napoleonic Wars. Rosalind? Katherine? Come on, girls, I can't believe you don't know.' And then we would have to listen while he reeled off not one, but two, three, four names of prime ministers serving during the war which lasted blah blah years. 'You should at least remember William Pitt the Younger.' It wasn't till a couple of years ago that it occurred to me that maybe my bragging father was lacking in confidence. I only worked this out because I lack confidence myself.

Anyway, there's Dad going on and on, leaving me no room whatsoever to voice my own terrors and fears. How would I know how to speak them? There's no space, no sufficient air, everything is already used up. Then the operator asked if I wished to extend the call. 'No thank you,' I said quickly, and hung up.

Wouldn't it be great if someone invented a machine where you could turn your parents off at will like that? I don't mean kill them or anything, but maybe a machine that allowed you to alter the frequency or the wavelength of the communication, perhaps something which let you fiddle with the dial until the quality of transmission improved. Something you could turn off when you wanted.

I always think one day the air between us will be perfectly clear. I always imagine on this day I will have a full, calm heart; the air will be free of debris, pure as an infant's first breath. On this day I will be able to speak everything that is in my heart and my father will have the grace to hear.


*Thursday*

Ken is back. He's got permission from the Department of Information to depict activities in munition and aircraft factories, which means he'll be spending a lot of time in Sydney. 'Depicting activities' means he'll be going into the factories, doing drawings and paintings of what goes on—he's not an official war artist yet, but he's getting there. Oh, I'm sure he can only go on to bigger and better things—he's so very talented.

*Friday*

Well, *we* are certainly going on to bigger and better things!! Last night I lost my virginity!!! It didn't hurt at all and there was hardly any blood. Ken bought *three* French letters and we used them all. Oh, the world turned slippery and soft, we were a dreaming huddle on the bed—now and then I raised my head for air and then I dove deep again, into the long sweet suck of him, the wet red slip of his inner lip, the tender open swell of his mouth. I know now what my body is for—I have used it all, every fibre and pore of it, every muscle. We drank champagne in bed and he pretended to launch me, like a ship. *Thwack* went the bottle, a playful knock against my scalp. 'God bless all who sail in her,' Ken said and we laughed.

I am launched.

I have sailed—I am away.

*Sunday*

Just when you think life can't get any better, it suddenly gets worse. Last night Ken and I met up with his friends at this pub in King Street—I recognised most of the faces from the last time (I couldn't see Val) but the first person who came up to me was Bitter John. God he's horrible that man, really nasty, and I will never talk to him again as long as I live.

Ken disappeared and Bitter John sidled up to me straight-away. As soon as he opened his mouth he started to make fun of me. 'Here she is! The flower of Ken's bosom!'

I was feeling really confident before we went in, someone with a life of her own. I had a new pair of shoes which I thought looked flattering; I was wearing a very smart suit.

'Bitter John,' I said, 'haven't you joined up yet?'

He smiled vaguely. 'My dear, the army would not have me on a platter.'

'Why not?'

He looked at me with disdain. 'Don't you find your ingénue pose a tad tedious?'

'My what?' I tried to keep smiling.

'Your adoption of the guise of wonder. Your girlish air of joy at the wonder of being alive.'

I kept smiling. 'But I am glad to be alive.'

He blew a ring of smoke into the air. 'And so full of charm and innocence.'

Anger surged in my blood. 'At least I believe in something,' I said with the sweetest smile I could find. My heart was pumping so furiously I thought Bitter John might see the movement of cloth at my chest.

'Oh, yes?' he said. 'And what do you believe in?'

He wanted me to explain everything I believed in! He wanted me to explain myself to him. I was furious, speechless; I was beside myself with rage.

He smiled down at me. 'Do you want to know what your guise of girlish innocence really means? It says, "Oh, don't hurt me, I am a good girl, I am so very nice!" It says, "Oh, I am defenceless, without weapons, please treat me kindly!" Meanwhile, your true black heart beats on, continuing to be as vicious as it likes. You're a fake, darling, a beautiful fake.'

Tears leaped to my eyes. 'Uh, oh,' said Bitter John, 'not the waterworks. Not the weapon of choice of every manipulative young woman.'

I rushed past him, into the street. Ken didn't know I had gone till later. When he found out, he left straightaway to look for me and eventually made his way back here to the flat. I wouldn't tell him what was wrong—he only knew it had something to do with Bitter John. 'He's a bastard, Kath,' he said, stroking my hair. 'I wouldn't waste a single emotion on him, beautiful.'

Long after we had gone to bed I lay there in the dark, thinking. I know that some part of what Bitter John said is right—the part about not being able to let the blackest parts of myself show. It's true that I cannot tell people when I am angry about something; it's true that I rail against unfairness and bad behaviour and meanness only in the privacy of my heart.

But how can I begin to learn to taste angry words on my tongue? The only way I know of transmitting anger and pain is through the vehicle of words—but *written words*. I cannot speak them—I am going to have to write a letter to the world. Bugger you, Bitter John.

You are not right about my whole identity being fake. *I am alive. I am here. I am grateful to be breathing, alive upon the earth at ten o'clock in the morning on Sunday, February 22, 1942. I am here. I am.*

*Letter to the world (Poem for Bitter John)*

*Here is the dark*
*syllable of rage,*
*the fearless muck*
*of my heart.*

*Here is the putrid*
*waste, the blood,*
*the slime:*
*every worst wish.*

*Here is the good girl skin*
*the clean hair*
*the virgin eye*
*the whitest fingernail*

*Keep them:*
*the dark, the light*
*the blessed and the cursed,*
*humanity's sad address, freshly posted.*

*London, 1953*

*Tuesday*

David came home last night with this: colleague on Fleet Street laughing hugely at the very idea of a 'cosmopolitan Australian'. 'An oxymoron if ever there was one, eh, cobber?'

Last week he happened to be visiting someone at the *Times* when one of the subeditors asked if anyone could help translate some Latin. When David was the only one in the entire newsroom who could do it, the rescued sub was open-mouthed. 'How astonishing! I had no idea they even *had* Latin in the colonies!' (It was *indignatio ubi saeva ulterius cor lacerare nequit—where fierce indignation can tear his heart no longer*—which I thought was wonderfully apt. The words form part of Swift's epitaph, which no one knew except David.)

How *dare* they patronise him—one of the finest writers they will ever chance their mediocre eyes upon. This is all so tedious and predictable—the British notion of an Australian,

I mean—but fascinating too. Find the English very, very interesting.

*Later*

Stiff little party for the children, some confusion on my part whether an invitation to 'bring the children for tea' meant afternoon tea (as in a cream tea) or dinner for them and drinks for the adults—what??? Turned up yesterday at a posh house near the school with a bunch of flowers and a bottle of good French wine, just in case. The hostess met me at the door and said, 'What an extraordinary girl. Turning up with a bottle secreted in your coat!' All the other beautifully coifed young mothers laughed kindly. ('Tea' means dinner for the children only, usually cooked by Nanny and eaten in the nursery; a cup of tea for waiting mothers is rare; apparently mothers usually drop the children off and disappear.)

Am interested in why it never occurs to the English that perhaps *their* way of doing things is the odd way to a non-English person, that other people in the world may have other ways and means. Find it all fascinating—this race superiority, this dumb arrogance of the blood; they are truly appalling to Americans—always going on about them having no sense of humour, no sense of irony.

'One finds the American sensibility so different to our own,' said the same mother at the nursery tea where I made the faux pas of bringing the wine. She was speaking (condescending?)

to the new American mother at the school who looked interesting to me—perky, slightly unconventional in a way I could not quite put my finger on.

'Yes, we have a more sophisticated sense of irony,' the American girl responded, smiling, and I immediately sat up and paid attention. She was wearing those new khaki Capri pants with sandals. Her hair was short and unschooled (everybody else, including me, sported a French chignon—mine held together with a hideous old doughnut ring the girls had been playing with—I found it by chance under the bed, covered with dust). 'I mean our sense of irony is more playful than yours,' the American girl continued. I was quite speechless with admiration: I looked over with fascinated horror at her effect on the gleaming English mother.

The hostess, Charlotte, was raising her overplucked eyebrows. 'Really?' she said, which meant, *You couldn't be more wrong.* 'And how did you reach that conclusion?'

The American girl, Rosanna, continued to smile.

'People so misuse the word "irony",' she said. 'You know, "Ironically killed on her wedding day".'

'Yes,' I said, 'when they mean "coincidentally" or "tragically" or "bizarrely". Or even, "luckily".'

'Obviously its use in the Socratic sense has been lost entirely,' Rosanna added and the hostess Charlotte exchanged an ominous glance with another mother.

'Ironically,' I said and Rosanna looked at me and laughed.

We are friends after this—the American academic and the

mad Australian mother who goes around with bottles of wine secreted about her person. In fact we fell straight into that particular shorthand intimacy which comes when two people meet and recognise they will be friends for life.

Rosanna is from New York and has been in Lionel Trilling's course in the Romantic poets at Columbia. She briefly wanted to be a poet herself but quickly decided she was not good enough; she was not heartbroken by this discovery, which only confirms to me that she made the correct decision. Her husband, Claudio, is a photographer, an Italian-American, quite famous, who is older than her and who established his name with an extraordinary series of photographs of the first prisoners released from camps in Germany. Rosanna came to England for postgraduate work in Middle English, having recently moved to London from Cambridge. They have a precocious son—the same age as Anna—called, rather alarmingly, Cody. (God, I sound like an Englishwoman!) All this came out on the way home (David and I still no car; Rosanna, big American-looking thing—Chevrolet?)

'You may call me Dr Weiss,' she said to the girls in the car. She was a terrible driver, made worse by the fact that she was trying to roll a cigarette at the same time.

'Where's your stethoscope?' Anna asked her, having recently learned the word.

'Here, give it to me,' I said, grabbing the cigarette papers from Rosanna's fingers and the pouch of tobacco from her lap.

I rolled the cigarette (badly), lit it with the lighter on the dashboard and handed it to her.

'What's a steth . . . stet . . .' asked Lil.

'Stethoscope,' said Anna. 'You can't say it. You're a baby!'

'I am not a baby!' wailed Lil. 'Mummy, Anna called me a baby!'

'Baby! Baby! You are a baby! Elizabeth is a baby! Poo-ey baby! Poo-head baby!'

At that moment a dog ran in front of the car, Rosanna swerved to miss it, and Lil hit Anna across the head. Anna began to howl and then Cody began to howl and then Rosanna stopped the car and put her head in her hands, at which point the cigarette caught a strand of her fringe. The car was filled with crying and the stench of singed hair.

'Ironically, the mothers could not remember what it was they were talking about,' Rosanna said.


*Tuesday*

In a blue funk last night because David came home very late, reeking of cigarettes and drink, having spent long hours with friends at El Vino.

Can it really be true that none of his women colleagues are admitted to the inner bar there?

What happens at this inner bar? Does it contain heady air we are not supposed to breathe?

O, to be lungful of smoke and soot, of all the world's best pollution.

Foolishly, recklessly, full of hope, took notebook with me to the park today. Thought I might be able to sit down on a bench and dash off a few ideas. Notes? Thoughts? Words for possible later use? Beware of poetry and springtime, beware of trying to record the glory of dappled things.

Wrote:

*Broken.*

*Feast.*

*Bee.*

But here is Anna. Here is Anna, rushing up and knocking my arm, so that my pen skids across the page.

'What, Mummy? What are you writing? Write down Cynthia's party. Are you writing it?'

She has been invited to Cynthia's party on Monday—can think of nothing else.

Poem: *Cynthia's Party.*


I am the bloody Pied Piper to my children, who are instructed by their instincts to follow me everywhere. They follow me to the bedroom, to the bathroom—yesterday even to the toilet, where I sat, captured like an Indian, my journal shamefully open on my knees. 'She's in the loo!' Lil cried triumphantly, pushing open the door—my best thoughts scattered, my skirts hoisted. Rounded up, corralled, cornered like an Indian by the cowgirls of instinct.

For too long I have been a thief in my own life, stealing out of bed before dawn, notebook in hand, slipping into a moment's cold freedom. In the chilly dawn I sit in silence, the children sleeping, the day not yet cracked, every pore open. If I sit very still I can hear the clock of the universe, the motion of eternity. In the blue time, the eye time, I claim a single fat tick of time for myself.

## Monday

David and I are wondering if he shouldn't leave his job; he thinks we should write a book together, for quick money. 'A biography would be perfect. Something that would give us a nice big advance, enough to get us started somewhere else. France maybe, or Spain.' It's a huge gamble—we have a lot to give up—staff flat, regular income, pension scheme, security— basically, everything safe. But neither of us wants safety, neither of us will make the proper mulch for pension funds.

I know there are people in Sydney who would kill for the London posting but what David wants most is to write fiction. But if he does give up his job we won't be able to stay in London—it's too expensive to live decently on little money, particularly if you have children. If we didn't have children we could live in a cheap room in Soho and pretend it was romantic, or a thatched cottage with a leaking roof in a village in Dorset. But having the girls means sticking to the daylight world, marking breakfast time and lunchtime and tea. Having the girls means thinking about schools and houses and responsible citizenship; it is the job of children to keep their parents on the straight and narrow.

Earlier tonight we had a fight about it—David wants to leave the job pretty much straightaway, then stay on in London while we write this proposed bad book together for some incredibly huge amount of money. The conversation got snagged on whether writing a bad book (even if it did make us rich) might not cause irreparable damage—basically my argument was that writing is so hard anyway, a form of locked combat, and I have been trying with all my will for years to learn how to write well—and failing, failing—surely it is too big a risk to start writing fast, and badly???

David said, 'A bad book can teach you what a good book is. It might prove a valuable lesson. Better to have a bad book to study in prison, for example, than no book at all.'

Myself—rather no book.

Myself—helpless perfectionist.

'You'll never write anything if you expect perfection,' he said. 'Better to have something on the page than nothing at all.'

I lost my temper: David has always written with effortless grace, words flow from him uninterrupted; I have always had to hunt down every word as if armed with a knife. 'That's all right for you to say! I can't hold an uninterrupted conversation, let alone finish a book.'

'Nothing stops a true artist,' he said, 'not war, not poverty, not the state.' The true artist will let his wife starve, his children go barefoot, his mother drudge for his living at seventy, sooner than work at anything other than his art." George Bernard Shaw.'

I glared at him. 'What if the artist happens to be the mother?'

He smiled. 'Darling, wet nurses are thick on the ground if you only care to look.'

I left the room.

Now I'm sitting here, nursing my anger (ha!), wishing David to hell. I heard him go out, to that grotty pub on the corner probably, and I hope he never comes back.

I've tried so hard to write the best I can. I've tried so hard these last few years to write anything at all. I can't try any harder or I'll die from the effort.

Goodnight.


*Tuesday*

Just looked at what I wrote last night—how deluded and irrational and insane. Christ, Katherine, what makes you think you have to take more desperate measures than David in order to get the work done? Surely writing is hard for everyone, why must you make special pleadings for yourself? Just do it, for God's sake. Write!


*Later*

Awful afternoon with the girls. All day I've been feeling dreadful about the fight with David. Tried ringing him at various times today—secretaries kept telling me he was out, meeting contacts—surely he wouldn't be sitting there, getting them to lie? Anyway, tried again when I got back with the girls—dumped them outside practically as soon as we walked in the front door, telling them to play in the communal gardens. Couldn't get through to him yet again—away from his desk—tried twice, three times, four. Eventually gave up—made the girls eggs and soldiers, bathed them, read three stories, exhibiting that fatal enforced female patience that marks the fall of my days. Was dying to get back to this story I've been trying to write, dying to tell David that I loved him: he is still the most interesting man I have ever met, I still feel I will never reach the end of him. I was desperate to talk to him, to have uninterrupted time in which to think.

In the bath Anna whined and whined about finishing her 'book'. 'Can't I do a tiny, tiny bit after this, Mummy, *please?*' Kept whining until I gave up and let her sit for half an hour at the kitchen table writing her book like Mummy—then Lil wanted to write a book too and they quickly began fighting over pencils. I shouted, they cried. At school the girls are learning about the jobs people do—a policeman, a doctor, a nurse—Anna's book featured a nurse from a country called Honeyland. On the stairs on the way to bed Lil suggested other jobs people might do—'a stringer' and 'a God-maker' being the most original—to which Anna laughed cruelly and Lil cried. They began to pull each other's hair, I gave each of them a hard frustrated slap, slammed the door and left them howling monstrously in their room. Oh, God, to be rid of them for a night, a day, a month. They are at that stage where both of them talk incessantly—the pitch of their voices grates on my ears, my nerves, my dreams. SHUT UP!! I scream in my head while clamping down furiously on my bad-mother teeth. The violence in my hands, my heart; too much the writer, too little the mother—no triumph in either.

And of course David does not come home, and the love that I felt for him this afternoon is slowly curdling. A few hours ago I wanted nothing less than to tell him I loved him and now I am furious with him again. It's ten o'clock and no word from him: David is on the loose again, on the spin, filling his lungs. Where is he, where is he, the wallpapered walls ask, where is he, where is my gun? So here I sit, having taken up the bottle, having drunk the lot, having looked at my sorry little story by the light of alcohol's sweet swoon. It is bad, of course, bad as can be, it has not captured even the smallest of truths. Is it worth it, I ask again: the breaking, the clawing, the grasp?

Is art worth it? No, the story says. No and no and no. The story, the room, the bank, the world—everyone and everything screams no.

But David says yes, David says yes, when he is in the same room, when he is standing here, between me and the merci-lessness of no.

Where is he?

Where the hell is he?

*Sydney, 1969*

David keeps asking me to read his manuscript. I keep refusing.

I am relinquishing my role as his personal audience. I am going to fold my hands tightly in my lap and refuse to clap.

I have passed up his offer to read it at first draft, in second draft; now the galleys are on their way.

Publication date: December 1.

*Monday*

Lil has a publisher interested in her poems. Why can't I feel happiness?

*The Island, Greece, 1962*

MONEY IN HAND
£220 (Account: *Ethniki Trapeza*)
£80 (Account: National Westminster Bank, London)

MONEY COMING
£250 (Payment for two pieces, *Harper's* and *Queen*; self)
£50 (Sale of furniture to Ellen)
?? (How much for David's new book?)

How arrogantly optimistic of us (me in particular) to think we could make a living here. Is optimism a disguised form of arrogance, some misguided notion that catastrophe befalls other people but never oneself?

David is making a kind of mercy dash back to London—going to look for a job, and taking casual subbing shifts while he is there in order to send us money. Rosanna and Claudio sent us a large cheque which gave David the fare to go and enough to live on while he is there—the cheque arrived completely unsolicited, entirely out of the blue. *Listen, guys, we don't want thanks, we don't want you to send it back, we don't want you to do anything except take the money and never mention it again.* Dear Rosanna. I took the ferry to the next island the following afternoon intending to bank it (all of us are sick to death of the sight of bread and lentils—the girls and I had fun planning the meal we would eat at Pan's, the new clothes we would buy—everything we own is so threadbare and faded). David and I usually take it in turns to go and withdraw our remaining cash from the little branch of *Ethniki Trapeza* (there is no bank here) and as it happened it was my turn. In truth it is always a treat for me—a night alone in a freezing bare room above the baker's shop. But when I got to the bank, a large cheque in US dollars from a New York bank proved too overwhelming. The manager was brought out, everyone in the bank came to look at this mysterious object; eventually it was decided that it must be taken to the head office in Athens to be formally presented like some rare gift from a foreign king. So—back to my little room above the baker's, no ferry back until the next morning—and a night alone.

I had dinner in the nameless taverna where I usually eat. '*Kalispera, Kyria Katerina. Ti kanis?*' It is hard to eat alone in Greece and after I had inquired into the health of Aphrodite's mother, the welfare of the children, how the Christmas celebrations were progressing, I was eventually left alone.

As I sat there—ouzo, *mezethes*, more ouzo—I started to weep. No heaving sobs, just lone slippery tears—of thankfulness, mainly. Rosanna, bless you—thank you for saving us, for giving us another chance. I thanked Rosanna and Claudio again and again but I also sat there drinking too much and going over in my mind just exactly how we had arrived at such an inglorious, broken point. We sacrificed everything trying to make a living from our books—have we sacrificed our children too? I can sincerely put my hand across my heart and say I was convinced I was delivering them a better life—a life rare and free, shot through with wonder. I thought I was giving them something richer and more beautiful than the life they would have had in London—grey and conformist, moving from leaden point to leaden point, from exam to exam, as if parts on some production line. Here they stepped into real freedom, here Anna learned the gifts of the sea, the shape of the earth, Lil has known the full force of her limbs, the breadth and width of the stars.

But we are so poor! Rich in all else but poor in cash—our stories, our words, all our books have brought us nothing. What pride can there be in needing to rely on the kindness of friends for the bread in our mouths? I know that some part of David is deeply ashamed, humiliated that he had to take Rosanna and Claudio's money—I know he feels that he has failed us. But haven't I failed too? Haven't I failed to write the book which from beginning to end tells the story of meaning to someone? What of those books of David's and mine which have languished, failed even to earn back the modest advances given to us by publishers? Where is the judge to decide if it is worth going on, whether our poverty is the world's way of telling us that what we are offering is not what the world wants, that market value, what the market will pay, is the only real value.

And what is the right moral response to Rosanna and Claudio sending us this cheque, enabling us to go on. Why should they, or indeed the world, owe us anything? We are the ones who chose this life for ourselves, no one else was responsible; we are the ones who took the risk and jumped overboard into the sea. The sharks are eating you? Should have stayed on the boat with all the rest, should have kept the girls on that grey boat, with food in their mouths, sure in the knowledge that they would reach some grey but certain destination.

I don't know any more. I just don't know.

*Sunday*

David is taking the boat to Athens in the morning. Tonight we got out his one remaining good suit, not worn for years— slightly moth-eaten, certainly unfashionable—but wearable. He intends to stay in London for at least three months. While he is there he's going to look at the possibility of a permanent job, of all of us coming over to join him.

I watched him going through his old dress shirts—he looked awful—bleary, bloated—the planes of his sensitive face showing everything, everything. How broken he looked. The bags under his eyes are swollen and puffy, filled, it seemed to me, with all the tears he will not cry; how I wished to cradle his large, prideful head. After he had packed he asked me to cut his hair—the girls were asleep and he drew up a chair close to the fire in the kitchen. This winter has been bitter—no doubt made more bitter by our winter coats having been turned inside out and restitched by me for the fourth year in a row. Anyway, at least it was warm by the fire and the glow from the oil lamps cast a beautiful soft light.

David's hair is sparse now, completely grey—I was pierced by the terrible intimacy of his exposed head. His naked ears; the private, aging skin on the back of his vulnerable neck: I could hardly bear to look. I love him so much, his natural bodily grace, the instinctive dignity he possesses. As I cut his hair I saw that time was turning him into a man approaching old age; I bent down and kissed the back of his poor defeated neck. What a sad, painful affair, the tangle of love—how hard our griefs, how infinite and various. As I kissed his fading neck I caught the particular scent of his skin, recognising it like an animal would know its mate: a sweet, musty scent that reminds me of some unknown plant I knew long ago. I wanted to say something to him about us being like animals or plants, living things sharing light and air, but when I opened my mouth I could not formulate exactly what it was I wanted to say.

'Thanks for everything, Kate,' he suddenly said, taking the scissors from my hand and kissing my fingers. 'I couldn't have done anything without you.'

I swear there were tears in his eyes.

'You are coming back, aren't you, Davey? You sound like you're saying goodbye.' I haven't called him Davey in years.

He smiled. 'I could never leave you.'

He stood up and we held each other by the fire, both of us struck fearfully wordless.

# Sydney, 1942

## Monday

Ken has been staying—well, not staying exactly, just throwing me on the bed at every opportunity and then falling asleep afterwards like a child. He comes to see me whenever he can fit me in between traipsing back and forth to munitions factories, then heading back to barracks. Since the Jap submarine attack last month we are truly at war—rumour has it that the subs were carrying bombs aimed at the Sydney Harbour Bridge. Just imagine—those massive concrete pylons bombed, falling into the harbour. I remember the first time Ros and I went on a ferry underneath it as children, not long after it opened, how looming and immense it looked. Our necks were bent right back, we glided under its monstrous weight, open-mouthed. The Sydney Harbour Bridge falling down—it would be like the sky falling!

All the time I wonder if those midget submarines are prowling beneath the surface of the ocean, dark and fast as a shark. How do they see down there on the bottom, where everything is cold and fleet?

Ken said this morning that maybe one or two subs might get through but the Japanese couldn't send the entire navy to mount an attack.

'It's too far,' he said, 'and they'd use their whole navy. Don't worry, Kathy, no slanty-eyed bloke is going to climb in the window. Anyway, if one does, the Australian army is personally here to protect you.'

And then he tickled me so hard I thought my stomach would burst from laughing. 'Oh, stop, please!' I pleaded, again and again. He finally relented and kissed me instead—he didn't have a French letter but we decided to risk it. We've been doing that a lot lately, and I have never missed a period—Ken knows how to calculate the right days—I am always on time and there are plenty of 'safe' days. I would do it EVERY day if I could—I love ripping off my clothes and lying length to length, toe to toe. I love sinking into him, the wet pulse at my centre, the curling dance of our tongues. I am transfixed by the sensation of him inside me, the bloom of him slipping sweet and hard. His skin is always so deliciously warm—he seems to have a body temperature at least ten degrees higher than anybody else. Sleeping with him is like sleeping with a furnace—I am forever flinging the bedclothes off, even though it is the middle of winter. He is lit by life, that's my theory anyway—a boy aflame!

I am going to meet his parents this week—I've already met his sister, Gloria, whom I didn't like very much I'm afraid. She's the superior sort, hardly says a word but still manages to convey the impression that she finds you wanting. She is what Atpay would call a 'type' —or what Mum would call a 'little miss'—anyway, the sort who always turns me into a blabbering fool—I rush to fill up the silences instead of staying silent and composed like her. She's very beautiful (looks a lot like Ken) and does some modelling work and a bit of typing and lives at home with her parents. Anyway, we're going to dinner there on June 8—we're going to stay the night since it's hard getting around at night now, and besides, Ken has to be at a factory out that way early the next morning. BUT we won't be sleeping in the same bed, he says—his mother will make up the spare bed in Gloria's room and Ken will stay in his old room. 'Don't worry, sweetheart, the floorboards won't creak when you sneak down the hall,' Ken said. 'How do you know?' I said. He just smiled and tapped the side of his nose.


*June 9* I'VE BEEN BOMBED!!!!!

Writing this down straightaway, before I forget anything! Have just rushed in—it's two o'clock in the afternoon and I've been trying to get home to write this for hours!! I'VE BEEN BOMBED!!!! TRUE!!!!

Here's everything, from scratch. 4.30 pm yesterday afternoon—Ken arrives to take me to his parents before it gets too dark. Quickly make love before we go (hair mussed up, lipstick awry, worry all the way on the bus that his parents will be able to tell straightaway that we have just done it).

Very nervous about meeting them—but you know how within seconds of meeting someone you know whether everything is going to be okay or not—well, within seconds I knew everything was going to be fine. His mother, Betty, has a kind face—she's surprisingly plump and pretty looking—rosy cheeks and dark hair all fluffed out around her head—not what I expected at all. She seemed too young to be Ken's mum, and kind of the wrong shape and look altogether—I was expecting an older version of Ken and his sister Gloria. (They both look like their dad.) Anyway, Ken's mum was practically *flirting* with Ken, her own son, laughing at his jokes and being all coy and girly. I couldn't believe it! She acts like she thinks he's the best thing since sliced bread, but it obviously gets on Gloria's goat—as it would on mine if I was his sister. (I'VE BEEN BOMBED!! I STILL CAN'T BELIEVE IT!!!)

Anyway—God, I have to write all of this down so I remember everything EXACTLY. Well, Ken's dad was a surprise too—sort of weak and wishy-washy, stoop-shouldered—the opposite to his son in every way, who is all big-chested confidence and self-possession. His dad, Ernest, kind of sat there and disappeared into the background, hardly contributing anything to the conversation, just smoking cigarette after cigarette and drinking endless bottles of beer. He looks like Ken and Gloria though, which seems to be about the only thing they have in common—except he is a washed-out version of them, insipid, like a photographic negative of a gloriously coloured photo.

Well, for dinner we had a roasted rabbit with all the trimmings, and beer for all of us, which left me feeling quite tipsy. Talked mostly about Ken's work in the munitions factories and his plans for after the war (he wants to go to Europe to study). 'All my life I've wanted to see Paris,' said Mrs Howard. And Mr Howard made the only funny remark of the night: 'The question is, does bloody Paris want to see you?' I laughed but Mrs Howard looked offended and I lowered my eyes—Ken kicked me under the table. After that Mr Howard didn't say another thing all night!

After dinner we sat around the piano, which Gloria played, and Ken and I and Mrs Howard sang. Ken's got quite a good voice, and I love singing, even though I'm not very good. I love the way it makes you feel like you have just run up a good hill, all that air and energy and rush. I sang my tuneless heart out and even Gloria smiled at me. When she started playing 'Abide With Me' all the others packed it in, but I love hymns too, so we did 'Rock of Ages' and lots of others till Gloria said she'd had enough. It made me quite like her—that, and the fact that I could imagine how she felt having a mother who so clearly preferred her brother to her.

Anyway, the kitchen for a cup of tea before bed, listening to the radio for the latest war news (the boy from the flat next door, who Gloria and Ken grew up with, has just been killed in Singapore), and then bed. Gloria and I went to the bathroom to wash our faces and change into our nightgowns, then I gave Ken a chaste kiss goodnight and he whispered, 'See you later, beautiful.'

No late-night confessions from Gloria just a curt 'Goodnight, Kathy', lights out, and before long some breathing that suggested she was asleep. (Although on those occasions when I've feigned being asleep, for one reason or another I can never work out how to breathe properly, having never had the chance to monitor my own breath when I am asleep!) How long was I supposed to wait? Minutes? Hours? I lay in bed trying to work out if it was safe to creep down to Ken's room, but when Gloria started snoring (politely, femininely) I took my chance.

Now—here comes the BOMB!! What happened was that I crept out of bed as quietly as I could and opened the door—which creaked like a door in a horror movie. Bloody hell, I thought, poised on the threshold, waiting for Mrs Howard to rush up the corridor. When no one came I left the door ajar and made my way along the walls in the dark, praying that I would feel the doorway soon. Ken was right though—the floorboards didn't creak.

Luckily Ken's door didn't creak either as I opened it and he was waiting for me in the dark. He had my nightdress up over my bottom and his hands on the curve of my naked buttocks within moments. I straddled him, my hair brushing his face, the smooth cups of his palms resting gently on each curved globe of flesh. 'A perfect fit,' he said, breathing into my mouth. He slid into me and just at that EXACT MOMENT there was this god-almighty crash and the wall above the bed fell down and this shell came through the wall and skidded right across the floor, right through the wall of his parents' bedroom, right through another two internal walls before coming to rest – unexploded!!!—on the communal stairs. A Japanese shell!! IN ROSE BAY, SYDNEY, AUSTRALIA!!! We didn't know what was happening—for one wild frantic moment I thought my father had come to smash down the door—Ken and I were covered in broken bricks and dust but we were in one piece, not a scratch, standing there in our nightclothes, speechless. I can't remember getting up from the bed, walking to the door— I remember everyone standing in the corridor, me suddenly crying, wondering if I had been smote by God, Ken telling me to shut up, me crying harder because he had never ever spoken cruelly to me before, his mother coming up and clinging on to him, shrieking hysterically, his father limping because his foot had somehow been crushed by falling debris. Gloria was there too and then all the air-raid wardens from the area, trying to work out how to move the shell so it wouldn't explode. And Ken shouting at me, 'It's not a bloody bomb, for God's sake! Everybody calm down, bombs fall through roofs, they don't come through walls!'

But I was terrified another one was coming and I didn't know where to go—did the flats have an air-raid shelter? Where was it? It was after midnight but everyone in the block of flats was up, gibbering, crying, wringing their hands. Then we were all herded off to a shelter somewhere, but I had recovered my wits enough by then to watch the air-raid wardens carrying the unexploded shell out, down the stairs, cradling it tenderly. I wanted to go somewhere, hide in the earth, cover myself with the safest dirt. We were all being told to keep calm, to follow instructions, not to panic. 'A bomb!' people kept repeating and air-raid wardens kept saying, 'There is no bomb! Keep calm!' and the children were crying, along with their mothers, every one of us wishing to live, wishing to evade extinction. By then I was angry with Ken—how was I to know it wasn't a bomb? How am I supposed to know the difference between a bomb and a shell? He was being the Big Leader, explaining to everyone in the shelter that it was probably a shell from the Japanese subs that have been around; we would have to wait to learn whether there was any serious damage. Then of course everyone was convinced that when the sun came up we would find Sydney in ruins, the Bridge gone, the Town Hall smashed. How many submarines were there? How many shells? We passed the hours scaring ourselves out of our wits, but then morning came, and as the hours passed, good news—no one killed, perhaps half-a-dozen shells at the most, only one exploded.

I've only just got back here now, the newspaper confirming all this under my arm, Ken gone off in a huff after I refused to kiss him goodbye.

And of course Mr and Mrs Howard could not have cared whether their favoured son was entertaining twenty prostitutes in his bed! They wouldn't have known which door I came out from in all the chaos, and frankly I don't think they would have cared if I was dead or alive. Mr Howard's gone off to hospital to have his foot dealt with, and right at this moment I don't care whether I see Ken Howard ever again. I just remembered something else he said: 'Stop being a drama queen, Kathy! Hose it down for God's sake, you're hysterical!' All my life people have been telling me to hose it down—you're too dramatic! Too stuck-up! Too pretty, too sensitive! Well, now I know what people mean—I'm too much myself. Ken wants me to be someone else, someone I'm not.

I've been bombed, Ken Howard. That's my story and I'm sticking to it.

## Wednesday

Mum is putting the weights on Ros and me to come home. 'I can't sleep at night for worry,' she said but then Dad got on the phone. 'The bloody Japs couldn't hit a target if you paid them, Kath. You're as safe as houses—your mother doesn't know what she's talking about.' Ros has just been here for dinner and both of us want to stay in Sydney—she's seeing some fellow who's on the same course as her, but the main reason she wants to stay is university. She tried explaining to me St Thomas Aquinas and his arguments for the existence of God, but it struck my head like complicated maths and I soon tuned out. She's always been good at maths, Ros—as well as everything else—and now she has this new sophisticated glow about her, as if she could tell the world a few things. She says she is never going to get married.

She already knows all about Ken but when I told her about the bomb and being in his bed, the first thing she said was: 'I hope you're using reliable contraception, Kath. You do know about diaphragms, don't you? I can give you my doctor's name if you like.'

She has tried to press this once before, when I told her about losing my virginity. There is nothing starry-eyed about my sister—I want to talk about love and roses and all she wants to talk about is sperms meeting eggs.

Speaking of which . . . I think that is Ken at the door. Should I let him in?

# The Broken Book

*Here I am, the girl of teeming stone, leaving school, accepting second prize. Life's runner-up! But will I cry and gnash my teeth? Will I show anyone I care? No, I will smile and wish the winner the best of luck, all the while plotting my mutinous revenge. I will pack my little kerchief of worldly goods, tie it to a jaunty stick, and set off for the city with a wave. Goodbye, Blowhole. Goodbye, Dad. Good riddance.*

*For a while I will work in a spectacle shop and curiously I will come to believe my 20/20 vision eyes are losing their powers. I will need to blink a lot while watching lesser eyes reading diminishing letters, for it is as if a film of unknown origin has descended upon my previously glistening young orbs. Every lunch hour I will try on various spectacles while wondering if I have spent my life trying to get to this blurred new point. Was I meant to grow up and lose my sight in a spectacle shop?*

*I will take my own flat in a seedy area of the city peopled* by artists and poets. I hope that I am a poet too, a carrier of coiled words, a vessel for dreams. Is a poem as real as a pair of glasses? Is a poem as real as a gun?

The war is on! Bombs, guns, planes—no poems, no poems. Instead, lectures from my father Percy Morley via the medium of the telephone, a trip with my mother Dorothy Morley to the best dressmaker in the Blowhole to kit me out for adult life. Four dresses for summer, three skirts for winter, two blouses; a coat, fully lined. Mum will come to look for flats with me, all the while tut-tutting at the lowly forms of life visible around us. 'That girl has no self-respect,' she will say, sotto voce, as a young woman passes us in the street, hatless, gloveless, stockingless, her hair swinging uncurled and free, a cigarette dangling from her unpainted lips. My mother has heard that the Witch of the Cross, Rosyln Norton, lives nearby. 'I don't understand why you are attracted to ruffians, Cressida,' she will say. 'These people have the Devil on their shoulders. Why don't you move somewhere nice?'

Where is the planet Nice, Mum? Where is this place where everyone is well behaved, their emotions neatly tucked in like a freshly ironed shirt in a clean pair of trousers? Where is this place where all the pain and rage and bile of the world do not exist, where no one kills another human being because of his religion or his race? I would like to live there, happy on a cloud, my dimming eyes adjusting to the light.

In the meantime I will decide to leave the spectacle shop because while walking to work I have seen a job advertised at *a cinema. A lot of theatres have closed because of the war, but a few picture houses struggle on. What is it about my beautiful eyes and wilful blindness? Why is it that as I take my place in the world I find myself blinking?*

*But one afternoon a brilliant light will unexpectedly fall. The light will come in the shape of a man, a tall, wide-shouldered man. The man will have a name and the hands of an artist, but he will be revealed as a true artist of the body. He will take my clay and shape it, he will knead me and break me, the first man to enter my body. He will write his name upon my skin; I will hand myself over as if on a plate and fail to notice the crumbs of other women around his mouth. The first man to join himself to me. My body proves itself to be a fast learner, taking to that ancient rhythm without lessons. I learn the art of suck and sigh, the wonder of the penis, the soft knowledge of testicle, lip, tongue. I am being mapped, traced upon the earth, my first man is showing me that I have joined that long line of girls becoming women, of women growing old, eventually becoming of the earth, humanity's mulch. I am joining hands with all historical women, with the future: I am taking my place.*

*Look at me, a member at last. A man has chosen me, the invisible girl, life's runner-up. A wide-shouldered man is telling me I am beautiful, that he is in love with me, that there are safe days of the month. A man who is cleverer than me, more everything than me, has finally chosen me first.*

*I will exist in this new world of bodily swoon for six months, eight months, ten. I will keep blinking but my eyes are always* peeled, my ears are always open. I will learn again that there are women much, much cleverer than me, grown-up women who are friends of the man who has named me. In their company I will blush and stammer, lower my diminished eyes, completely forget what to say. I am practising my first adult form, trying on my shape in the world.

And then the days will come when the day does not come, the day of blood, of hot red rush. I will wait for the blood, I will wait and wait. I will sit at my table, a calendar before me, and count and recount the days. I will try to see through time, the walls of my body; I will try to see the workings of God. But my body is dumb, my body does not flow, as if clogged. Now I am both dumb and blind, not privy to the secret interior life inside my own skin. I will suddenly become conscious of this secret alternative physical reality, this other unseen physical self I cannot reach to speak sense. I will sit in the dark and plead with my body to release its flow and save me. But my body won't answer; it gives back the sensation of dumbness, of something dark and unknown, beyond which I cannot reach. I can't believe my own body is betraying me, making its own secret plans. I am the teeming head here, I am the captain! Do not destroy me, not now just as I am about to step out and take my place, not when my whole life is before me.

I will cry in the arms of the visionary man, who will coo into my beautiful ear and rock me. He will take me out to drink champagne to cheer me up and tell me not to worry too much. 'You don't know you're pregnant for sure,' he will say but I know, O, I know. I am a body occupied, claimed land, my breasts are responding to some genetic message from my body's new captain, some cunning mutineer.

I will forget to do my job properly so that the cinema manager, Mrs Close, will ask me if something is on my mind. 'You've been very distracted, Miss Morley. Everything all right at home?' I am frequently late for work, or late back from lunch because I have been sitting in the park going over and over dates in my head. I can't concentrate on anything but the drama going on underneath my own skin. The days keep coming, more and more of them, taking me further and further away from a miracle.

Then the fateful day will come when I finally find the courage to go to the doctor, a doctor I have never seen before, whose offices I pass every day. He will ask me to take off the skirt my mother recently had made for me when fitting me out for adult life. I will lie upon the high cotton-covered bench where the doctor will put on a pair of rubber gloves and stick his fingers into me while palpitating my uterus. 'You are at least sixteen weeks pregnant, young lady,' he will announce. 'I take it you are not married?'

I am not married, sir, I am not married. I have not even begun my grown-up life. I am a teeming girl who has just left school, a girl who has long supposed herself to be above anticipatory mistakes. I am that girl who intended to do everything, to write poems, to be a witness to Life. I am that girl who wished to rouse the sky.

But right now I find myself crying on the examining bench, crying tears that are coming so fast they are rolling down the side of my face and into my ears. Get away from me, Doctor, let me get up, let me get out of this room into the air. Let me run somewhere safe, somewhere far from this news, let me run so fast it won't catch me. Let me reach the telephone, where I will ring the man of visions, who will tell me he is sorry but he cannot speak right now. Let me sob, let my heart crack, let me bleed, O please let me bleed.

I will turn up unannounced at the door of the man of visions. He is about to go into the army and is staying with friends, in a flat in the suburb next to mine. He will take a long time to answer the door and when he does he appears to be doing up the collar of his shirt. It is late, I know, too late for a young woman to turn up at his door carrying a secret. 'Hush, darling, it'll be all right,' he will say kindly, taking me at once in his visionary arms. But who is that coming out of the room behind him? Why, it is Lorna of course, you remember Lorna, I think you met at the King's Arms? Of course, Lorna, the clever girl of words, his old chum! She will say, 'I was just saying goodbye before he is lost to us—I was just off myself!' Cheerio!

And when she has gone, I will make a scene and the man of visions will assure me I am jumping to conclusions. 'She's just a friend!' he will say and I will leave the house trying to *believe him. I am trying to believe you, Man of Visions, I am trying to believe that Lorna is your friend.*

*But all the while I am walking home (will walking make something come loose?) I am thinking: that girl Lorna had the tag of her blouse sticking up from the neck of her cardigan. That was definitely a girl with her blouse on inside out.*

*I will turn up at the door of my foe, my sister Hebe, too late at night for a young woman to turn up with a secret. 'Oh, God, you poor thing,' she will say but not before she tells me I should have been more careful. Not before she tells me I should have listened to her advice and protected my ovaries and my heart. 'What a goose,' she will croon as I cry. 'Poor little Cress.' She will make me a cup of tea and toast just the way I like it, thickly spread while the toast is still hot. 'I don't know how you can bear to eat it like that,' she will say, 'it'd give me indigestion.' So Hebe waits till her toast is stone cold and then spreads a thin film of butter. 'Now,' she will say, 'what are we going to do with you?'*

*It is far too late to risk a trip to a woman she knows who extracts mutinous strangers. What are we going to do with you, Clever Clogs, teeming as you are with ready life?*

*London, 1953*

## Sunday

Rosanna is having an affair. Not her first either—apparently she and Claudio have this understanding that they both need time apart from each other, and in this time apart both are free to take lovers. Rosanna thinks that deep down Claudio does not quite believe her to be as free as himself. 'Every now and then he goes crazy,' she said. 'Last year I was spending the night with a lover in his rooms at Soho when Claudio came knocking on the door in the middle of the night. I don't believe a man brought up a Catholic with the idea of sainted motherhood can completely evade his past.'

I listened to all this with a feigned air of sophistication, as if it was nothing to me to hear my best friend in London is having an affair. We were sitting in her living room, where Claudio's fabulous new series of photographs of London and Paris were carelessly stacked against the walls, and all the windows were open to the thick wet summer air. It is a beautiful room, gracefully proportioned, with high ceilings and an enormous marble fireplace. Rosanna was slung over a velvet sofa like a discarded garment, all slouch and crumple. She was smoking one of her endless ready-mades; we were drinking martinis, preparing to pick up the children.

'Aren't we the naughtiest mothers in South Ken,' she said, 'drinking, smoking, having affairs. Do you think Mrs Dance will expel us?'

'Probably,' I said, pouring myself another drink from the pitcher at my feet. 'Is this all mine?'

Rosanna didn't answer, she lay back on the couch with her eyes closed. 'William is the finest lover known to man,' she said, 'sorry, woman. He goes on and on for hours—when he finally comes it is unbelievably exciting. And I thought British men were supposed to be duds in the sack.'

I sat there listening, glad she didn't have her eyes open. I wasn't embarrassed, I didn't think she was bad, I just couldn't understand how she could bear another man other than her husband to enter her body. I am an Old Testament woman myself, I am wedded for life, my body belongs to no one but my husband, David John Murray. I am the human swan, mated for good, repelling all others.

Yesterday I watched my husband reading his new short story for a recording at the BBC. He's had two stories accepted now, which has fuelled his desire to give up journalism and launch himself into a novel. As he read, I sat in the control room and watched the sensual curve of his upper lip, the dark command of his open mouth. I claimed his chest for myself, the hair greying at his temples, the collapsed skin over his eyes. I claimed him then, I claimed him afterwards too, in the pub with all the other writers where we went for a drink. I claimed him as he sat among the faint; as he told endless stories and charmed the women. *This one is mine*, my heart said, *this mouth, these lips, this tongue.* He was telling an exaggerated story about a reading he did at Oxford where the other writer he was reading with was blind drunk.

He was miming being drunk, the writer's failed aim for the microphone, his mistaken belief that the first row of the audience contained a urinal. 'Oh, he didn't!' cried a pretty lady poet. 'I don't believe you!' My husband stood up and started opening his fly. 'Stop! Stop!' everyone shrieked. *This raconteur is my husband*, my heart said, *this man of story is mine.* When we left the pub I took his arm and said, 'Don't kiss any other girls, will you.' He bent over and kissed the top of my head. I stopped walking: 'You know that if you do I'll take a knife to your heart.' He laughed as if I was joking.

I could not bear to place my lips against another man's mouth, I could not bear an unknown man's fleshy stalk to touch me. Our children came from that private place where David has been, our children travelled that dark wet route on their way to us. Seven years we have been together now, seven years since another man touched me: never another again.

'Would you ever have an affair, Kate?' Rosanna suddenly asked, opening her eyes.

'I don't think so,' I said. 'I'm still in love with David.'

'That doesn't matter,' she said. 'You can still love your husband and have an affair. Is the sex still good?'

*When we lie together it is as if we share a skin.*

'Pretty good,' I said, my lips involuntarily curling up in an adolescent smirk.

'In my humble opinion a bit of fantastic extramarital sex does wonders for the marriage bed,' she said. 'You should try it. Do you think David has ever had an affair?'

I sat up. 'Never! He wouldn't have an affair in a million years.'

Rosanna slowly rose too. 'Come on, it's time to pick up the kids.' She crossed the room and took my glass.

'I wouldn't be so sure, honey,' she said, 'that's the one thing you can never take for granted.'

I smiled and we went out the door together, the new woman and the old, the woman of the future and the woman from the Old Testament masquerading as a sophisticated modern woman of 1953.

I can't believe David would ever be unfaithful.


*Monday*

Humiliating, cringe-making scenes from my literary career. Oh, God, can't bear to think about last Tuesday; days later it is still causing me to wake in the night, in horror and nauseous remorse.

Last month my first novel with a 'prestigious' London publisher was published. No flashy launch for me, but as a consolation prize I was invited by my publisher to one of its famous parties, where the poet of our century, Mr Thomas Stearns Eliot himself, was going to be present. I was beside myself with nerves—Eliot, the man who single-handedly ushered poetry into the modern world! Apparently he lives like a book himself—composed as a poem, nerveless—I wondered if I would get the chance to speak with him, and if I did, whether I would have the nerve to open my mouth.

At the party everyone stood around in clusters, looking over shoulders for someone more famous, more celebrated. Saw Cecil Day-Lewis, Rosamond Lehmann, Cyril Connolly, and lots of others I didn't recognise but would know their work if I heard their names. Felt myself degenerating by the second into my public, more fluffy self, my smile freezing, every utterance becoming more and more stupid. I'm so much more acute than my social self suggests; no one would ever guess from my trite and meaningless conversation that my intelligence is bright within, appraising, actively working, more unflinching than could ever be expressed in the open air. What is this social self but a false self sent into the world as a form of protection? I wanted to flee.

General atmosphere all round of drunk desperation, fake bonhomie; overheard a well-known editor laughing about there never having been so many hostages to fortune collected in one room at the same time. HOSTAGE TO FORTUNE—the corruption of the writing life—the next book will make my name, the next book will ease the perpetual agonising over money—hence, the envy which builds up for those who have been struck. Cannot remember who said that literary fame is like lightning—never know where it will strike, but once it strikes, you know without doubt you are hit. And then I saw TS Eliot himself, standing in a corner, larger and taller than I had expected, his shy lovely eyes hovering on the face of a woman I did not recognise. I knew at once that even if the chance should arise I could not possibly say a single word to him.

Somehow found myself in an argument with a celebrated male writer over 'women's writing'. (I am too embarrassed even to record his name.) He said while he had the utmost respect for it (immediately hackles went up—why is there no category called 'men's writing'?), he believed that essentially writing was an occult thing for women, and that his tastes in books were exclusively homosexual.

'Surely for women art must always be a thing apart,' he announced. 'Women *are* creation, after all; one might argue that creation for men is a compulsion to better a woman's ability to give birth. I believe men are essentially jealous.' Several people nodded their heads, women included. I listened, dumb-founded.

'Women are life,' said another man, whom I did not know.

'And presumably men are death,' I said, my heart jumping.

Everyone turned to look at me. I willed myself not to blush, but my heart was thrashing.

'I'm not sure that's what I meant,' the man I did not know said, 'but, yes, there is something in that. Men's need for war, to go off and fight. I believe creative energy in men is drawn from the same source—energy and action. A woman's instinct is to withhold, to protect and nurture. Women do not have the same instinct to act, to create, that men have.' He stopped speaking and looked at me. 'My dear girl, I wouldn't lose any sleep over it—anybody who has the audacity to look like you could not possibly be a serious creative artist. You're far too beautiful.'

Several people laughed approvingly and everyone looked at me, waiting for my reply.

I thought: a woman's instinct is to make art, to break herself upon the page until the bloodied page breathes.

'I'm afraid I am an unnatural woman. My instincts are creative not maternal.' I turned and walked quickly away.

I felt like a bloody idiot. I WAS a bloody idiot. I blindly groped my way to the bathroom, trembling, buckled by hot shame. Trying not to cry, I rushed down the empty corridor of the famous London publishing house. Women writers! Everywhere: rushing, mad women writers, bawling into their handkerchiefs.

And now comes the *pièce de résistance*: I soon learned that the man I had walked away from was the most famous literary critic in England, the man whose word could make or break a book. David laughed himself stupid but, personally, I never wanted to leave the house again.

Then, last Tuesday night, after swearing I would never go to another of those nerve-racking parties, we went to another nerve-racking party. (I've been stuck at home with the girls for months—then two parties in quick succession at which I disgrace myself!) The first person I saw as I entered the room was the esteemed critic leaving by another door—we were in a private room upstairs at the Ivy, and he hadn't seen me come in. My poor book had won exactly one review since publication—squeezed in with four other books in a job lot of 'first novels', reviewed by another first-time novelist—and when I saw the most famous literary critic in the whole of England walking out the door, something went off inside me, a personal cataclysm, an interior earthquake, a private explosion—anyway, something happened, and I started to RUN towards him—RUN!!—as if I had a tail on fire. I ran towards him, out the room and down the stairs, panting horribly, aware of my own humiliation as I ran, not thinking of anything else really but my own shamelessness, and of course I was making so much racket on the stairs (I was wearing heels), he reeled around in what I can only describe as terror. The mad beauty descending on him! The woman writer without a maternal bone in her body! I was smiling idiotically, goofily, as I came towards him, realising I had no idea of what I was going to say.

'Hello, there!' I called out in my most jolly voice. 'On your way out?'

But it was myself who was on the way out, of course, myself who was digging her own grave in broad daylight, by the light of the silvery moon. I was going down swinging, the woman writer whose children were asleep at home without her, the woman writer who believed herself capable of war.

'Ah, yes,' he said, shaking my proffered hand, 'the authoress with unnatural instincts.'

I laughed weakly, stupidly, showing all my teeth: a perfect picture of simpering femininity. 'Katherine Elgin,' I said, 'pleased to meet you.'

He was already looking at his watch. 'I'm afraid . . .'

'Oh, please don't let me stop you. Which direction are you headed in?'

I was going to pretend to be going his way. I was going to pretend to be the nicest possible woman in the whole world in the hope of a splendid review—did you know that I would walk on nails to reach a reader's eye? That a book only becomes a book when it meets a receptive eye?

Just at that humiliating moment my husband appeared at the top of the stairs. 'Kate?'

The waylaid critic of international repute was already speeding on his way, nodding his goodbyes as I turned towards my husband on the stairs.

David supposed me to be making some secret assignation—he did not catch the famous critic's face—he supposed me to be caught in the act of making plans for a future rendezvous with another man!

All the interminable way home in the taxi he went on and on about my flirtatious ways, about how I continued to flaunt myself about in the most humiliating fashion.

'I don't understand why you need to do it,' he said. 'You're beautiful! You could have any man you wanted! You don't need to prove it again and again!'

What does beauty have to do with anything? Beauty is for girls and men: it is nothing to a woman who wishes to make art. Beauty matters only to women who have nothing else but beauty: then it is a terrible, perishable thing, a flame already going down.

I told him I did not want a lover, I already had the only lover I needed. We stayed up for hours, talking and drinking, finally collapsing into bed. When he came he cried out as if in pain. 'That was wonderful,' he said and immediately fell asleep.

## Thursday, Reading Room, British Museum

Mrs Dapp is picking up the girls from school—thankfully don't have to rush back. Got an idea for a novel which has been niggling me—but how to write a novel about the relationship between Australians and sport? How to approach it? (How I love this room, the glory of its domed glass roof, its benches, its little green-shaded reading lights—the fact that centuries of other greater writerly hands and eyes have sat here before me—what an honour, what a privilege, that my own paltry hands can join them. Am rereading Gissing's *New Grub*

*Street* in bed at night and falling in love with it all over again—so much of it takes place in this very room where that poor woman of ink-stained fingers, Marian Yule, toils anonymously for her father, where she gets headaches from reading too many books. So many books! So much compressed human effort! In this room one might suppose for a moment that the effort is worth it, that books are not an isolated consumer preference or an idle way of passing the time, but a real and actual way of participating in the world—a vivid, living, breathing means of communication.)

Anyway, must go and check to see whether my communicating books have arrived—is there a single book in the world this marvellous place does NOT possess? I've ordered mountains of stuff about sport, Australians and football. The Great Australian Football Novel???? Now there's an idea!!

NOTES

*AUSTRALIA: Official handbook issued by the Australian National Publicity Association, June, 1941.*

*Social Conditions*

'*As a nation the Australian people are wholehearted in their fondness for outdoor sport and recreation. In this they reveal a characteristic of their Anglo-Saxon forebears, since the British have always been noted for their enthusiasm for competitive games.*'

What about the upcoming Melbourne Olympic Games? Pat writes in a letter this morning that the place is already going crazy, with lots of articles in the paper about the games being Melbourne's big test to see if it can take its place with pride as one of the great cities of the world. She's working for a new theatre company (she says the Melbourne theatre scene's much better than Sydney's) but she swears she's leaving town when the Games are on. *I've bloody had enough of it already, Athykay. Is the Queen going to come? Will the Olympic Village be open in time? Can we show our international guests that we are a swell, sophisticated people? Who the hell cares? Christ, it's enough to make me get on the first ship to London!*

Hmmm, maybe I should go back and watch it all for myself. Maybe David and the girls and I should move to Melbourne instead of dreaming of Greece??? But how could I get a novel out of a hundred or so athletes converging on a city for several days and then going home again? Plot? Details?????


*After lunch*

Getting tired, headachy, just like inky Marian.

Is writing a branch of memory? If I could remember everything, could I write like Proust? (Ha!) Writing is an attempt to capture temporality. Sense of felt life.

Is it true, as Rosanna suggests, that living in the world of books can sometimes deaden you to the cries in the street?

More particularly, can it deaden you to the cries in the room?

## Friday

How little we know of what will befall us.

How lucky to live without knowing.

How unlucky of me to choose to walk from the library down through Covent Garden to the Strand and then on to Fleet Street because it was the most glorious day and I thought I would surprise David instead of going straight home. How unlucky to catch sight of my husband walking a little way ahead of me down Fleet Street, his arm around the waist of Evelyn, the prettiest secretary in the office, to see them stop and engage in a kiss so fervent that David's hat fell off when Evelyn took his head in both hands. His secretary, for God's sake! That fact alone is almost as humiliating as the fact that the lips which pressed themselves so long upon my own came down upon another woman's mouth.

How cruel to see a lying word alive on my husband's tongue.

*Story*

(LONDON, 1952–53; WRITTEN BY KATHERINE ELGIN'S
ELDEST DAUGHTER, ANNA B. 1947)

Miss Caroline from Honeytown
By Anna Murray if you want to buy this book you have to put
a cross on it

Once upon a time miss caroline woke up in honeytown and
when she walked down the street her shoos got stuck in the
honey and then she cood hardly walk and there was honey trees
and honey houses and honey money and miss caroline's Mummy
was cross with miss caroline and she shouted at her get your
shoos out of there now and miss caroline cryed and cryed and
she cood not get her shoos out of the honey

The End

By Anna Murray

# The Island, Greece, 1963

A famous lady English novelist has appeared in our slovenly
midst. Antonia Godwin is the celebrated recipient of some
bountiful prize for a first novel, which sold trillions of copies
and is now being made into a sumptuous film. She is among
us like royalty among commoners; apparently the fame of our
little artistic community has spread and the word is out in
London that our humble island is the perfect place to come to
finish a book or a play with absolutely no distractions. No cars.
Only the soft music of donkeys' feet. What rustic charm!

She arrived at our table last week, on Friday, with a little
entourage of hangers-on. 'What bliss it must be to live here
day in and day out,' she announced in an actressy toff's voice.
(Let her come naked in winter, when the sea is like an oil slick
and every taverna along the waterfront is closed, forcing us to
huddle in the back of shops among the sacks of lentils and
scavenging cats with pus-filled eyes.)

David was being his most winning, affable self, drinking glass after glass, disarming her by asking after a well-known poet whom they both knew. 'Oh, we must know many people in common!' she said, obviously surprised that such scruffy would-be artists as ourselves had once mixed in such exalted circles. 'You write too?' she asked David, assuming, I suppose, that I must therefore be the writer's wife. She is tall, haughtily beautiful with an aquiline nose, long legs, large breasts. I was looking closely at her Italian sandals, the cut of her dress, the careful way she had swept up her hair. She is here to write her 'Greek novel'.

David was soon entertaining the whole table—the distinguished lady writer; her entourage; the French pianist and composer, Stephanie, who has been living here almost as long as us; and all the other expatriates with whom we share this island. The painter from Seattle (very good, have no doubt that he will one day make his name). The painter from Sydney (very bad). The folk singer and poet from Canada via New York, Jerry Rothschild, whom everyone believes to be 'the real thing'. And me, of course, the one who always meant to write the best book I could.

David was telling war stories (the lady novelist and David were both in America for the same part of the war) and then the conversation turned, as it always does, to life and art. David was being his best, most eloquent self; his drunkenness had not yet tipped over into something more malicious. How embittered he has become since he came back empty-handed from London—these past few months have been the worst I can recall. We no longer go out together happily as a couple—that is, unselfconsciously, without some kind of strain. If we don't brawl shamelessly during the time we are in public then it happens afterwards, when he presents me with a long, disgruntled list of what I said or did wrong.

Last Friday was no exception. The night was brilliantly clear, the first warm night of spring: every star was blisteringly lustrous, the sea one black slice of shine. The water in the harbour looked glowingly luminous, a lapping, glossy dark thing at our feet. I suddenly found I desperately wanted the visiting English lady novelist to know that I was a writer too, the author of two slim, out-of-print novels once published in London. I heard myself putting my oar in, so to speak, my voice sounding ridiculously posh, not a rogue Australian vowel to be heard. For some reason now lost to me I started telling a joke about one of the Queen's courtiers coming through customs at Sydney airport, how the customs official took his passport and said, 'There's no "t" in courier, mate.' Everyone laughed politely and David shot me a contemptuous look. I sat back in my chair and shut up.

I know all about life and art, mate, I wanted to shout, I know every last piece that makes up art's whole, the way my husband and I fight night after night, causing tears to roll down each side of my face and meet as if in a bow under my chin. A ribbon of tears tied prettily around! What life! What art is this?

'You,' my husband shouted when we got home, 'you have

only two modes of being—the pompous I-am-a-neglected-genius mode or the unconfident I-am-a-defenceless-victim mode. Which is it now? Are you the unsung genius? Or the put-upon victim of men?'

I forget why he was shouting this. Oh, yes, it started when I lost my temper because he was late meeting us at Pan's restaurant earlier in the night. It was the first time in months Anna had agreed to come to dinner with us—and he had to go and muck it up by being late. How can you be late getting to a restaurant which is five hundred yards from your front door? He was working, he said, and had arrived at an important scene in the book and couldn't stop; he'd told me three times already to expect him any time between quarter past and half past. 'What? Eight or nine?' I said, knowing I was making a mistake by going on about it but I could not stop. Within minutes the whole thing was a mess. 'Do you want to bloody eat dinner tonight or shall we just go home?' he shouted, slamming his glass down and shattering it, at which point Lil started to cry. I tried to redeem things as best I could, cleaning the glass up, trying to calm everybody down by making a few desultory stabs at conversation, but the evening was wrecked. The four of us sat there, eating in miserable silence, Pan's awful food sticking in our throats.

What shameless people we have become. I am as thoughtless and lacking in self-discipline as my father—how I used to hate the way he let his emotions run loose without a thought for anyone but himself—and yet here I am, forty years old, as shameless as him. I'm sorry, Anna, I'm sorry Lil, I'm sorry. No money, no love, no way out. Just more and more of this.

What is the process by which two people become less themselves over time, reducing bit by bit that which they are able to reveal to each other? What is the butcher's dark art which makes couples take so stealthily to hacking? When does the particular moment come when each feels himself to be wronged and embarks upon a deep and hidden course of retribution?

Sometimes I think that I have never truly known my husband. Sometimes I think that the veil which exists between ourselves and other people is never rent, no matter how intimate the connection. I wonder, too, if love itself is nothing but a form of self-hypnosis by which we invent the people with whom we fall in love through some greedy private act of self-gratification. I know my husband was once a dreaming boy in St Kilda, Melbourne, a skinny boy who was no good at football and wrote poems about the moon long after he should have been asleep. I know his father came back from the Great War full of fear and anger, that he badly beat David and his brother, his mother too, until the day David turned sixteen and broke his father's nose. I know that like myself David feels as if he built himself, that he arose, sourceless, as if from air. But what do I know of my husband's veiled interior, of the infinite mysteries which make him, still dark to me after so many years?

Sometimes I think I know him best from his fiction, which allows the illusion that the veil has been lifted to reveal the working consciousness within. Surely I cannot have mistaken fiction's art for human truth? Could it really be that David's truest story is one I will never read because it was never written down?

Once I could tell David everything. Once he held me while I cried for everything lost to me, while I released to him every last secret. Once he took great pains to remind me of everything I still contained, of everything I could find within.

Once he loved my vitality, my ability to talk to anyone, my spirit of invitation to the world. Now he hates my vitality, my ability to talk to anyone, my spirit of invitation to the world.

Let me count the ways in which I have failed him. Let me count the ways in which we have failed each other.

## Today

A moment's peace, a moment's reprieve. David came down from the studio (we finally cut a hole in the ceiling and have run a ladder up—effectively attaching him to the main body of the house). 'Do you want to go for a walk?' he asked, surprising me. I was peeling potatoes for dinner but wiped my hands straightaway. How humiliating my belief in the possibility of redemption, how poignant my battered heart's ability to hope: what is this human facility to be punched again and again but still long for the bruise to be kissed?

In the street we walked side by side like two exhausted soldiers. Gone, gone, the days of holding hands, of conversation that is arbitrary, trailing, running off in unexpected directions. We are all plod and effort now, all manufactured speech, both of us have memorised the list of all those things we cannot speak about. I thought of mentioning the lady novelist but I imagined there was danger there, an undercurrent below the line of sight. I ran through other topics in my head but every single thing was suddenly perilous.

'What a magnificent day!' I said. David grunted, as we were already climbing another hill.

'Antonia is leaving in the morning,' he offered. 'Apparently she has had a change of plans.'

'Oh,' I said, 'I hope it was nothing I said?' I offered this vapid remark as a kind of conversational tool, knowing it to be the most stupid of devices.

He cast me a contemptuous glance. 'I'm afraid that not everything in the world relates to you, my dear,' he said. I thought this remark might just as easily describe himself.

'She is very beautiful, isn't she,' he continued, 'she obviously takes a lot of trouble over her appearance.'

'Unlike me,' I said.

He gave a great burst of laughter. 'You! You don't give a damn about clothes or fashion or what you look like. You only care about being a genius. Have you looked in the mirror lately?'

'Why?'

He stopped climbing and looked hard at me. 'I think the expression is, "You have let yourself go".'

My hands instinctively shielded my face and his mouth flickered into a kind of smile. 'There's nothing worse than a beautiful woman hanging around when the party's over,' he said.

The air left my lungs. I heard the pulse of my blood.

'Oh, don't panic, darling,' he said, turning around again and starting to climb. 'You can live among the ruins of your beauty, like a Roman statue whose arms have fallen off.'

I sat down on the stone steps, trying to breathe. 'How can you be so cruel?' I said, beginning to cry.

'Oh, it's that time again, is it? Drama 101!'

I picked up a rock and would have thrown it at him except Antonia herself appeared from a side lane at that very moment.

'Hello there! Isn't it the most perfect day?' she said. 'I am tempted to write to my publisher to say I am never coming back.'

My eyes were filmy with tears but I still managed a social smile. Where did that smile come from, with my heart so full of my own misery and disgrace? 'We don't have the choice,' I said to her, 'we're stuck.'

Her glance took us both in; she made some kind of appraisal of the situation, and smiled. 'But what a place to be stuck,' she said. 'Lucky you.'

Lucky me, still longing for the kiss upon the bruise, still hoping to be noticed and loved. Lucky me, offering up my ruined statue's face in stupid, never-ending hope.

In bed last night, feigning sleep, David came in, took off his clothes and crawled in beside me. Instead of lying stiff on his side of the bed, he snuggled into me. We lay, cradled like egg and cup, and a single tear slipped from my eye to the pillow.

'I do love you, you know,' he said, 'still. Despite everything. Because of everything.'

I did not want to say the wrong thing. 'Even though I'm an ugly old hag?' I tried to make this sound like a joke.

'Oh, you're not that bad. Angelo wouldn't say no to you.'

'Thanks,' I said, 'considering Angelo is about one hundred and three with one eye and no teeth.'

He laughed. 'You'd make a lovely couple!'

I kicked him under the bedclothes. 'I'm really not that ugly, am I? Are you still attracted to me?'

He kissed my hair. 'Of course, of course.'

I did not want to bring up the fact that we hardly ever make love. I did not want to bring danger into the room, our other harder selves: I did not want to be the first to lift the knife.

'David, are you attracted to Antonia? You must be—you know what men are like.'

He laughed. 'Do I? I don't even know what I'm like.' He kissed me softly on the nape of my neck. 'Darling, if I had a drachma for every woman I've been attracted to, I'd be Aristotle Onassis.'

I took a breath. 'Would you ever have another affair?'

He sighed. 'Oh, sure, I can really see me sneaking off without the whole island knowing.'

I thought: it doesn't matter now if he has another affair, the circle was broken when he took to his bed a pretty nineteen-year-old girl one summer in London. Whatever was safe inside the circle, whatever was whole and unblemished, was released. I lay quietly beside him.

'Oh, the number of times I've fallen in love,' David said dreamily, his voice soft in my ear.

'What do you mean "fallen in love"? What do you mean exactly?'

I listened to him breathing. 'Feeling lighter on my feet. A general sense of happiness because that person is alive in the world.'

My heart started a little dance, from shock. 'How many times have you felt that?'

'Oh, I don't know, dozens. Twenty, thirty, I don't know, I've lost count.'

'But you can't have! You can't have fallen in love thirty times. Surely you are describing a crush, or a fleeting feeling of attraction for someone. You are not describing falling in love.'

He removed his arm. 'Why not? Just because my experience is different to yours doesn't mean it's not real for me. Honestly, Katherine, you are the vainest creature alive.'

'My vanity has nothing to do with it. You're a writer, you know how to use the correct word. Falling in love is a life-changing experience, which most people are only lucky enough to experience once or twice in their whole lives.'

He snorted. 'Oh, I see,' he said, 'and how many times have you been in love?'

'Twice,' I said. 'Exactly twice.'

He lifted himself up and hissed into my ear. 'What a lucky man I must be. The much-desired Katherine Elgin, choosing lowly me. May I ask if I am the first or the second?'

He got out of bed and stalked to the door, slamming it on his way out.


I think David began to leave me when my whole self was trained upon the girls. They took the milk from my breasts, the sleep from my eyes, the juice from my body. There was nothing left for him; I was too tired from holding them all day to hold him.

It was in those early days before we left Sydney for London that David first began to go. The secretary merely met him at the door.

He didn't want a wife whose eyes were elsewhere, on small children, on her work but not on him. When we first met, David said he had always wanted to live with another artist. It was his dream to have a mate who, unlike his first wife, understood what it meant to speak of writing as a vocation.

But he didn't expect me to cling to work despite child-rearing, domestic burdens, the gift of love. Perhaps in his deepest self he does not believe a woman can be an artist.

Now David thinks my compulsion to write is evidence only of neuroticism.

I am beginning to think he is right.

## Monday

I have to face the fact that this experiment of ours has failed. David knows it, which is undoubtedly why he is so continually bad-tempered, and I know it too, but neither of us dare yet say it out loud. Very bad sales for his last book, his London agent suggesting his publishers might not be interested in his next one, our last remaining money running out. I dare not tell him I have just heard from Cape that they are not going to take my novel.

This morning on the way to the market Lil spied a pair of cast-off tourist's sandals outside Cassandra's house. *'Ella, Mama, ella! Paputskha!'* she cried, rushing towards them like a starving girl to food. It wasn't the fact of her running towards them which struck me to the quick, but that she worked out in a flash that the shoes were abandoned and she was in need of new ones. They are too big for her but she will not give them up and has been clomping around the house all afternoon. Here is the hard truth: we no longer have enough money to go to Athens to buy new shoes for our children.

We will have to go back to Australia like whipped dogs, our tails hanging. We will have to go back and admit that the nay-sayers were right, you cannot slip out from under the net and survive. It's true, the world makes you live by the rules or else it makes you pay and pay. It turns you into home owners and mortgage payers and pension savers and insurance holders, it makes you live near good schools for the children.

The girls know something is fatally askew: yesterday Anna asked me who David was married to before he was married to me. 'Why do you want to know?' I asked, hearing an unfamiliar note of anxiety in her voice.

She shrugged. 'No reason.' I explained that a long time ago David used to be married to a woman called Jean but that sometimes marriages did not work out and people decided to leave each other.

'Is Dad going to leave you?'

I crossed the room and took her in my arms: she stiffened.

'I'm sorry if our fighting is upsetting you, darling. We're going through a very difficult time,' I said.

'Is he going to leave?'

I touched her hair. 'No, sweetheart, he's not going to leave.'

She looked fierce. 'I wish he would. I wish he'd go away and never come back.'

'Oh, Anna, you don't mean that. You'd be very sad if he did. We all would.'

She pushed me away. 'Would you? Would you really?'

We stood looking at each other. I could not explain the dark and complicated plaiting of David's life with mine, or the source of my desire to keep holding on, obscured now even from myself. I know it has to do with claiming something of my own, of wanting something that can never be taken. I want a stake in that which endures, in that which weathers loss, pain, the press of time itself. I want some pledge from eternity, Anna, some sign of life's ceaseless, unforgiving motion.

# The Broken Book

*Take care, do not come too close to me, the grey dust of my failure will coat your clothes, the stink of my ruin will curl in your blameless nostrils. Do not look me in the eye, do not look upon my faulty works. I have lain down with dogs and got up with fleas, just as my good mother feared; I have shown myself no self respect whatsoever. Look! My mother is crying, my father is shouting, my sister is imploring everyone in the car to calm down. Calm down, folks, I haven't shot anyone! Calm down, my fellow Australians, I am after all only a foolish girl who is mistakenly in the family way.*

*'Cressida, I thought you were smarter than that,' my father will say. Too smart to get pregnant? Or too smart to sleep with a boy in the first place?*

*'Oh, Percy, what are we going to do?' my mother will wail and I will shoot a look of pure hate at Hebe. Why did she have to tell them? Couldn't we have dealt with this by ourselves?*

*Why do I have a sneaking suspicion that there is the tiniest glitter of malicious triumph in my elder sister's pretty blue eyes? She did not confess to me that she had already told them, all the way down in the train from Sydney she did not say a thing. It was only when we stepped off the train and onto the platform and I saw my parents' faces that I knew straightaway they had already been told. My mother's eyes were swollen from weeping; my father's hot head looked ready to explode.*

*'Get in the car, young lady,' he said. 'Hebe, follow me.'*

*I followed their backs, my mother sniffling into her handkerchief beside me. 'How could you do this to me?' my mother said, sobbing quietly as we walked. Do what, I thought, for as far as I knew I had not done anything to her. Was she pregnant too?*

*In the car in the back seat I pinched my sister Hebe and managed to hiss at her, 'Why did you tell them?' This was easy to hiss as my mother was weeping loudly and violently in the front passenger seat, repeating between sobs, 'Oh, Cressida, how could you?' (Even I could tell that this was a rhetorical question.) My father was going on and on in his booming endless voice about what young people were coming to, how the war had ruined the morals of an entire generation, how the world was never going to be the same again. He was saying, too, how he would never have dared to go against the wishes of his own parents and something else and something else but I was too busy pinching Hebe and trying to hear her justification amidst the terrific noise of the Morley family being dramatic in the car (Austin, rust-eaten due to merciless sea air).*

'I had to,' I heard her say, 'you were too far gone for an abortion. What else were we going to do?' I don't know, Hebe, I could have jumped off a cliff; I know a perfectly good one just off Booby's Point which plunges a hundred feet into the sea. I could have swallowed arsenic like Emma Bovary and heard the gay singing beneath my window as I lay dying. I could have plunged a knife into the man who was fucking Lorna and a pretty woman called Kay at the same time as myself. (Correction: not the same time in real, actual time, of course! A foursome is beyond even my puny reach although I am obviously now a full-blown slut.) I could have packed my little bag tied to the stick and started a whole new life. O, that upcoming tiny scrap of humanity and me!

Instead, here I am, the catalyst for my family's ruin, the human instrument of my family's defeat. I thought you didn't care what other people thought, Dad? I thought you were one of Australia's rare free thinkers. How could I know that sex is the one thing you fear, that evidence of a working wet triangle between your daughter's legs is the one thing you cannot bear to face?

And then we are inside the house, quickly, so no one will see. Hide me, this evidence of your failure, your second daughter who has brought you nothing but shame. I'm sorry! I take it all back, the kissing and the joy and the unbuckling of my eighteen-year-old heart. To be innocent again, a sexless child, a girl without breasts, devoid of a single pubic hair. Can you give me a cuddle, Mum, please, can I sit on your lap? Can I get my favourite doll and will you read me a story, can you grate an apple and bring me a glass of flat lemonade like you used to when I was sick? Why am I crying, why am I useless as a child, why do I long to shut my eyes and wake up again to find everything as it was before my fall? 'Mum, I'm so sorry,' I say to my mother, sobbing in her fleshy arms, and she will stop crying herself to put her soft mouth on my head to croon, 'Ssshh, ssshh. There, there, Cress, it's all right.' I can hear my father crying, too, a sound I have never heard before in my life. Despite the fact that I have never heard this sound, a kind of embarrassed cough, I know straightaway without doubt what it is. I'm sorry, Dad, I'm sorry, I promise I'll never do it again.

And then there is a knock at the door and everyone straightens up, adjusts their face, runs from the room. A family's secrets are visible to no one, not even a friend standing in the same room. Here is Comrade Martin, the family friend from down the road, bringing around the money collected from the local community to send to headquarters in Sydney and then on to Russia's glorious Red Army. See my father's social smile, his hearty grip, the public self so effectively divided from the private. Do unmarried girls get pregnant in Russia, Comrade Martin? Does anybody care? I am trying to imagine some unknown girl far away in the snows of Russia, pregnant, possibly cast off.

So it is arranged that I will give notice on my flat, my job, my life, and tell everyone that I have been offered a wonderful new job helping the war effort somewhere in the country. I will give notice on my boyfriend too, the one who deflowered me, the one I mistook for my personal vision. I will write him a long letter of bitter accusations and grief; tear-stained, bloody. He will surprise me by replying, offering to help in whatever way he can but at the same time making it clear that I must understand him to be a man of ambitions. 'I do not see myself ever supporting a wife and children,' he will write. 'I intend to dedicate myself to art.' I might suggest that having a wife has never stopped a male artist before; indeed, many a male artist has been allowed to work through the kind agency of a wife. Why can he not dedicate himself to me instead? Am I not a work of art myself, like him an artist of the body? Am I not a nascent poet perhaps, whose poems he once declared to be promising? Might not we both dwell in the house of art and love, our baby asleep in a white basket between us, witness to our every act of happiness?

Cressida, dream on. Be sensible, young lady, live in the real world, not the world of What Might Have Been, do not try to live in that sweet world of your own making. Come out of the poem, walk off the page, keep your dimming eyes open. This is reality, love, here, in front of your nose, in that swelling lump beneath your dress. The prince has bad breath, the prince does not want you, the prince has written himself out of the story. O, Cressida, all alone in the cold, nowhere to hide, tipped out of the warm story into cold life. Here there are no princes, no happy endings, no summing up. Here there is only your belly, and inside it, a real human baby who is yet to read a single book.

*The Island, Greece, 1956*

Ena, Dio, Tria, Tesera, Pente, Exi, Efta, Okto, Enia, Deka, Endeka, Dodeka, DekaTria (Deka + Tria), DekaTesera (Deka + Tesera etc). Any number from 1 to 1 000 000 is always a combination (e.g. 500 = *Pendakosies*. For more than a thousand you say the number plus the word *Chiliades*). Phonetics: Forget about the alphabet for a moment and concentrate on the sound. E.g. How much does it cost? *Poso kani? Me lene Katerina. Me lene Katerina.*

My name is Katerina. As a birthday present the girls and their friends sang me the formal Happy Birthday song for my birthday yesterday—as opposed to the informal version, I suppose. *TriandaTria*. Thirty-three years old. Between them, Anna and Lil translated as they went:

*Long may you live Kyria Katerina*
*And may you live many years*

*May you grow old*
*With white hair*
*May you spread out everywhere*
*The light of knowledge*
*And may everybody say*
*There, is a wise woman.*

Well, I am certainly spreading out everywhere. I am certainly growing fat on cheap Greek wine, *psomi*, Greek words. My poor head, not one more word, please. Not one more twist of the tongue. Both David and I are *still* taking lessons from Thanasis, the mayor. Our second year of him coming to the house for our lessons, wearing his one and only tie, full of bluster and self-importance. The girls are often around, sniggering in the background, Lil cannot comprehend why adults have to sit down with their books and pencils just like she does at school. 'It's easy, Mama! Just talk!'

Just talk, she says. Just free your stupid English tongue. Isn't English strewn with thousands and thousands of Greek words? Hasn't Greek given us the words for science and medicine and botany and technology? Hasn't Greek given us the language of poetry and art? *Ne, Ne! Poso kani? Poso kani?*

## Wednesday

How I love our beautiful whitewashed house with its bright blue door. How I love the cool damp of the kitchen, the giant flagstones still cool underfoot even on the hottest day. It takes days and days of 100 degree heat for the whole house to grow murky with stifled air, but still the kitchen is dark and cool—some nights I creep down with a blanket to lie alone on the cold, hard floor. I have my kerosene stove, my stone sink, no running water yet (the town well is directly outside the front door—we are frequently woken in the mornings by that chatterbox Soula, and often kept awake by her drawing up the bucket with her chums late at night). I love my kitchen, its battle-scarred table, its earthenware jugs and woven baskets, its little anteroom to the side. A hanging cupboard with a wire mesh door, just like we had all those years ago at Kurrajong Bay. No refrigerator yet, only occasional blocks of ice from the island's only fridge, located proudly in the main room of Kostas's shop.

I don't think I have ever loved a house more. Two entrances, one at the front near the well, which opens into the largest room, with its glorious wooden fireplace. Then into a room which has the other entrance door, placed at the side; then into the kitchen. No connection between the upper and lower floors yet, all of us have to pile out the side entrance (which is enclosed in a courtyard) and up the outside stairs.

Ah, but the roof! The most amazing ascension into the blue, the whitewashed stone houses all around, the hundreds of steps behind and around leading up even higher. The infinite swoop of the sea and the sky, the knowledge that we are but fleeting, elemental as water and air. On the roof at night I feel the pain of trying, of all my moments rich in hurt and joy and incompleteness, heavy with struggle. Up there I try not to yearn for that which is lost but to count what is near. What is near is my daughter Lil's milky skin, my daughter Anna's vanishing self. Anna is leaving us second by second, growing into her mature self and the child is dying: the fat baby hands, the tiny teeth, the boneless nose. Let me hold her soft bones one more time before she goes, let me hear her undeveloped voice, her irritating pipe. Let me record how she is before she leaves, my disappearing girl, evanescent, swift as life. Alone on the roof at night I count each day's fleeting gifts.

I note the dignity of Stavros the donkey boy passing beneath the house, the dark of the streets, the moon revealing his slow progress. Stavros, the boy born with cerebral palsy, son of the donkey keeper, making his shaky way up the path beneath our house. The sound of the donkey's feet stopping, myself peering over the stone buttressing wall of the roof, watching Stavros removing the hessian bag attached to the saddle, slowly and shakily taking from it the wooden handled broom to sweep up the crumbly mass of donkey shit into the bag. What dignity, what grace. This is the community which embraces the shaky dignified boy, the drooling crone, the retarded girl. This is the place where the boy who stole money from Kostas's shop so shamed his family that they felt the only recourse was to move away. Seven years later, everybody still talks of the only robber the island has ever known.

This is the place, too, where my fat-bottomed neighbour Soula believes she has the right to walk into my house,

unannounced, at any time of night or day. 'Katerina! Katerina!'
I hear her bellow at the very moment I am trying to capture
the perfect word. She wants to give me some eggs, still covered
in feathers and shit, or teach me how to make *tiri*. I don't want
to make bloody cheese, I don't want to cook and clean any
more than I have to. She believes my children to be improperly
looked after—hasn't Anna been baptised yet? Why don't they
go to church? She doesn't know it but she is teaching me to
speak, she is teaching me how to answer back. What are the
words for *I am busy, you old sticky-beak, leave me alone*? I was
amazed to learn that she is in fact two years younger than
me—I thought she was at least ten years older. Perhaps it is
because she is already a widow—her husband, a fisherman,
was lost at sea. He may be gone but his presence is everywhere,
from Soula's eternal black widow's weeds, to his stony photograph
on the wall and on the mantelpiece, to Soula's insistence on
quoting his long-gone words. Also, his three children: beefy
twelve-year-old twin boys, Theo and Mikos, and bossy little
Cassandra, Lil's best friend. Cassandra is bound to grow up
and turn out exactly like her mother; at eight she is already a
plump Greek housewife, all jowly chin and disapproving presence.

Must stop. Speak of the devil. *Soula! Tikanis?*


## Thursday

Let me sing of the pleasures of freshly washed sheets. Let me
recite the alphabet of a clean scrubbed house, the tiles newly

mopped and gleaming, the beds neatly done like a sum. Praise the cut mountain flowers mourning their roots, the captured bright froth of them blossoming in the jar. Sing of the swept fireplace newly bereft of its ash skirt; the last of summer's plucked fruits and the sea's stones on the windowsill, the life of art, the art of life. Still life, life stilled, the earthenware pots, never before so round and whole, still life created by this most lacklustre of ordinary housewives. The rewards of the toil of my fingers: the polished glass, the made beds, the straightened cushions, all brought to momentary order. Life will wreck it all; tumbling life will cause it to crumble into disarray, but pause for a moment, *regard!* Happiness dwells in the walls of the house, happiness lives in the whitewash, in the skin of its living, breathing walls.

Rosanna and Claudio and Cody arrive on Sunday. Yippee!


*Friday morning*

Haven't had a minute since the lovely Rosanna *en famille* appeared. She has cast her eye upon everything: our house, our marriage, the girls, our Greek friends, our little expatriate circle—I have felt ourselves to be on display, that I have to have everything in perfect order to justify our choice to live here. Why should that be, I wonder, when I know Rosanna to be the most generous of friends, the least judgemental of women? I suppose it has more to do with me proving myself rather than anything to do with Rosanna, with me needing to show that my choices have as much validity as anyone else's. We had a party for them during the week and *everyone* came: the mayor, his wife Maria, all the teachers at the school, every shopkeeper, our new friend Stephanos, the cultured, well-travelled banker from Athens who has just bought the house next to ours as a weekender, and his wife, Katina. Even Lieutenant Manolis came, the fussy senior police official here who issues the residency permits for all foreigners living on the island. He spent the early part of the evening looking like he might arrest someone, but by the end of the night he was dancing with the best of them. There was much showing off, much raucous dancing and plate smashing; at one point Pan climbed on top of the roof and played his *lyra*. Afterwards we sat in our little walled garden, the night luminous, the air scented with all the flowers we have grown. Stephanos lingered on, although his wife had left; David and I sat close together, the tips of our knees touching. Rosanna was holding Claudio's hand.

'You guys seem really settled,' Rosanna said, 'happy.'

I turned to David. 'We are.' He smiled at me.

'I could never leave my country,' Stephanos said, 'my country is who I am.'

David lit another cigarette. 'Perhaps that's because you're Greek, Stephanos. Not all of us are born so fortunate,' he said.

'I disagree. I have travelled to many other places which are just as beautiful, where I have felt that I could live. But I always hasten back to Greece because I do not want to become a divided man.'

Claudio, who had been silent, suddenly spoke. 'Everyone is divided, Stephanos. To be human is to be divided.'

Stephanos sucked on his cigar and considered this. 'Perhaps. But one can certainly reduce the number of divisions. One can stay where one is born so that there is one less thing to feel divided about.'

'I don't feel divided living here,' I said.

Stephanos turned to me. 'But surely you are merely suspending reality? Surely the idea of returning to your native shore hangs over you like an unanswered question?'

'I never want to go back,' I said, 'never.'

David laughed at my ferocity. 'I wish I could feel as certain as you, darling. I can see there might come a time when one feels one doesn't belong here—but neither does one belong back in Australia.'

'Citizens of the world then, that's what you are,' said Claudio, raising his glass to us.

'Belonging nowhere,' said Stephanos. 'Take my advice, my friends. Go home while you still can or you will end up having no home at all.'

'Oh, I don't see any reason why they should go home,' Rosanna said. 'From where I sit I think Kate and David are living in paradise.'

David and I smiled at each other, convinced for the moment that it might be true.

## Wednesday

Ever since Rosanna left, everything has fallen apart. Perhaps it was the strain of feeling I had to show her the face of perfection, but I don't think her leaving and my little trough of despondency are necessarily linked—I think it's more to do with life's natural peaks and troughs. Last night with the girls was awful, awful . . . What a gulf between one's dream of motherhood and its daily practice.

Am I a hothead? Is David a hothead too? Of course! At our worst both of us are full of passionate intensity, easily roused, our nerves practically standing up and waving—why should I be surprised that our children are like us, all teeth and blood? Last night things got out of control so quickly I felt winded, as if I had been unexpectedly punched.

Anna and I have always had a difficult time of it. Is she too like me, or not like me enough? I can spend all day comfortably with Lil, but with Anna, everything I do is wrong, wrong, wrong. Yesterday started badly; she kept waking up in the night complaining about an earache. This is the very thing that always makes me want to rush back to civilisation—what if anything should happen to the girls? What if they should need a doctor in the middle of the night? There is no hospital here and only one 'doctor', a retired ancient specimen from Athens who is very deaf. Last summer I was almost blind with the most appalling conjunctivitis and Soula's peasant remedy of the sap of vine leaves had no effect whatsoever. 'You must cry the fullest tears to wash out the eye,' the old doctor told me while I sat there foolishly hoping for antibiotic drops.

In the night, cradling a weeping Anna, I prayed that her ear was not so badly infected that her eardrum would burst. I had some ancient aspirin tablets left over from London and I gave her two in a big glass of water, hoping that children were allowed to take aspirin. I couldn't remember! I was panicking, thinking I would get the first boat to Athens in the morning.

In the morning she was perfectly well. No temperature, no earache, the whole thing was probably the result of a nightmare from which she could not properly awaken. Anyway, she was fine by the morning, a bright happy colour, but clearly she did not want to go to school. 'Can I stay home with you, Mama?' she asked in such a plaintive way that I mentally put aside my work and agreed. I wondered—not for the first time—if she was happy here, if we have placed her in jeopardy through selfish desires of our own. When she is older will she curse me for a childhood spent flying through the air, hanging on to my aspiring coat tails? On the surface at least she seems happy enough, slipping effortlessly into this life of the elements. She is still young enough, too, to regard me as her moveable house; wherever I am is her home. Well, anyway, Lil was already running off up the hill to school before I had time to think, holding hands with portly Cassandra without a backward glance. David was off, up the ladder to his studio on the roof, which left Anna and me.

'What would you like to do today? We'll have a special day to ourselves, just Mummy and Anna,' I said, stroking the last of her wispy, disappearing baby hair.

'Can we have a picnic?' she asked. 'At the cove?'

It was wet, cold; the last thing I felt like was a picnic. 'I'm afraid the weather's terrible, darling.'

'But you said it was my special day!'

'It is, I just don't want you to get a cold going out in the rain.'

'You never let me do anything I want!'

I continued to stroke her hair but she flung me off. 'You're a liar! You said it was my special day!'

I examined my conscience: was I saying no because of my fear of her catching cold or because of my own dislike of going out in the rain?

'Oh, all right, let's go,' I said, already growing bad-tempered. I got our boots, our raincoats, our rain hats, and started packing up a lunch. This is the time of year when food is at its worst— the last of the summer fruits are going, the winter vegetables are yet to come. So, *psomi*, a withered old tomato, some *halva*, two boiled eggs. I was in the kitchen getting this together and Anna was at the table, bleating.

'Where's my special book that I was writing? Lil's taken it!'

'She has not,' I said. 'I put it away carefully in your room. Why don't you start putting your own things away?'

She pushed her chair back and rushed from the room. 'Where did you put it? Where?'

'On your chest of drawers!' I yelled, growing more

bad-tempered by the minute. I heard her slam the outside door, then I heard her thundering about upstairs. She must have been flinging open cupboards, slamming drawers shut, generally behaving as if she had misplaced the bloody crown jewels.

'Where? Where?' I heard her screaming, through the floor. Then she came thundering downstairs again. 'Where did you put it, you *vlaca*!'

I put down the knife. 'Don't call me *vlaca*, please. It's rude.' (Roughly, it means 'stupid' or 'dummy'. In its mildest sense at least—it can also mean 'moron'.)

'I can't find it! You've lost it!'

I slammed the knife down, wiped my hands and stalked out of the kitchen, out the door, up the outside stairs, to her room. Her papers were exactly where I said they would be.

She came into the room behind me, glowering.

'Can you apologise please?'

She looked at the floor. 'Sorry,' she said in a surly voice, barely more than a whisper.

'Properly,' I said.

'Sorry,' she said, looking at me fiercely.

'Let's go,' I said, in a full-blown bad mood by now.

As soon as we left the house she said, 'I'm hungry.'

I kept walking. 'You've just had breakfast! I'm sorry but you'll have to wait.'

'It's not fair!' she said. 'I'm hungry and you said it was my special day!'

I tried to breathe, slow and deep, the bloody rain all the

216

time washing down the back of my neck. 'It's not far to the cove, Anna. I'm sure you can wait.'

'You *vlaca*! You never give me anything!'

And with that she ran off down the lane, full of righteous, wounded anger, her little back stiff with pride. I stalked after her and in this way we finally came to the cove. We walked without speaking past the figs at the corner, past the rocks and the cave where we swim. Our feet followed the curve of the road which runs around the island, the sandy, rocky unpaved road where we walk all our days. I tried to raise my eyes to heaven, to the beauty of the sea, to the figure of my little girl striding so purposefully ahead. Why do I find you so difficult, I asked her yellow raincoated back, why do I find it easier to mother your sister rather than you? Was this why I was so instinctively jealous of my own sister? It's not that I love Anna less than Lil—in fact because my love for Anna is so hard won it sometimes feels infinitely more precious—but, treacherously, I enjoy Lil more.

As we approached the cove I caught up with Anna and said, 'Don't ever talk to me like that again.'

She looked at me, surprised, as if she had forgotten what she said. She nodded, momentarily cowed.

We got there, we sat on a rock, we ate our lunch. Anna thawed out, as she always does, gathering sticks to throw into the waves, a dried fig leaf which we used to make a little boat. As we launched it into the sea I said, 'One day, when you are very old, you can tell your grandchildren that you once sailed a boat with your mother into the Saronic Sea.'

She looked at me blankly, a young girl with no use for time. We knelt together on the wet gritty sand looking at our frail boat as the rain fell. Suddenly she turned to me and said: 'I don't care if I die, Mama, because then I can go to heaven and sit on a cloud.' She stood up, gave me a kiss, and ran towards the water.

Well! What happiness is this when Lil comes home from school and immediately bursts into tears because Anna triumphantly gloats that she has been to the cove with Mama? 'It's not fair!' cries Lil. 'I never get to go!'

Isn't this the cry of humanity itself? Isn't this the cry of the world? *It's not fair! I don't have enough land. Enough success, enough money, enough love!* Surely this is the crux of all humanity's woes—economic, religious, social, political, personal—that someone, somewhere, feels that there is not enough to go around? In Lil's cry, in Anna's; in the faint, long-ago childish cries of Ros and myself, someone feels themselves to be standing too far outside the warming light.

From worse to worser. Daddy has gone off to the waterfront to join the other stateless geniuses. Mummy is home with the children, gritting her teeth. 'You were the one who wanted them!' he said, smiling, a joke with a wire in it.

'Bye, Daddy! Bye!' the girls cried as we settled around the fire, ready for stories. Earlier I had promised to take both Lil and Anna to the cove for a picnic on the weekend, in order to shut Lil up. 'I'm going to take Scruffy,' Lil said. 'He'll get wet!' Anna replied. We were reading *The Little Prince* on the sofa and Anna said she intended to become a nurse to tend any pilots who should fall to earth around us. I was just getting to the part where the Little Prince describes his people, when there was a knock at the door. 'Sit quietly and read please,' I said. 'Anna, keep reading to Lil.'

'I want to read too!' Lil was saying as I left the room.

It was Stephanie, the French composer from the house on the corner. We have known each other since we first arrived, yet somehow we have never become friends: I always know it is her at the door because hardly anyone ever knocks. 'Excuse me, Katerina, but I was wondering if you could borrow to me any kerosene? My stove has exploded! It is good that I have a second appliance!'

'Oh, mine does that all the time,' I said. 'Come in.'

I led her into the kitchen, even though I could hear a fight breaking out in the other room. She began a long story about how she normally never ventures out alone at night; she heard another girl was raped last summer by some of the naval cadets from the island's naval academy. I was listening to the sounds in the other room, only half listening as I filled her tin.

'Excuse me,' I said, 'I'll be right back.'

When I opened the door to the front room I saw a feathery rain. The girls were having a pillow fight and had split some cushions; duck feathers or goose feathers or whatever feathers they were flew up to the roof, down to the rug, landed in their hair like confetti. They had knocked over and broken a pottery vase, my favourite blue one I bought in Dieppe, a picture was off the wall and the clock on the mantelpiece was in danger of falling too; every cushion, every rug, every sofa cushion had been ripped from its moorings to fly with the feathers round the room.

'Put those cushions down!' I yelled. 'Now!'

They ignored me and continued to whack each other with abandon. 'Anna! Elizabeth! Stop at once!'

I was screaming now, at the top of my voice. 'Right! That's it! We are not going to the cove on Saturday! Did you hear that?'

They stopped immediately and Anna flung herself, shrieking, prostrate on the floor. 'Oh, please, Mummy! We didn't know! We didn't know!'

'You didn't know what?' I screamed. 'You didn't know you weren't supposed to wreck the room?'

At which point the childless French girl opened the door to the screaming mother and her weeping children. 'Get upstairs now!' I yelled at them, and they ran screaming from the room. Why must girls scream so much?

'I had better go, I think,' said Stephanie.

I tried to smile. 'Yes, yes.'

I followed her to the door then turned on my heel and flew up the stairs like a mad woman. 'Anna! You are eight years old! Old enough to know better!'

Why were these words so quickly in my mouth? Haven't I heard them somewhere before?

'I hate you! I hate you! I am never going to bed, ever!' Lil was shouting, refusing to move from the top of the stairs. Anna was there too, holding on to the railing like a chained suffragette willing to die for her cause.

'Let go of that railing and get into bed!' I shouted.

'No! You *vlaca!*' Anna said, clinging on.

'Anna, I will give you five. One. Two. Three.' I was trying to count slower. 'Four . . .' Usually by four she had stopped whatever it was that she was doing.

'Five! Right, that's it!'

I was up the stairs like an avenging angel, wrenching her arm free. She turned herself into a starfish so that I could not carry her up the stairs; Lil was simply standing there screaming at the top of her lungs. I was blindly wrestling with my eight-year-old daughter on the outside stairs in the cold rain, trying to manhandle her into her room; my other child was screaming hysterically. Why was I surprised that Soula burst through the side door, her kind Greek heart bent on rescue?

'Katerina? Katerina?' she cried, in all her black presence, in all her puzzled face and Greek neighbourly closeness. My Greek completely deserted me and I started bellowing to her in English,

'Thank you for your assistance, I am all right, I do not need your help, thank you!'

Reluctantly she closed the door, by which time I had managed to frogmarch my daughters up the stairs. Lil still refused to get into bed; I flung her down upon the bed, pushed a blanket over her, and tucked her in. She pushed it straight off, I tucked it back in, she pushed it off and attempted to get up again. I tucked her back in but this time I physically held her down, a grown woman holding down a seven-year-old. I was unhinged! I was slapping her hard on the bottom with my open palm and she was screaming. Anna was sobbing in bed and then I was sobbing too, the three of us, howling at the moon. I crept into bed with Lil and she was still weeping, her little chest heaving with hiccups.

What kind of mother am I, to be so quickly reduced to such murderous rage?

For much of today I have been sitting here wondering where everything went wrong, at which particular point I might have prevented the whole thing from happening. Was it at the start of the day, when Anna said she was hungry? Should I have simply given her something to eat? Should I have found her papers for her, even earlier than that; should I have calmly surveyed the room when I opened the door on the pillow fight and not lost my temper like I did?

My children have shown me to myself, at my best and at my very worst. They have revealed my fullest self, in all its failed entirety, myself writ large, or rather myself writ painfully small. Motherhood has forced me to cast my eye back towards my own childhood, to the day Ros and I were fighting so much our mother threatened to ring the children's home on our new telephone to ask them to come and pick us up. We continued to fight and it was only when she picked up the receiver that we flung ourselves hard at her feet.

Once I thought my mother was monstrously wicked for doing this, but if I'd had a telephone last night I would have picked it up and unhesitatingly pretended to summon the police.

I wonder why I have not been in the right frame of mind to practise spreading out everywhere the light of my knowledge. Right now Kyria Katerina feels like she will never practise anything again.

I am DESPERATE to get back to my book.


*Friday*

Soula is taking the girls for the night—she'll give them dinner and promises to take them all to the cove in the morning (that'll be a sight—I don't think Soula has walked further than the port since 1947!).

'Do I have to?' Anna wailed as soon as I told her.

'Yes,' I said, practically pushing her out the door.

'I don't like it at Soula's.'

'Why not?'

'I don't like Theo.'

'Oh, Anna, he's a perfectly nice little boy.'

'He tried to kiss me.'

I leaned over and ruffled her hair. 'He won't be the last, you know.'

She wrested her bag from my arms and stormed off down the lane.

I love her but the house is so blissfully peaceful without her. Right. Back to work.

*Sydney, 1969*

## Tuesday

David has just gone, the house is quiet; the girls have taken him to a publisher's party. 'Come on, Katherine, it'll be fun,' Anna said, 'you can bask in David's reflected glory.' I waved them off, pleading a headache, intending to write this before taking yet another long hot bath and heading off to my dreamless bed. The bath is my sanctuary.

Word is out that David's forthcoming book is marvellous, a certainty for every known literary prize. It is a sequel to that other triumphant book which made his name, that book of remembering which I once helped him to remember. On the rare occasion when I accompany him to a social event, strangers approach to tell him his book is a masterpiece, then they turn to me to say I have revolutionised the essay form. I am ashamed to say that I feel miserable whenever anyone compliments me on my column.

These days David is constantly being marched off to glamorous events, to meet actors and politicians, to have expensive lunches with literary editors; he is frequently asked to join the advisory boards of Australian cultural bodies. Because of my column I am sometimes asked to various things too—to speak at lunches for middle-class North Shore matrons, for example, who have never had to worry about money in their lives. Sometimes I feel like a terrorist within their midst and wish to depart from the script to tell them the real story. I have my fans, too, it seems; David says it is never done to insult one's fans, no matter how few.

At these events, during questions after my 'amusing' speech, I am frequently asked if I am flattered by my husband's literary portrayal of me as his muse, as an unearthly goddess whose beauty rivals that of the sun. I laugh modestly and hope they won't be too disappointed by my actual human form, by the jowls at my chin, by the film across my once extraordinary blazing eyes. If only David knew what an image he made of me which I can never live up to. I have begun to say no whenever I am asked to these events: I feel a strange embarrassment about my collapsing face, as if I were stepping out in public sporting a particularly ripe cold sore. And besides, appearing to be anything but flattered by David's portrayal would seem unattractive. Bitterness is the least appealing of emotions.

Everyone wants to know what I think of David's new book, how I feel about being portrayed as that fallen beauty who broke her poor husband's heart by having an affair. At least I assume that's how I'm portrayed—I still haven't read it. He keeps pushing it in front of me, where it remains unread on the table or my desk or wherever he has put it, like something crouching and menacingly alive.

How does anyone know what is in his book anyway, apart from the handful of people in his publisher's office who have read it?

I hate being the subject of gossip. I hate the way gossip is a form of Chinese whispers. I have trusted perhaps two or three people in my life, for the rest it is silence and cunning. Even Ros has heard campus gossip about his new book and asked if I'd read it: she can't believe I haven't. 'How can you stand not to?'

This from my sister who once accused me of betraying her trust for writing about a character who resembled her in my first novel. If I remember correctly, Ros said I had destroyed her life, embarrassed her in front of her friends, turned her into someone she wasn't. 'I was never that mean to you, Kath. Never!'

'Are you telling me that, or are you telling the character who you think is me? The character in the novel isn't me either, you know.'

She sneered. 'Oh, sure. You used dialogue that actually happened. Sentences I can remember saying.'

I recall arguing with her that fiction was not life transcribed, yet fiction unquestionably took life. 'Of course you were never as mean as that character in my book—and I was never as innocent or as put-upon. I made us both more interesting.

Characters in books walk around as if floodlit, Ros; you can see inside their heads like you never can in real life. Fictional characters are always meaner or crueller or more innocent—they are like figures in an allegory, far more radiant than anybody is in real life.'

She wasn't convinced. 'Whatever you think you made of me, I own the copyright to my life. Don't you think it's a question of who owns the story? Who says you have the right to use my sentences in the first place? God, the ego of writers! You think you own the whole bloody world.'

I told her I believed everyone owned the story, for all of us make it. She rolled her eyes, 'Yes, but don't you see that writers have an unfair advantage? Not everyone *can* write the story.' She went on to say that there was something morally corrupt at the heart of fiction: we argued long into the night. Of course, now I am terrified of what she will make of the Hebe character in *The Broken Book*. Might that be one of the reasons I can't finish it?

But right now it is my turn to sit on my hands while my husband ransacks his life and mine. David will chop me and gut me, fatten me up like the sweetest of fish. I will float up, newly rinsed. I will no longer be myself but will emerge transformed, for that is art's job. But how much is art worth?

I am but a single moment, the briefest of flickers. I can only hope that when I am gone, something of that flicker will endure in art's bright flame.

Why do I feel strangely exposed then, as if I was publicly naked? I know that his cruel mermaid is no longer me because

I, too, once made the sleekest of fish from the plainest of bones. I know that his cruel mermaid is not me, but the question is, will anybody else?

And where is my own bright book? For so long, through so many failed attempts, I tried to capture the experience of felt life in a net of meaning—some glimpse, some nuance that would reveal something at the heart of life, its mysterious core. But all my words have been stillborn things, too frail to support the great hopes I held for them. For so many years now I have begun a story, a novel, and then stopped. I have begun everything with the most radiant of hopes and been disappointed again and again—I have captured nothing. Everything has fallen short of my intentions. *The result, unhappily, was not correspondent with her efforts.* All the labouring of my fingertips has come to naught.

Surely now is the time to ask myself whether David's success has been bestowed because he is the better writer. I was only ever half good, a minor talent, while he has proved the real thing.

I am carrying in my pocket a handful of the poorest words, a writer of ash and air.

*Thursday*

Another tooth broke off this morning. The second in two months. Jagged pit in back of mouth. Tunnel to nothingness.

229

At night my hips ache, arthritis in the bone. I lie sleepless in my single bed between the twin peaks of pain, imagining the curved crest of each decaying hip bone, the fallow skin slung between.

The greed of the grave: so much human effort, following the wasted dead.

## Midnight

What does it matter that the world lacks one more book, that some book inside myself remains unwritten? The world will not cease to roll for lack of it, there will be no cold waiting hole in the fabric of the universe.

What value has my life had—have I been brave, kind, good? Should I have been more engaged in the public world instead of caught up in the vanity of believing I was making a testament to life through writing? Have I been generous enough to my husband, to my daughters, to my friends? It sometimes occurs to me that I should have tried harder to hold onto what was mine, that I loosened my grip too easily without a fight. I let something go when I shouldn't have, failed some test I didn't know was mine.

Strength is leaving me, all desire to pull myself to my feet. Darkness has descended, some shadow I spent too long trying to evade.

# The Island, Greece, 1964

An extraordinary night—dawn is breaking as I am writing this—have just now crept back into the house. I've been walking all night with Jerry Rothschild—we walked right down to the little bay on the other side of the island, where we swam in the phosphorous sea. Everything was rendered strange and magical: when I lifted my arm from the water light streamed from it as though I was some fork of heaven's lightning. We struck out for the open sea—surprisingly Jerry turned out to be as strong a swimmer as myself, he used to swim as a boy across cold lakes in Canada—my body fell into swimming's remembering, the hypnotic swing of arms and breath, the rise and fall of the sky and the stars. We finally stopped when we were a long way out and began to tread water: our feet cycled down upon the spinning sea, stars moving upon the surface all around us.

'You belong here,' Jerry said, 'this is your home.'

His voice is deep and sonorous as if it dwells further inside him than other men's. I floated on my back and looked up at the extravagant full moon.

'I hope you mean the island and not the sea. I'm tired of being mistaken for a mermaid.'

He laughed, a sound rendered impossibly loud amidst the quiet murmur of the Greek sea. 'I mean the island, madam. You belong here.'

'Do I? I wonder if any of us do. I feel like I belong here but I doubt if Soula thinks so. Or even the island itself.'

'The island loves you. The rocks. The stones. *Thalasa.*'

From my throat came a dark and bitter laugh. 'Is that remark meant as irony?' He asked what I meant; I told him that after almost ten years David and I had finally decided to go back to Australia.

'Why?' he said but I didn't answer him, diving deep instead into the waiting arms of the sea. When I came up he had already started back for shore.

When we arose dripping from the water, light streamed from us, turning us into temporary gods. 'This place makes you feel like Zeus,' he said, handing me my dress. 'Your clothes, Aphrodite. How can you bear to leave? Anything else will seem a half-life after this. It isn't an easy life here but it is a vital one.'

I was slipping my dress over my head while he spoke, suddenly conscious of my nakedness. In the gleam of the moonlight I thought my body looked strong and whole, I felt again the power of my limbs. For a broken statue I felt amazingly restored.

'Italy is beautiful, and France too,' Jerry said, 'but neither have the tragic majesty of Greece.'

I looked at him. 'I know. Here you are aware of being in the cradle of creation. A place of legends.'

Behind us the mountains were black and still; I could just make out a monastery clinging to the end of a bony promontory. The silence was broken occasionally by the distant clink of goat bells, the cries of unknown birds.

In the strange luminous silence that earth was revealed as immortal, I imagined I felt the breath of the divine. For a brief moment it seemed possible to perceive the outline of existence, humanity's arc of birth, fruition, decay. We stood without speaking, rendered sober by the earth's air and the salt of its sea.

I was only with Jerry at all tonight because I made the mistake of dancing with Peter (the homosexual painter from Sydney). We were at the little *kafenion* at the cove; there was a wedding party, *lyra*, bouzouki, dancing. I begged David to dance with me but he wouldn't.

'I do *not* want to dance with you, Katherine! I do not want to dance with a drunk woman with smudged lipstick making a fool of herself.'

'I'm not drunk. I'm enjoying myself. Come on, dance with me. Please?'

He leaned across the table and put his head close to mine. 'You are embarrassing me. Stop acting like a fifteen-year-old slut.'

Anger rushed at my throat. 'At least I haven't been sitting there all night like a bloody corpse!'

For a moment I thought he was going to hit me. Instead he rose from the table and promptly left. Stephanie, who was sharing our table, politely looked away but Jerry Rothschild looked me full in the face.

'Is he always like that?' Jerry said.

'Not always,' I said, 'he's having a bit of a hard time. You'll have to excuse him. Anyway, I probably am embarrassing.' I sat there, mortified by my stupid behaviour.

He looked hard at me. 'Do you always defend him?'

'Yes,' I said, 'as a matter of fact I do.'

He said nothing, but went on looking at me. Jerry Rothschild is handsome in a faded, effortless way; he has what I think of as Jewish good looks—a Roman nose, brown eyes, a curly, intelligent mouth. He has dark, tightly sprung corkscrew hair, greying at the temples, and looks vaguely Italian. ('I'm a Rothschild,' he says by way of introduction, 'from the poor side of the family.') He is tanned, sexy, confident with the ladies—in short, exactly the kind of man of whom I generally disapprove—too sure of himself, too proud of his reputation as a *roué*. Apparently the only thing he takes seriously is his work: he has already published two well-received volumes of poetry and is hard at work on another.

'What are you frightened of, baby? Your old man? Or being alone?' he asked.

I let the 'baby' pass; it was late, it was true that I had probably had too much to drink. 'Oh, Jerry. What business is it of yours?'

'I dig you, Kate, I really do,' he said.

I laughed. 'Oh, please. You make me sound like a garden.'

'A beautiful garden,' he said, placing his hand over mine. He picked up my hand, raised it to his mouth and kissed it.

'I am a married woman,' I said, snatching my hand back.

'Spoken like a true professional,' he said, leaning forward to kiss me. His mouth felt odd, strangely shaped; it felt like my first kiss.

I tried to break away but I felt myself falling towards him, my nipples swelling. I was kissing him but trying not to; I suddenly felt fully awake, fully aroused.

'Come for a walk,' he said, pulling me up from the table. 'I promise to behave like a gentleman.'

I followed him out blindly, without thinking at all of where I was going. I *was* pretty drunk actually, drunk enough to be past caring.

It was only when we were outside in the air, in the night smells of the island, that I properly awoke. He was walking back towards the harbour, no doubt towards the tiny whitewashed house above the church he has rented for the past year, next to Pan and Rita's.

'I can't go home with you,' I said, stopping.

'I know. We're going for a walk.' He continued up the path, turning off to take the narrow trail that led up and over the hills.

'It's at least five miles this way,' I said, following him.

'We can swim at the bottom,' he said.

I was already cradled in alcohol's sweet forgetting so I kept walking, turning up my head to that full and bony moon. I felt again the island's mysteries, I felt my drunken soul begin to grow.

We walked and walked, mostly in silence, until we came to the swimming cove. Jerry stripped off and dived straight in; I hesitated only briefly and then followed.

The walk and the sea and the moonlight have completely sobered me. Sitting here writing this in the soft pink dawn of the morning I am claiming a moment's happiness before I turn back into a mother and a wife.

# The Broken Book

*All Angels Mother and Baby Home.*
*Lauriston Road, Scone, New South Wales (Tel Scone 141).*
*Before and After Care Home. Accommodation: 24 mothers*
*and 12 babies. Length of stay: 6 weeks before, 6 weeks after*
*confinement. Age of mother: 15 years and over. First pregnancies*
*only. Extra-marital cases considered. Controlling body: Scone*
*Moral Welfare Association. Application to: The Matron.*


*Is this not the place of cream teas then? The place of pretty*
*thin cups and slices of lemon and whipped fluffy cream balancing*
*on scones? Is this the other scone, the capital S Scone, the finest*
*place in the whole of New South Wales for morals? Citizens of*
*Scone, be on the alert: loose women are walking the upstanding*
*streets of your town!*
*At least this one is, the one with the uncurled hair and the*

swollen belly, me, Cressida Morley, Clever Clogs. Yes, me, on a rare afternoon out, two weeks to go and still counting. Is that a twitching curtain I see before me? Or is it my imagination that allows me to suppose more righteous eyes than mine have looked upon me and found me sadly wanting? Perhaps it is my own shame which allows me to suppose people are exchanging covert glances as I pass, whispering to each other, 'Look, there goes another one.'

I am learning to walk with my head down, looking up only when I must. Is that a car coming? Shall I cross the road anyway without looking? Sometimes I do this, make a vow with myself: I am going to cross the road without looking and if a car happens to come, So Be It. It is a kind of dare, a challenge to God, a test to see whether I am alive or not. I suppose I must be: I eat, I walk, I am a kind of ship, a cargo ship who used to be a girl. I am alive because the cargo I carry is alive too, a twisting, nervy, elbowing presence beneath the engine of my heart. 'You're doing very well,' the doctor said this morning, listening to the cargo hold, a cold trumpet against my warm skin. 'All this will be like a bad dream one day,' he said kindly, patting my arm. 'Now get up, there's a good girl.' Doesn't the kind doctor know that bad dreams end with the coming of the morning? Doesn't he know that every morning when the light comes into the sky I am still here?

I am still here, alone in my bed, alone in the room with those other four ships. All of us have turned our faces to the wall except for the other Cressida, the other girl who shares *my name. The other Cressida is trying to pretend we are on some jolly lark, that life hasn't stuck out its malicious foot to trip us. She is resolute in her black humour, always cracking jokes despite the fact that none of us finds being alive particularly funny. 'Oh, come on, we're not dead yet,' she will say with a gimlet smile, 'don't let the bastards get you.'*

*O, but I am dead, you see, that former girl of teeming stone is gone and in her place is fossilised rock. I am nerveless and bloodless, I will never cry again, I am renouncing happiness forever. There is a fossil where once there was flesh, there is the shape of my former self recognisable in the rock. But do not mistake me for a living thing, do not mistake me for a beating heart.*

*I am gone, away, look, there in the rock is a net of bones, a veil of finest carving. Tooth, fingernail, bone, the pearly shells of my once fine ears. Silvery, frail, fleeting as a shadow, the faintest mist of my former breathing life.*


*The life of a once-teeming girl, the new life of the rock. Your job will be to make tea for the staff, to help with the washing of dozens of sheets, the pegging out of nappies, the sweeping of floors. Your job will be to get down on your knees and polish the new linoleum. Sore back? Should have thought of that before, my girl. Your job will be to keep away from the nursery where all the new babies are kept before they are given away. A new baby anyone? Only one previous careful lady owner! Your job* will be to block your ears in the night from the new babies mewling, to stop yourself being so surprised that the crying does not all sound the same. One cries like a kitten, a scratchy mewl; one bellows as if he were cross. Your job will be to make your face as impassive as a piece of cloth, as bland as a row of regulation white nappies. Your job will be to look away when you stumble across a former girl crying on her knees, and to drink up your milk to help your baby's growing bones. Your job will be to smile when your mother Dorothy Morley and your sister Hebe Morley come to visit you, just the once. 'You're a good brave girl,' your mother will say, patting your hand. The kind doctor said that! Or a variation on that theme: what a good, kind girl I must be! Then why do I believe myself to be in exile from all decent citizens? Why do I believe that if I took myself back to the streets of the Blowhole my mother would drop dead of shame?

Cressida, it is about time you understood that there are two worlds: the public and the private. The public world is the important one, missy, the only one that really matters. (You know, the one that organised the current war, the one that men run.) This is the world with the rules you must follow, the true world that decides what is important. Girls and their love affairs are not important matters of state; girlish first person narratives are not what the public world wants. The public want heroes, men of history and action, real men on which to hang a proper myth.

Cressida, you are the embarrassingly small private world

*of need and ache and want. Put yourself away, cover yourself. Can't you see that everyone else in the public world is modestly dressed?*

*Here it comes, the shore, the docks, the creak of the pier. Here comes the disembarking, the unloading, the frenetic activity down below. 'Matron! Matron!' I will find myself crying. 'Oh, Matron, please come!' And she will come with her torch and her no-nonsense-please voice to shine her light upon the sheets which are wet. 'It's only your show, nothing to cry about,' she will say, helping me to my feet. I cannot stand. I cannot heave myself up. I am doubled over, my hands on my knees, God's fist pushing up and up, that mighty cruel fist shoving and shoving. 'Come on, Cressida, surely you can make it to the door?' the matron will say and I will sob, 'I can't! I can't!' She will press a bell and another sister will come and go away again to fetch a wheelchair. I have lost my legs, my wits, my courage, I am a stupid girl having a baby in a stupid bloody country town called Scone. I am the one who was in labour on and off all day, not bloody on enough to be taken into the delivery room to relieve me of my burdensome cargo. I am the one who was told to keep doing my chores, that it would make the baby come faster.*

*I am the one who was pouring tea only this morning for a squadron of good Christian ladies. 'Sugar?' I was asking, offering the tray while Matron said, 'Labour tends to be more distressing and more prolonged in the unmarried.' The ladies of the Scone*

Moral Welfare Association gravely nodded their heads and not one of them even glanced at me.

My labour is distressing, it is, you were right; by which law must it also be prolonged? Does my uterus know I am unmarried, is this God's way of showing me who's boss? I am being wheeled, crying, into the delivery room while the fist of God works in mysterious ways. I am all alone in a high white bed, left alone for hours and hours; I am shaved, scrubbed, penance for my sins, sackcloth and ashes. Ampay, where are you now? Hebe, please, can't you come; Mummy, can't you come to hold my hand and make the pain flee? Man of visions, how could you do this? Whose pain is this, this pain like a fist, straight up my soft centre, shoving up, not stopping, coming at me again and again? Which former teeming girl is this trying to crawl out of her own burning skin?

Why, this is your punishment, Cressida, dirty girl who lets men touch you down below. No escape for you, just pain and the white empty room; Matron coming in every now and then, a young sister sitting sometimes reading in a chair. You mean to ask what it is she is reading but somehow you will never get the chance. Pain is in the room, pain is stalking you, pain is who you are and you will ever be.

And then the doctor will arrive and your baby will unexpectedly slither out from between your legs like a wrongly delivered parcel. That reading sister will have put down her book and with one hand she will attempt to cover your face. Sister, are you trying to stop my tears, or to cover my witnessing eyes? 'Stop it! Stop it!' I will cry, becoming hysterical. 'Let me see the baby!' And the doctor will be visited by a moment's mercy and lift her up, life afloat, a misshapen fruit, scaly, dark, with the exact face of her father. Her sex, pink and swollen, little plum, the skin on her face and body peeling strangely as if she has been too long in the sun. 'A bit overcooked,' the kind doctor will say, wrapping her up.

Overcooked, my body her oven. Who is she and how did she get here? I don't know who she is anyway. She looks too cross, too mean, she does not look like I expected her to look. What did I expect? A little Cressida, myself anew, a bright new teeming block? O, Clever Clogs: a baby girl, who looks exactly like her betraying father. Clearly he has cleverly betrayed you again, delivering to you this fresh reminder of his once-loved face.


Should the unmarried mother who is about to give up her child breastfeed or not? This has long been a problem for all moral married women of good character and in the good town of Scone opinion even now is divided. For the moment it is the bottle, at once. No contact with the baby, cabbage leaves for all those rock-hard grieving bosoms!

So I will lie in bed, a cabbage leaf over each fallen breast. My breasts are aching, engorged with milk, no mouth in which to gush. Whose turn on the breast pump, to cream some of the milk off, but not too much to encourage breasts to refill? Go on, Cressida, pump away, get that sorry wrist working. Do not look up if groups of good Christian ladies come to walk through the wards, making sure that everything is running smoothly.

Look, that other dirty girl also called Cressida is smoking in bed. Her baby was born last week and Cressida already wants to go home, but not before telling me she could not be bothered to ask the doctor if her baby was a boy or a girl. Smoking in bed! The good Christian ladies who happen to be passing cannot believe their eyes. Cressida blissfully fulfils all their notions of a wayward girl—her mouth is slutishly lipsticked, her hair curled and impossibly blonded, her nails long and outrageously painted. Look, she is sitting on the bed, cool as a cucumber, staring back at them.

'Cigarette, sweetheart?' she will ask one of the ladies in the doorway, offering up her silver cigarette case. The ladies will run, skedaddle, all of them, trotting fast to Matron as quickly as their little legs will carry them.

There is only Cressida and myself left in the room and both of us are silently waiting for the mighty squall of Matron.

I happen to know that Cressida is only sixteen, although she looks at least twenty. I happen to know that she last worked as an usherette like me, that she comes from a family of factory workers in Newtown. I happen to know that she cries in the night when she thinks every witness is asleep.

I am the witness who knows that last night she snuck out to the nursery even though she told me she didn't care if her baby lived or died. I am the witness who knows this fact because I snuck out trying to see mine.

'Cigarette?' she will ask hopefully and I will shakily stand up, holding my cabbage leaves under my nightie, and stagger over to her bed. I will take a cigarette and sit down on the bed where we will wait together for Matron to come. Matron, do not forget that we are at war! The two Cressidas and all the rest, us empty ships, each one of us representing a private war-damaged country.

My disappearing daughter has a name but I have made a secret vow never to tell it.

*Sydney, 1943*

## Sunday

Haven't written anything for a long, long time—haven't felt like it really. It was my birthday yesterday—I'm now twenty years old. Just think, when I am twenty-one I will hold the keys to the door.

I'm not going to have a twenty-first party, I've already decided.

## Tuesday

Ros says I've been staying with her long enough. 'It's time you faced the world again, Kath.' She was with me this afternoon when a passing soldier gave me a long appreciative whistle— she had to hold me back from punching him in the face. 'Kathy, ignore him!' she said, tugging at my wrist when I wheeled around to face him. 'I suppose you think that's a compliment,' I shouted into his startled eyes. 'I'm not a dog, you know!'

'Come on, Katherine,' she said, 'let's go.'

When we got home she made me a cup of tea and I burst into tears. 'Oh, come on, Kathy, *please* cheer up!'

I glared at her. 'You only want me to cheer up so you'll feel better,' I said, knowing I was being mean. I have been staying here ever since I left Mum and Dad's two months ago—I knew that if I had to stay in Kurrajong Bay for one second longer I would kill myself. One morning I actually went to the beach and considered it. I am very good at holding my breath and I saw myself swimming further out and further out, beyond the breakers, swimming on and on until I got so tired I would sink.

'Listen, Kathy, I know you've had a terrible time,' Ros said, putting her hand over mine, 'but it seems to me the time has come to make some sort of decision. It's been almost a year now. Are you going to let this ruin your life or are you going to try living again?'

I looked at her; I was waiting for something. 'You *will* find someone else to love, you know, you *will* find someone who deserves you. You've just had the most incredible bad luck.'

I thought: that's one way of putting it.

'Look at you! You're the most gorgeous girl in town! You're beautiful and clever and everyone loves you. Oh, Kathy, if you only knew how jealous you make people feel. I've been jealous of you from the moment I first laid eyes on you.'

She looked so earnest and pleading that I smiled. Actually,

I began to laugh. 'But I've always been jealous of *you*! You're the one who's beautiful and smart, much smarter than me!'

She started to laugh too. 'The Elgin sisters mutual admiration society. Look at us.' We were sitting at the table, laughing and crying, our fingers laced.

'I'm your biggest fan,' she said, 'and if I ever lay eyes on Ken Howard again I'll kill him.'

I couldn't stop laughing. 'Oh, that would really top it off for Mum and Dad. I can just see the headlines. AVENGING SISTER GETS LIFE FOR MURDER.'

We sat at the table for a long time. At some point Ros started talking about having a party, my own personal Facing-The-World-Again party. I sat there, a smile on my face, but really in the privacy of my head I am still swimming out to sea.

## Sunday

It's five o'clock in the afternoon and I am in bed. I couldn't open my eyes until midday, and I have been sick twice, my poor stomach trying to relieve itself of the gallons of alcohol I poured into it last night. I can hear Ros and the clink of bottles, the sweeping up of broken glass. She has just brought me a raw egg beaten up in tomato juice which is her hangover cure. 'God, it smells like a brewery in here,' she said, flinging open the window. Anyway, I feel a bit better now, well enough to write this anyway.

*Everyone* we know in the whole world was here last night,

*everyone.* (With one obvious exception.) Even Atpay was here, on leave from Far North Queensland, looking very soldierly and professional, straight off the train. Ruth Parker was here, and all these other girls I hadn't seen for ages from Kurrajong Bay, and Beryl and Ray and Clem and Jack and Bernie, and Ros even managed to track down Val, who brought her new girlfriend. I don't know if Val has heard anything or not but she was her usual warm, kind self, and her girlfriend is a knock-out, a Rita Hayworth lookalike who spent the entire night fending off the unwanted attention of the blokes. 'I like girls, darling,' she would say sexily, which only seemed to spur them on. Ray followed her like a puppy all night.

I couldn't bear anyone knowing what has happened, *I could not bear it.* Surely Val doesn't know?

It was great to see Beryl again, she said she'd wondered if she'd offended me, disappearing as I did without even saying goodbye. 'Everything all right?' she asked, her eyes looking sharp. I looked away as if the traces of pain might be upon my face like a telltale ash. 'Oh, you know. . . Ken . . .' I managed before my mouth started to wobble.

'I thought as much,' she said, looking for somewhere to put down her drink, about to give me a hug. I reared back from her, stiff, my palms sweating; my looming tears fled, my mouth turned into a smile. 'Beryl, I'm *fine*! I'm perfectly fine! You always said he was dangerous. What are you doing, anyway?'

I cannot stand the thought of anyone pitying me. I will not be pitied, I will not be the girl for whom everything went wrong.

It is embarrassing, being seen as weak and hopeless and fallible, being known as the kind of girl who is useless about life and men. I will not stand and be pitied for my tragedy: *I will never ever let anybody know.* I am going to sew up my past and put it in a sack. I am already making the finest stitch, so fine no eye will be able to detect there once was a visible rip.

## Thursday

I've just come back from an evening on the tiles with Ray, a bit drunk as I write this. He wants to go to bed with me. 'Oh, come on, Kathy, you must have known I've wanted to from the moment we met.' I got really cross with him. 'I thought we were friends, Ray. Why do bloody men ruin everything?' I stormed off and he ran after me. 'Why are you acting all insulted? It's a compliment, Kathy.' Everyone was looking at us but I didn't care. 'It's not a compliment. Don't you understand?' He was trying to stop me walking, standing in front of me, tripping me up. Eventually I had to stop because he kept falling over. I started to laugh and we both sat down in the doorway of a shop which was boarded up. 'It's not a bloody compliment, you know,' I said when I stopped laughing. 'You're thinking of yourself, not me.' He took my hand. 'I think you're the most beautiful girl I have ever seen,' he said, 'beautiful as a princess, more beautiful than the starriest night sky.'

I started to cry. What's the use? What's the bloody bloody use?

*Wednesday*

I'm going to join up. Two days ago I ran into Pat unexpectedly at Central Station.

'Where are you off to?' she asked and I started to cry again. She shooed everybody away and we sat down on a stack of bags while I wept.

'Oh, Athykay,' she said after a while, 'I know something awful's happened. If you ever want to talk about it, you know I'm your best friend in the whole world.'

I attempted a smile; she squeezed my hand.

'But if you don't want to talk about it that's all right too. Rulytay.'

I managed to laugh.

At that moment I decided to join up. Atpay came to the recruitment office with me.

I'm moving into barracks tomorrow.

# The Broken Book

*Cressida Morley off to war, a girl at war finally in uniform.*
*That hat! Worn just so, at the perfect jaunty angle: eyes right,*
*Gunner Morley, forward march. Practise throwing yourself*
*upon the ground, practise lining up the enemy in your rifle*
*sights. Learn to tell which way is up, how to operate the ham*
*radio, how to read the map. Learn to like living with a squadron*
*of girls, dormitory style. Breakfast. Everybody out.*

*It will be your sister Hebe who will suggest the Australian*
*Women's Army Service, for aren't you already a woman at*
*war? Hebe knows you for what you are, she recognises a bombed*
*woman when she sees one. Hebe will pass a recruitment poster*
*in the hall at the university where she works pruning young*
*minds. 'You've got nothing to lose, Cress. Why not?'*

*Why not indeed? You have already knitted a small white*
*cardigan for your lost daughter, taken the overnight train to*
*Scone and walked from the station to Matron's door. 'It's a*

birthday present,' you will say and Matron will smile kindly. 'Will you make sure she gets it please?' When you have gone Matron will add it to the pile of other gifts delivered or sent by former girls who do not know or perhaps have forgotten that all contact between mothers and their relinquished babies ceases on adoption. All the cardigans and dresses and bonnets and bracelets will be collected to be taken to a charity.

Not much to live for? No comfort in tears? Roll up, join the war effort, join the millions of men and women all over the world having their lives shaken. Join the comfortless tears of old women in Poland; the mother of young Sid Becker of Mareeba, Far North Queensland, who has just heard her son is dead. Join those three brothers far away in Germany, believing themselves to be walking to freedom through the snow. One will die, one will eventually find himself in Israel, one will find himself alive in America. Look! Their tears are joined, a human sea, from the smallest tear of that former girl Cressida Morley to the largest tears of entire peoples and nations. Which of us is wise enough to measure the sorrow in a single tear? Is this particular tear more bitter than that one? Where are the scales on which to weigh the grief of a bad marriage versus the pain of losing an arm in war? The giving up of a child versus the loss of a brother? Our sorrows are private, yet all our sorrows flow towards the one human sea. Let none of us judge another's sorrow, let none of us attempt to weigh the pain of another human heart. Too dark the light that is shed there, too dark to read the mark upon sorrow's scales.

*In darkness, then, make your sign upon the paper, sign your name upon the printed page. Cressida Morley, former teeming girl, now officially of the AWAS, one of our dear, brave girls. We promise not to ship you off to the fields of war yet, at least not if we can help it. It is men who must steel themselves not to tremble when faced with a command to run towards other men armed with knives and guns. The weapons aimed at you will be harder to see.*

*Up at five! Peel those potatoes, clean those latrines! What shall we do with you, a strong young woman with no visible defects, perfect eyesight and quick reflexes? Can you type? Can you keep a secret?*

*You shall join all those other gunners at the gun site guarding the harbour then, you shall learn to man the guns at dawn, to stand guard with your fixed bayonet at night when the moon is full and all the Southern Hemisphere's stars are fixed too, unfathomable as the deepest space in which the planets are suspended. You shall learn to watch the night water, to write a poem in the thinnest night air. Does a poem exist if it is written in air instead of pencil?*

*You will grow to love army life, the jostling of your thoughts, the busy minutes and hours which do not allow you the privacy in which to be sad. It is hard to be sad in public, hard to look inward when your eyes are being trained to look out. Man the view-finder, Gunner Morley! Quick! Fall out!*

*Oh dear, here is your uniform:*

*1 pair trousers*
*1 green pullover*
*2 shirts*
*1 tie*
*3 pairs socks*
*1 pair boots*
*1 greatcoat*
*1 hat*

*Khaki breeches do not make for glamour, do they, but on you they look divine. On you, men's eyes will still turn to look; on you, all male soldiers in the vicinity will still know how to whistle. So many soldiers, so many men.*

*Now is the time to sing the strumpet song, time to declare yourself queen of the kingdom of men, empress of all you survey. Now is the moment you will come into possession of your fullest powers and learn the ancient song of women who have ruled the world of men, of women who have divided and conquered. Wield your beauty like a knife! Slice through those soldiers! You are the queen of American men, Australian men, Canadians, English men, young and old. You are the owner of something they want, the body incarnate. On leave from the army you will dance with handsome American airmen on polished sprung floors, drink cocktails with indistinguishable numbers of Australian soldiers in khaki. One man will slip you his telephone number at the railway station while your companion for the* night isn't looking; another soldier will come up to your table at the jazz club while your partner is in the toilet. 'You must have dinner with me. Promise?' And he will push into your hand a note with his name and address. Cressida, you had no idea you had it in you.

Do you sleep with any of them? Do you bestow on any of them your magnificent favours? So many men, so many penises: thick squat ones with little hats, thin bowed ones, pointed ones, incy-wincy ones no bigger than a pencil. Penises, arise! All of them aimed at your softest centre, just like your mother supposed. Blush for shame, how many did you say? At ten you stopped telling, at twenty you grew tired of those repetitive voices saying how beautiful you were, how much they wanted to kiss you, sleep with you, marry you. What is it that you get from these penises? Love? Attention? Promiscuity's saddest hope that causing a penis to rise in homage must therefore afford you some value? The fleeting triumph of having some nameless man choose you? What hollow triumph, what failure of self. Surely that is not a sorrowful tear still hoping for the true man to come along to see the true you? Surely you are not still dreaming of salvation?

Cressida, how long before you stop counting? How long till the day arrives when you sleep with two men in one day? The one you went home to bed with, the one you will meet a few hours later for lunch. Your ovaries are protected by a tight rubber cap now, snug against the entrance to your womb. Such a watery trickle still from the river of men.

Walking down the street you think: I have slept with two

*men in one day. You scan the passing faces to see if anyone can tell, if the river of men has left some visible trace upon you. But the flush of triumph is withering fast, turning into a feeling of cold, hard pain. How to staunch the flow of sadness that has been inadvertently released, how to crawl somewhere warm and safe, somewhere noble and clean?*

*It is upon waking the next day that you remember the warmth of the book. It is upon waking that you become the girl in the story who says, 'Every morning is the same. I place my feet upon the floor. I walk to the bathroom, wash my face, look at myself in the glass.*

*'I want to be the girl who sees the world, who marries the right man, who wakes each morning to something new and exciting. I want to be the girl who dared to dream, who flew so high she felt the breath of angels.'*

*It is then that you remember a book is a house with walls and a door, which only you can open. You remember you can go into this book and lock the door and no matter how hard or long anyone knocks, you are the only one who has the key. 'I know!' you cry. 'My book will be my boat, my wings. My book will be the engine of my hopes!'*

*My name is Cressida Morley and when I am twenty-three years old I will begin the long and arduous business of writing myself into existence. In writing my first poems, my first stories, I will begin to write the story of myself.*

*I am that former teeming girl who feels herself to have burst from the carapace, who through building the words of the story remembers the pleasures of the physical world: the hard white chop of teeth into steak, the thrust of an iris in spring, the push and shove of a baby's head rending me open. In the book my eyes can bear to remember the swivel of her head upon her new neck, the grief which is like a throb beneath my skin. In the book I see again her velvet, boneless feet; the tiny triangle of her upturned face. I see that she was little more than a puff of cloud upon the pillow, only hours alive to the air. In the broken book of life my disappearing girl is here again, right here under my heart.*

# The Island, Greece, 1964

## Midnight

I suppose I should feel furtive, or guilty; instead I feel the most insane sense of liberation. How did I ever suppose I could never sleep with another man? It felt like the most natural thing in the world.

When we were girls Pat and I used to wonder what it would be like being pregnant; we couldn't imagine what it would be like having a baby inside you. We supposed it would feel alien, unnatural even. When I did get pregnant, I couldn't get over how known it felt, almost like a bodily memory.

Sleeping with Jerry is like that. It's exciting and rough and tender and charged but it also feels fine, entirely within the realm of the known. (Of course there was the initial shock of everything being different—his skin, his mouth, his smell, the whole shape of him—but I soon got over that.) Whoever would have guessed? So light-hearted, so free of angst, the complete and utter opposite of being with David. I was reminded of what being happy feels like; it's a holiday from life.

Now I am wondering about other things I thought I could never do, other crimes I am capable of committing. I fear I am capable of anything.

I am relieved, too, that Jerry doesn't appear to be taking it seriously. I don't need undying declarations of love; I am too old to want to claim another scalp.

'I'm not going to ask you to leave your husband,' he said afterwards, when we were smoking cigarettes on the balcony.

'I am mortally offended,' I said. 'It's the least you can do.'

'I just want to fuck you,' he said, pulling me towards him and kissing me softly on the mouth.

In the morning we sat around drinking coffee laced with Mataxa while he read his poems. They are pretty good. He has a kind of secondary career as a folk singer (he plays guitar) and my hunch is that is where his real talent lies. His songs, delivered in that extraordinarily deep and resonant voice, were outstanding.

I finally walked home late this evening, so I've got time to clean up the house and prepare some food before David and the girls get back from Athens in the morning. They've got another three dental appointments after this, which doesn't allow much time to conduct the rest of my love affair.

It's going to be short and sweet, a romance rather than a marriage. How nice to feel strong on my feet again, my eyes clear, seeing everything for exactly what it is. I like talking to Jerry and he enjoys being with me.

How lonely I have been.

I don't even want to think about David.

## Monday

It is surprisingly easy to lie. 'Lie' is perhaps the wrong word; it is easy, rather, to evade subjects, to deceive by omission. I haven't told David anything that is untrue; I have simply left things unsaid. We live with the unspoken: there are entire continents to which we do not go.

I spent the morning with Jerry swimming at the cove. When I came back at lunchtime, David asked whether I had enjoyed myself. It was no lie to answer yes.

We've been together only one other time since David's return; a hasty coupling against the rocks one night on the way back from a dance. David was asleep when I got in: I slipped into bed beside him, and lay sleepless until dawn.

## Saturday

Today the house is silent. The girls have absented themselves, sensing pain; at midday, David is still in bed and I have only just got up. I have a small, egg-shaped lump on the back of my head, painful only if I press against it. There is a terrible calmness in the air.

I can't believe it was me who suggested a drink on the waterfront last night. We've been trying to avoid that malicious evening gathering for months; it was doing us more harm than good, drinking with those childless Peter Pans every night, those untested geniuses who could prove their genius at one stroke if only they could finish their novels or their paintings or their poems. They all believe that if they had the time or the money or the right circumstances they would produce a masterpiece. A bestselling masterpiece, too.

It was me who suggested we go. I've been feeling increasingly desperate, hemmed in, and the thought of other people, *any* other people, seemed preferable to spending another night alone with David. He's been working feverishly, only stopping at sundown to begin serious drinking. For weeks we've been locked together in speechless misery, sitting on the roof each night before catatonically falling into bed. I needed air, comfort; also, I suppose I was hoping to get a quick chance to talk to Jerry.

'Come on, let's go down to Pan's,' I said. 'We can have one drink and leave if we don't like it.' For a moment I longed for London, for any big city with anonymous faces and crowds and endless choices.

We threaded our way through the dark lanes, past the dimly lit houses. We paused a moment outside the little church where Lil was baptised; the sound of chanting rose up from inside, a full-throated yearning for God. The moon was full and I felt again the strangeness of existence, the absence of answers.

'Do you ever wonder what we're doing here?' I asked David, not looking at him.

'I think about it every day. I wonder who I am, and what I'm doing. But most of all I wonder about you.'

I looked at him; he held my eyes fast.

I glanced away.

I should have known the signs were ominous. David only ever seems to notice me when he senses some part of me is withdrawing.


Everybody was there: Christophe, the dapper little painter who claims to have dined with Satre at the Flore and the Deux Magots, Stephanie and her sister Mathilde who is visiting from France, assorted American and English would-be writers and poets, and, of course, Jerry. He gave me a wink as I sat down in a chair I judged to be far enough away from him.

'Attention everyone, Mr and Mrs David Murray have arrived. To what do we owe this unexpected honour?' It was Harry, the smart-arsed ex-public school boy who claims to have had an affair with Auden. Everybody looked up for a moment.

'We thought we would grant you the pleasure of our company,' said David. 'You may need an example of erudition.'

Harry snorted. 'And how is The Great Australian Novel going?'

'It's going,' replied David. 'How about your poems?'

'I should have a collection finished by the end of summer. I think the best publisher for them will be Faber.'

'Katherine's first book was published by Faber,' David said. 'You might like to talk to her.'

Harry looked at me with scant interest. 'Your books are long out of print I hear. I imagine you have a stack of first editions mouldering away in some cupboard.'

Jerry unexpectedly let out a laugh. 'You'll be lucky if you get into print, Harry. Your poems are execrable.'

Harry gave him a contemptuous look; by now the attention of the rest of the table was elsewhere. 'And of course the world is absolutely littered with top-class poets from Canada,' Harry said.

'Why don't you go home and polish up your masterpiece, man? You don't want to waste precious time.' Jerry lifted his glass to him.

'And you don't want to waste time making eyes at Mrs Murray. Mr Murray wouldn't like it.'

I gave a weak laugh and was careful not to look at David. There were other conversations going on; I wasn't sure if he had heard; besides, he knew as well as me the malicious nature of island gossip. Half of what you heard was untrue, the other half was ridiculously embroidered.

Nonetheless, I was careful not to speak to Jerry. I spent the rest of the evening talking to Christophe, who gave me a long lecture on the nature of the artist. 'The artist must live for himself alone,' he announced. 'His art must be his entire life.

Look at Proust, Flaubert, Stendhal—solitaries, every one. The true artist must never form attachments.'

I thought of Tolstoy and Picasso and Hemingway—men whose lives were littered with children and wives—but suddenly found myself too tired to argue.

At some point I looked across at David. He was sitting there, not speaking, watching me closely.


When we got home, it started. Why was I flaunting myself again; why was I so susceptible to calculated flattery; what hollowness was at the heart of me that I needed to debase myself in such a way?

'Debase myself?' I shouted. 'Listen to yourself! You sound like a puritan.'

'And you sound like a woman with no shame.'

I stepped closer to him, speaking into his face. 'I've done nothing to be ashamed of,' I said calmly. 'Have you?'

'I've always told you everything,' he said. 'I told you straight-away about Evelyn. My life is an open bloody book.' He gave me a little push so that I stumbled backwards against the wall. He stepped closer.

'You keep everything secret. What other dirty little things don't I know about, Katherine? How many men have there been? Ten? Twenty? Fifty? Of course, you started young, didn't you? You had a head start.'

He was shouting hard into my face; I pushed him away. 'What's that supposed to mean?'

'You got your degree in men. It's your *métier*.'

'How dare you! I haven't looked at another man since I met you.'

'You were too tired from the legions you'd already had. Besides, I didn't say anything about looking, darling. You're cleverer than that. Secrecy's your thing, isn't it, covering your tracks.'

His voice was low now, snarling with contempt. I started to cry, in helplessness and despair. 'You've always excelled at crying, too. Tell me, do you ever cry when no one is watching?'

He still had me pinned to the wall. 'Does your boyfriend know your dirty secrets? Does Jerry know?'

Instinctively, I shoved hard against his chest. 'All right! All right! I did sleep with Jerry. He was kinder to me than you could ever be.'

He pushed me violently against the wall; my head gave a sharp crack against the stone. His teeth were bared like a dog's; for a split second I feared for my life. Then, without warning, he suddenly let me go; both of us sank to the ground.

He collapsed in my arms, his shoulders heaving. When at last he stopped, we sat wrapped around each other on the cold floor. In the dark, we held each other for a long time; from somewhere I heard the sound of a cock crowing, the creak of a bed. My limbs were aching; I was growing cold, but I dared not move. We sat there, wrapped around each other for an hour, more; at last, very quietly, I began to speak.

'It's you I love,' I said, speaking into the top of his head. 'No one but you.'

'If only that was enough,' he said. 'You won't let me in, Kate. After all these years, you still won't let me in. Your heart is a secret. What are you frightened of?'

I didn't answer. How can you prove you love someone? How can anyone make the invisible visible, turn ghostly love into solid, breathing matter?

'It's you I love,' I said softly as he stood up. 'You.' He held out a hand to help me to my feet.

My sleep was troubled and full of dreams. I dreamed that David asked me to jump out of an aeroplane with him. He was the one wearing the parachute and I was meant to jump with him holding me in his arms.

I was supposed to trust that he would keep holding me. In the dream I understood this is what love asks of us: it asks us to jump, to believe in the power of silk and ropes and a lover's willingness to keep holding us up.

I woke unable to remember whether David held me fast. I remembered only the sensation against my face of cold and rushing air.

*The Island, Greece, 1965;*
*Sydney, 1965*

I cannot bear to write about leaving the island, I cannot bear the finality of words. David slipped away without fanfare two months ago to set up everything in Australia, leaving us to weather the full Greek departure: bunches of flowers, a speech from Thanasis, Pan on his *lyra*, photographs, the agonisingly slow arrival of the boat to Athens.

Soula was distraught, her fat cheeks wet with tears. Jerry was hovering somewhere in the background while Cassandra sobbed hysterically in Lil's skinny arms. I shut the door of our house for the last time, on the lemon tree I planted, on the plum tree, on the walls I whitewashed myself. And then the last sight of the cobbled crescent of the harbour.

The island receding, its unforgiving hills, its heartless rocks, my island in the grip of the sea.

Do not make me look back. Let me raise my eyes to the sea ahead, to the eternity of the unbroken sky. You have broken my heart, do not make me write the final word.


## On the boat to Sydney

I am trying to wake up, trying to imagine ourselves wreathed in glory, of David's news that he has won Australia's most prestigious literary prize. Money. The prize at last. Too late. Alas, too late.

His telegram from Sydney came the day before we left. *Darling, we have triumphed. We have finally proved the nay-sayers wrong.* But what have we proved? What have I proved, here on this ship, trying to wake up?

Nothing but good news from Australia, he writes, entirely forgetting that we cannot afford to pay our own fare back even at the moment of our triumph, entirely forgetting that only a few months ago when he finally learned about Jerry he could not bear to look into my eyes. Has he also chosen to forget that the girls and I are entering our homeland as assisted migrants, that the garlands on our triumphant brows are bound with dried tears? If he could only see Anna's cautious face now, her wariness and fear about what lies ahead in that country she no longer remembers. What does she remember, I asked the night before we left. *Reaching up to open a door. A mulberry tree in someone's garden. The scratch against my bottom of a grey stone sink in which I was being bathed.*

269

She does not remember my father, my mother; she does not remember the flashes of the cameras as we were leaving; the glamour of our new season's coats. She is eighteen years old, tall, with fully grown breasts, she intends to go to university to study maths. She is cool, intelligent, a virgin; she is Greek, Greek, Greek. I wanted a girl better than myself, more polished, more accomplished, *more*. She is all that, my icy maiden, completely fluent in Greek, Latin and English, not bad in French. She knows how the sky works, the laws of the sea, she knows much more than me. Please let her learn, too, the republic of the heart, let her be richer and wiser and luckier than her faint mother.

And where is Elizabeth, my Lil, the prettiest of jewels in my crown? Off playing amid her beauty, casting her pearls among boys. Look at her, dancing along to somebody's tinny record player on the top deck, pretending not to notice the boys. Look at her, the artist, the poet, the one whose eye is already bent upon the poem. Use the poem, Lil, don't use your beauty, please use the words of the poem.

*Sydney*

As the ship came through the Heads I saw the arc of the Sydney Harbour Bridge, and yellow and green ferries on their way to Manly. I had to sit down in fear that I was going to faint. Anna looked at me anxiously; for her sake I smiled.

'Home,' I said.

There was a small posse of cameras and journalists to meet us. I saw David standing in the crowd on the dock long before he saw me; he was wearing a new suit which looked too big on him, his face anxiously knotted. When I saw his face again I understood all over again that I loved him. We have fought too long, side by side, to surrender now.


## Ros's house—first impressions

So this is Ros, *in situ*, Australia's first female tenured professor of English relaxing at home. These are the gum trees, the lawns, the big houses; this is the rumoured land of plenty. The super-markets, the washing machines, the televisions, *modern life*: like Sleeping Beauty I have awakened. Everything is so easy, everything you could ever need is so close at hand. First impressions: the Australian accent, how it grates on the ears. Everybody strikes me as loud, rowdy and uncouth, sloppy in speech and manners. I hear myself speaking and I sound like the Queen, all received pronunciation and rounded vowels. Even Ros's voice sounds harsh, I have never heard anyone say the word 'fuck' so many times in so few sentences. When did everyone start saying 'fuck' all the time? Ros seems like a woman perilously close to being too much like a man—Australian women have a kind of brusqueness about them, some knock-it-off quality, as if somehow lacking in gentleness. Certainly my dear Ros has it in abundance, a pull-your-socks-up manner, gruff, not comfortable with too much emotion. When we met for the first time in fourteen years, the first thing she said to me after giving me a cursory hug was, 'Our car's got a flat. We'll have to catch a taxi,' before hauling several suitcases up under her strong arm and marching off.

And poor Ros is cursed with me. A sister whose eyes are a vale of tears, whose heart at any minute threatens to burst its banks. How frail and old our mother looks sitting in one of Ros's ghastly new modern chairs, how bent her arthritic back, how unreliable her memories. I had to flee the room when I took her hand in my own and felt the flimsiness of her bones. I tried to speak but could not: I sat holding her hand for as long as I could before rushing from the room.

In Ros's green tiled bathroom I cried for everything. No father! How great the gaping hole in my mind's map of Australia—my father once took up the whole map, straddling the country. Without him everything seems unnaturally quiet: no harassing, booming voice, no immense figure to block out the light. I remember copying in my journal a letter Kafka once wrote: *Dearest Father, You asked me recently why I maintain that I am afraid of you. As usual, I was unable to think of any answer to your question, partly for the very reason that I am afraid of you, and partly because an explanation of the grounds for this fear would mean going into far more details than I could even approximately keep in mind while talking.* I cannot seem to keep anything in my mind: this new world presses too heavily upon me.

When I composed myself I went back into the lounge room and drew up a chair close to my mother.

'Do you still see anyone from Kurrajong Bay, Mum?' I asked softly (she has been in a nursing home around the corner from Ros since May).

'Kurrajong Bay? Oh, yes, I went there for a holiday once with Arthur. We went first class all the way.'

She has forgotten everything. She has no memory of that wooden house with the verandah covered by great arcs of jasmine, of the scrubby buffalo grass in that backyard with no fence, that garden which ran down all the way to the sand dunes. I wondered if she even remembered who I was. Did the long pile of days that we lived apart cause her to forget me? Should I have stayed to share the hours with her so that our lives would have remained bound by the commonality of shopping and dinners and slow Sunday afternoons, by the circumstantial captivity that tethers most lives? It occurred to me that in freeing myself I sidestepped my obligations, turning myself into the kind of daughter a mother might fail to recognise. It is too late now to reclaim those lost hours, and for this my heart feels drowned.

And Ros looks so like our father. Who would have thought that she would carry him on—his hands, the cut of his jaw, the set of his shoulders. I cannot look. I am forever rushing from rooms, an endless flood spilling from my eyes.

*Later*

My noisy, foul-mouthed countrymen and women—Ros's husband Peter must be the foulest-mouthed man I have ever met. He is an academic too—like Ros, never wanted children— and when both of them are sitting on the back patio drinking beers and smoking their heads off—the girls drinking weak shandies with us—it is all I can do to stop myself rushing up to Anna and Lil to block their ears. The girls continually talk to each other in Greek, a private code. They have already made friends with the teenage boy next door though—the vogue is for 'pool parties' and they have already been invited twice. The smell of Ros's Sydney backyard on a summer night—newly mown grass being watered, the buzz of cicadas; somewhere, the burned meat and onions of a barbeque. In the mornings I wake before dawn and creep out to turn my head up to the transcendent arch of the Southern Hemisphere's great sky, imagining the Greek sky beginning to darken.

I cannot sleep, I cannot sleep; everything is awake inside me, every dream, every thought, every fear. My head is crowded with the past, with people long dead or long gone. In the streets of Sydney I am forever peering into faces, looking for something, or someone. I am exhausted by everything. I cannot stop my mind from wheeling endlessly on its own anxieties, my heart is endlessly knocking in my chest as though I have had a terrible fright. Whatever happened to Beryl? To Ray? To that boy in Kurrajong Bay whose name I no longer recall who once kissed me?

Do our bodies remember everything? Do our eyes recall every once-loved face which passed before them? I cannot for the life of me remember the particulars of Beryl's face, I cannot remember the girl I was in that long-ago wallpapered room. I have forgotten so much, so many people! I have forgotten who I was. When I recall myself at nineteen, at twenty-two, I am recalling another person entirely, a kind of relative of myself, but no longer myself. All those dead selves piled up inside me, all the girls I used to be—how can I stop the dread that visits me at night, the fullest knowledge of the weight of my mistakes, the nameless anxiety that something awful awaits me. David is growing frustrated with me, forever asking how I am feeling. 'You've got that look again, Kate.' Success seems to have momentarily quelled his bitterness towards me but he is fast losing his patience (it is only when he is drunk that I glimpse again that closed-in, hunched look he gets when he is about to turn nasty). I cannot seem to help myself, I cannot compose my own face. I cannot stop fading out from wherever I am meant to be, from privately travelling far away. I am looking everywhere but upon the present moment, I am imagining everything but the shape of the future. How can I steady myself upon the earth so that I might safely push the girls out into life's waters? I am so frightened—surely I have not lost my faith in the value of survival, surely I have not travelled all this way only to lose that?

*Sunday*

The quality of Australian light, somehow harsher than Greece; the self satisfied nature of everyone—'Greece is beautiful but I bet it's not a patch on Australia,' said the man who stamped my passport at the dock. 'Welcome home.' What is it about Australia that already defeats me? The fact that there doesn't seem to be anything to struggle against? That meat and beer and neat lawns and full employment are laid out on the table and one need only reach out the laziest of hands? The struggle is over! The struggle to live a life singular and beautiful, away from Australia's sad suburban rectitudes, away from this brawny place that has no use for poets. Even our rocky island needed its poets, its stories and myths, even our former rocky home knew the purpose of a line from Aesop.

Everything is so familiar, and yet strange. The smell of the place, the light, the faces of the people—known, known, known. Yet many things are different—more Europeans, more European writing on shop signs, the ability to buy freshly roasted coffee beans. But still—ladies lounges in the pubs, bars where women cannot go—but at least the pubs close at ten now. I remember men at Kurrajong Bay in the pub after work guzzling as much beer as possible before six o'clock closing—at the very hour when people all over Europe were just beginning to dress for a pre-dinner drink.

Pat came up from Melbourne to see us—she's now a big shot in the theatrical world. She brought her husband George who runs an art gallery, a Frenchman who arrived after the war. Although we'd never met he soon seemed as familiar as Pat, who hasn't changed one bit—after a few seconds of awkwardness between us Atpay and I resumed our lifelong conversation as if my years away had never been and I had momentarily been gone from the room.

Pat and George are the most vivid people we have met so far—they said we would notice all sorts of differences since we had left, that the social and cultural climate of Australia was changing fast but they found themselves nonetheless mixing in a smallish circle of like-minded friends.

'Quite a lot of Australians still reach for their guns when they hear the word "culture",' George said.

'Yes,' said Pat, 'they still suspect you're a wanker, or a poof.' We laughed but I felt a sense of foreboding.

A general sense here that everybody is sleepwalking through their lives. Our island was hardly a bustling metropolis but everyone did their job with a particular kind of attentiveness, whether it was threading weave into the backs of wooden chairs or scraping up donkey shit. Even the men drinking ouzo or canned retsina sitting apparently idle around a table in Pan's taverna were doing a kind of job—sharing information, gathering news, living inseparably from every other man and woman around them. Life was a repetitive organic system, closely bound with the earth's seasons and the rituals of the Church.

Am I romanticising my past already? Is it too early to say that I fear my life in Australia will be dry and passionless, that

I fear everything good, every sense of the possible, is now behind me? 'Don't look back, Kate,' David said to me this morning, 'you'll turn into a pillar of salt.'

A letter in Jerry's distinctive curly hand arrived this morning. I threw it unopened into the rubbish bin. What use to me is the past?

## Monday

I've been offered a job. The editor of the *Herald* called to ask whether I would be interested in 'a little column'. I met him at a publishing party for David's book—quite a nice, civilised chap I thought—and he telephoned yesterday to say he had thought of me over the weekend and wondered if I would care to write something 'literary' for the *Herald*. He had in mind something like a fortnightly essay, in which I was free to write whatever I liked. Be witty. Controversial. Political. Anything I like.

A few ripe words then, succulent with meaning. A column, no less than 1000 words, a nice fat regular cheque. David, of course, being happy himself, was full of happiness for me. 'It can only be a good thing, Kate, an excellent way of keeping your name about. Thousands of people read newspapers—only a handful read novels or poems. It'll make your name. You'll be more famous than me!'

What happens to names which fall beyond the public's line of sight? Is a poet still a poet if her poem remains unread?

I have striven all these years to reach the nameless poem. It appears I have been travelling fruitlessly in a circle.

Journalism will put food in our mouths, my name back on the table; journalism was the place I began and it appears to be the place where I will end.

Why is it that I see this opportunity only as my failure?

I will write the column. But I will mourn the nameless poem.

*Sydney, 1969*

Can't do anything any more. Feel very frightened.
Can't feel love. Trying to hold on for the girls. Finishing this.

*Sydney, 1946*

May 15

*Knuckle, lip, ankle, flesh:*
*If I were a man I'd be him.*
*Our kin of bones*
*Our seamless skin:*
*Body of my body*
*Flesh of my flesh.*
*Our bony harmony, our common tears:*
*A single tongue, unleashed.*

His orgasm—soft and unfrozen—the sweetest, most silent orgasm I have ever known, a gentle sigh; if you breathed too loudly you'd miss it. As though everything has stopped: time, the movement of the earth, everything but the gentle throb in my dark centre. I am lost in the smell of him, the sugared oiliness of his skin, the surprising plump softness of his mouth.

Thank you, God, for the feel of my bare feet on the cold lino, for the balance of construction, the way my body of nerves and blood is held up. Thank you for the wonder of movement, for the settling of my shoulders, the swing of my arms, the bliss of animated life. Thank you for the breath of in and out, the hidden bloom of lung. Thank you for the sight of sky, of sun; for the sight of his wounded face.

# Sydney, 1951

We are sailing out through the heads of Sydney Harbour. I am alone here with my journal on the upper deck—David has taken the girls back to the cabin.

You should have seen the look on Dad's face as we were leaving—he was trying so hard to look nonchalant. Mum was hysterical, waving frantically, alternatively clutching and sobbing into her handkerchief like some mother in a bad movie. Dad refused even to wave: he was all dressed up, in his best suit and hat, his face completely impassive. I wonder when I will see them again.

'Goodbye, Katherine,' Dad said, kissing me stiffly on the cheek before we boarded the ramp. 'I hope London bequeaths you melodious days. Remember, "Life is just a stuff to try the soul's strength on".'

Is this Shakespeare? Tennyson? Davey will know—he knows everything—every poem, Latin, the workings of love.

I'm ready for life. I can't wait for it to try its hardest upon me, to try to force me once again to my knees. My soul feels like it has the strength of a thousand armies.

Am I not still standing? My arms full?

I feel equal to the bluest of peninsulas.

I plan on sitting in the opera house at Covent Garden, on plunking myself down at one of those famous tables in the reading room of the British Museum, on listening to the BBC till my ears break. I plan on drinking a cocktail at the Savoy, of turning up my eyes to the glory of St Paul's. I am going to take the girls to the Victoria and Albert and to concerts at the Royal Albert Hall. I am going to map the particulars of one small existence, write a testament to all the coming hours.

I am going to fill this book, and fill it and fill it with all the wonders I am about to see. I am going to write poems, stories, novels, the words of my children: I am going to write the story of my life.

What a gift life is, what a strange and terrible responsibility it is to live.

Let me be equal to it, let me feel its ecstasies and terrors.

Let me give everything it is within my soul to give, plunge headlong into the fullest rush of life.

Let life begin!

# Part Two:
## Anna

*Canberra, 2003*

I've been coming to the library every day for a month now. Being anal retentive I like to sit at the same desk. Preferably in the same chair. I get here early so that I can make sure I get my table. Only once someone else was sitting at it. I gave him my frostiest look.

Lately I have become worried that I am starting to forget my mother. I am beginning to forget how she looked the last time I saw her. I can't remember her last words to me. I think we discussed something banal like a new boyfriend or the results of an exam, I don't know, I no longer remember.

I am older than she will ever be. I have lived longer without her than with her.

I don't know what I expected in coming here. A means of reviving my fading memory perhaps. An explanation probably. One day I just decided to come. Since I live in Sydney, it took some arranging. My partner was helpful, my sons as understanding as teenage boys can be.

My desire to come no doubt has something to do with the fact that my eldest boy is preparing to leave home. I have always regarded myself as a practical woman. Not the type to succumb to extravagant emotion. Overly controlled is the usual complaint.

But lately I have begun to feel sad. I have been feeling that my life is coming to an end. My father died last year. The university has offered me early retirement. I have been thinking a lot about my mother.

A couple of days after my mother's death I could still smell her in her bedroom. In her sheets, her clothes. There was hair in her scabby old hairbrush. Everything she ever said to me was crystal clear. Now it is not so clear.

My father couldn't go near her room. When we were sorting through her things he stood in the doorway. He wouldn't come in.

He was the one who found her. He couldn't wake her up. It was only when he shook her and felt how cold she was that he realised she was dead. He saw the bottle of pills and the whisky on the bedside table. Then he saw the note.

For all its florid emotion it was next to useless.

*My darlings forgive me*
*I am sorry I am having trouble writing this. I have loved*
*you all so much.*
*Now I cannot feel anything except pain I am so sorry*

*Cannot write any more forgive me*
*Katherine*

The note is not in the library's collection. That is because I kept it. In the confusion of the moment my father didn't notice that I took it. I suppose he later assumed it had been thrown out.

Anyone can read it and still be none the wiser. It doesn't explain anything to me, or else its explanation lies only in the absence of her saying anything.

The meaning I took from it was that my mother loved us, but in the past tense. She had loved us, but previously, not now. Her small, inadequate note recorded the memory of love.

I could not believe my ears when my father telephoned that morning. 'Anna, it's me. I've got some terrible news. Can you come over?' I thought something had happened to Lil. 'Dad, is it Lil?' He said, 'No,' and straightaway I knew. 'Oh, please, not Mum. Tell me it's not Mum.' 'Yes,' he said, 'she's gone, darling. She's gone from us.'

They were taking her away when I got there. She didn't look dead, she looked asleep. I had this weird feeling she was going to open her eyes.

Elizabeth and I went with our father to the Glebe Coroner's Court to hear the coroner's verdict on our mother's death. *Yes,*

*I am David John Murray, author, husband of the deceased Katherine Anne Elgin Murray, late of 15 Stephen Street, Warawee. Yes, my wife had been drinking heavily the night before her death; yes, she had been depressed for some months. Yes, she was an author, aged forty-six years.*

At this point my father wiped his eyes and the coroner asked if he was all right to continue. My father said, *Yes, I'm fine.* My father went on to say that his wife had had trouble sleeping, that she had suffered from insomnia for the last couple of years, since returning to Australia after a long exile in Greece. *She had at least three current prescriptions for sleeping pills from various doctors in Pymble, St Ives, and neighbouring suburbs.*

Lil cried but I did not. I listened carefully to everything that was said. I saw that my father looked wrecked, as if he had not slept for months. It was news to me that he loved my mother.

After the coroner returned his verdict that Katherine Anne Elgin Murray had died on or about October 27 from an overdose of sleeping tablets 'self-administered while in a state of severe mental depression and while considerably affected by alcohol', my father stood and nodded. 'Thank you very much,' he said. 'Am I free to go?'


It sounds macabre but after my mother was buried I could not stop thinking about her decomposing body. We had a small funeral. My aunt Ros and uncle Pete, my grandmother Elsie. My grandmother didn't know what was happening. She looked frightened, turning around, twisting her fingers. She's long dead herself now.

For months afterwards I kept thinking of my mother down there in the dark. Did she still have her skin?

I kept thinking foolish thoughts. She was missing out on summer. Her jasmine was in flower.


Sitting here and reading everything my mother wrote has not made anything clearer. Despite all her words she had the same inability to analyse her emotions as the rest of us. In fact she was more wilfully deceitful than most. She specialised in romance, in emotional obfuscation.

My mother was so carried away with her private epiphanies about art and life she failed to notice what was under her nose. At her worst she bristles with vanity, drenched in self-pity and artistic self-regard. If I was a psychoanalyst I would say her grandiose persona as an 'artist' was the death of her. Only a narcissist could imagine having a soul with the strength of a thousand armies.

For someone who believed she had dedicated her life to truth she was astonishingly self-deceptive. For all her navel-gazing, my mother couldn't see how much like her father she was. Ros says she was exactly like him, self-centred, egotistical—I know that when she was writing one of her precious fucking books everyone was supposed to think it was the most important thing in the world. Sometimes when I came home from school she would look straight through me, her thoughts fixed on some character in her head. I once ate an entire freshly baked cake while she worked beside me at the kitchen table. Lil and I twigged early that we could get away with anything when she was writing.

My mother believed her status as an 'artist' gave her the right to everything, including the private details of my life. When she was doing the column, she had no compunction whatsoever about using my experiences, or Lil's. She wrote about 'the youth of today', the boys I went out with, the length of my mini-skirts. She had no idea how she hurt people.

My mother had a way of blocking out anything she didn't want to deal with. I was interested to see how she recorded my dislike of our neighbour, Theo. I think these days the term for what he did to me would be called sexual abuse. He used to lock me in his bedroom and pin me to the bed. He was twelve years old, but big and strong, and I was helpless.

I note my mother's unfailing romanticism about Greek island life. How could anyone think that living in the sun meant a life without shadows? The laws of life are just as unbeatable on a Greek island as anywhere else.

Sickness, bad faith, old age. Everything comes to us in the end.


For a long time I could not forgive my mother. Not only for killing herself but for leaving Lil the most terrible of blueprints.

My sister killed herself three years after my mother. Pills, alcohol, the same. I thought any vestige of love left for my mother was gone.

When someone dies by suicide there is an irresistible impulse to see every event in their life as a missed clue. For years I tried to read Lil's life backwards from her end, as if everything that went before was changed by that last, defining act.

Now I think she was just unlucky. She was a happy child, a happy young woman, until our mother's death. I think Lil's death was an accident: I might have dropped in unexpectedly or her boyfriend Paul might have changed his plans and stayed the night. Like me, like the rest of us, she would have gone on to learn that even unbearable sadness can wax and wane.

My father never re-married. He had a couple of long-term girlfriends. The last one, Robyn, I grew to like. I told her I understood completely when she decided to leave him.

My mother's death had gradually turned us into curiosities. We were early victims of celebrity culture. Before long, everybody wanted to know everything. Articles were written, books. A burgeoning women's movement claimed my mother as one of its patron saints. My father was reduced to the demon lover, and it was generally supposed that without him my mother's life would have been happier, her genius fulfilled. I once read an article which suggested that, had she lived, my mother would have been an active campaigner for refugees and women's rights.

I've got no time for all that crap. Celebrity culture rests on a false premise: that if every action is brought to light, truth will out. I agree with my mother. Everyone is a secret. In the end, no one knows anyone else.

Words cannot cover or reveal everything. A book will never save your life. I note that as my mother got closer to suicide, words failed her. For someone for whom writing was like breathing, this meant she lacked the means to go on. The mechanism by which she lived was broken.

It seems to me she finally discovered not everything in life can be written down. There will always be gaps in the narrative, mysteries impossible to record. I see that my mother never once wrote the word 'envy'. She lacked the courage to write some things down. Her journal often tells a different story to the one she thought she was writing.

I grew up surrounded by people turning their emotional lives into fiction. Yet my mother went to great lengths to point out the distinction between life and art.

The library describes her unfinished novel as 'autobiographical'. This suggests she gave birth to an illegitimate child. If I was the kind of reader to read a novel as disguised fact, I would say she did. But nowhere in her journal does she write of such a situation, recording only that something awful happened, about which she does not intend to speak. My instinct tells me she knew regret and sorrow but caused by what it is impossible to say. I am old enough to know everyone holds within them some accumulation of pain, some complex mix of disappointment, longing and grief.

I'm going to ask Ros. She'll tell me.

My late grandfather, Arthur Elgin, was never a communist. He was a lifelong Mason, a fully paid-up conservative. Apparently he loved sport. What my mother did not embellish was his personality: Ros says he was an egomaniac of the highest order, and never stopped talking about himself. Ros, who has just turned eighty-three and is still as sharp as a tack, tells cruel stories about him boring everyone senseless reciting the hundred and one quatrains of *The Rubáiyát of Omar Khayyám* while dressed in his underpants.

But if my mother's fiction does not tell the whole truth then neither does her journal. Many things are missing. Incidents from my childhood, for instance, from Lil's life and mine, which she never recorded. I remember for Lil's eighth birthday she went to Athens to get materials so she could make a beautiful blue papier-mâché doll. Inside the doll she secreted hundreds of pink sugar-coated chocolates. She hung up the doll from the plum tree in the walled garden. Every child was given a big stick with which to whack the doll. Chocolates rained upon us. It is one of the highlights of my life.

I remember, too, something my mother once told me about writing. She said it was like seeding a pearl. The writer puts in a tiny piece of truth, smaller than a grain of sand. The grain then irritates its environment into producing an artificial pearl.

The problem now is the impossibility of ever finding the original autobiographical grain. How could I ever begin to sort through her life and her fiction for truth?

I am a mathematician, not a writer. I enjoy the solidity of figures, the way everything operates under provable laws. Writing never appealed to me. It's neurotic, frankly. Living once, then living it over.

I have always known each breath is singular. Once you have expelled a breath it is gone.

I waited a long time before I had children. For ages I wasn't sure I wanted them.

It was Chris who helped change my mind. Like me, he belongs to a generation which believes it knows more than its elders. We flattered ourselves that knowledge equals power and supposed we could avoid our parents' worst mistakes. I was thirty-eight when Sam was born; forty when I had Alex.

I would like to report that I have proved a better mother than my mother was. Before I had my sons, I reckoned I would make a more attentive, caring parent. I believed I could give my sons everything I didn't get myself. I was therefore surprised when I found myself looking at my oldest son one day, thinking,

'Why should you have it any easier than I did?' At that moment, I hated him.

Last April I went back to the island for the first time in thirty-seven years. I am the only member of my family ever to return.

A couple of things propelled me. I knew it would probably be our last holiday together. Sam was leaving school; at fifteen, Alex had reached an age where he preferred his friends to us. Then my father died.

I wanted to go back.

It was misty as the hydrofoil came into the harbour. No old white boat now. No *Sirius* taking several hours from Piraeus, stopping off at various islands on the way. Instead a two hour bumpy trip by hydrofoil.

I had been scanning the horizon for some time. All at once the familiar shape of the island rose up. My breath caught.

The harbour looked the same. I had not seen it since I was eighteen years old. Then, someone had given my mother flowers. Lil was holding a new hand-sewn handkerchief embroidered by her best friend Cassandra. She was crying.

As the hydrofoil came into the port everything rushed back. The houses, the hills, the colours, the smells, the same sounds. 'Are you okay?' Chris asked. 'Yes,' I said, 'I'm fine.'

On the quay of the port my feet recalled the feel of the cobble-stones. I put my head down and walked.

I told no one I was coming. I still occasionally correspond with Lil's friend Cassandra. At fifty, Cassandra is a grandmother several times over but I have not heard from her in some years.

I did not look up. I did not expect to be recognised. Nonetheless I felt exposed. I followed Chris and was aware of the excitement of the boys, who had mysteriously dropped their air of inner-city teenage surliness to exclaim over the donkeys, as my sister and I had once done.

My heart was racing despite myself. The smell of petrol and kerosene and oil and salt and fish and donkey shit and rotten vegetables brought everything back.

We found ourselves in some anonymous room. Our bags on a mock marbled floor. The shutters opened onto a sports ground I did not remember. Boys were playing on a football pitch I had never seen.

Behind the field were the rocky hills of my youth. I saw olive trees, cactus, donkeys, the weak spring sun. Chris said, 'We don't have to stay you know, Anna. We can leave on the next boat.' I shook my head. My eldest son came up and offered his hand.

It was too early in April for warmth. Sometimes we needed sweaters. In the days that followed I passed unnoticed, indistinguishable from every other tourist. It was still quiet, out of season. I saw the effects of international tourism, how much cleaner and slicker everything looked. I noticed the plethora of shops selling tiny wicker donkeys, evil eyes, *komboloe*.

On warmer days Chris took the boys to the coves where I swam as a child. While they were gone I walked endlessly. I walked up to the school where I once stood at the wire fence shouting down messages to my father working in his studio in our house below.

Out of the corner of my eye I saw our house. Quickly my eye veered away. I turned and began to walk, fast. I continued up the hill. I passed the church where Lil was baptised, the houses where I knew all the children who once lived inside. Every house was freshly painted, probably owned by rich Athenians for use as weekenders. Derelict houses had been renovated; walled gardens where pigs and goats and chickens had been kept were laid out with expensive tiles and pot plants. Every time anyone passed I put my head down.

One afternoon I came by accident upon our house. I had momentarily stopped to rest. Turning my head I looked up a lane and saw the edge of it.

I stood very still. It seemed unbelievable the house had survived us.

I walked towards it. The well outside was no longer in use. All the windows were new. Everything was closed, every window and shutter and door. I quickly glanced over to the house next-door which used to be Soula's. Whoever lived there was not in.

I circled the house. Round the walled garden where I saw the tops of lemon trees. Past the plum tree planted by my mother. I went around the back of the house and down the other side. The window to the kitchen was open, protected by a new metal grill. I squatted down and peered in. The cool of it hit me in the face: its deep cave smell, its dark quiet. I could see straight through to the walled garden at the other side.

I stood up. I moved quickly back down the alley where I had come. I was trying not to run.


Every day the house kept drawing me back. I could not stop myself from walking towards it. I sat on my heels in the alley and made out our old bedroom, Lil's and mine. I noted the window where we had once yelled out obscenities to Theo. From where I had thrown water bombs at my sister.

As I got braver I took to sitting on the stone steps of what used to be Soula's house. Not once did I see Soula. I did not see anyone in our house either. It appeared closed up for winter.

I wondered who owned it now. When we left we handed over responsibility for its sale to Thanasis, the mayor. I believe he sold it for a pittance to someone from Athens.

I wondered what had happened to Soula. To Theo. Perhaps they were dead like the rest.

When I was with Chris and the boys I began to point things out to them.

I took them to the cove where we used to swim. The steps leading down to the sea had rusted away. My mother used to hoist herself up from the sea using those steps.

One morning Chris took the boys on a climb to the mountains. I bought a copy of the *Guardian International* and sat down at one of the indistinguishable new cafés. I was wearing my sunglasses for the first time, trying to drink a terrible cup of coffee made with Nescafé and UHT milk.

I happened to glance up. Coming straight towards me was Kyria Soula. Soula grown old, but still recognisably Soula. She moved slowly, still a far way up the lane. Straightaway I knew that squat and solid shape to be hers. I sat very still. As I watched my hands began to sweat. How old was she? Seventy-five? Seventy-six? I know she was younger than my mother. Age had descended on her like it never would upon my mother.

She came closer and closer. That same large, square bottom that had descended so many times down the ladder from our upper rooms. That same fleshy face.

I barely breathed as she drew closer, as she passed within inches of my face. I felt the curved ridge of the chair against my back. I came eye-to-eye with that living memory: I needed only to reach out a hand to stop her.

I could not move. She passed by, not glancing in my direction.

As she passed I noticed one of her eyes had filmed over. She had a wall eye, some kind of blindness.

But her face, her hands, her great solid bottom were the same. She was walking the same earth, the same streets as she had always done. She had lived here, rooted to the spot, turning into a mother, a grandmother, no doubt into a great-grandmother. Eventually she would turn into earth. Into the dirt of the cemetery on the hill.

I did not turn to watch her walk away.

On our last morning I made a pilgrimage to the locked house to say goodbye. I intended to place my hand one last time against its walls. If I had not made peace with the past, at least I keenly felt the full weight of my sorrow.

As I rounded the corner I looked up. A window was open. A sheet was airing. A clean white sheet was hanging from the very window where we used to hang our hairy old blankets. Lil used to say they were made of yak hair.

Against my will my heart jumped up. Just like my mother I did not stop to think. I rushed to the door and knocked.

I heard someone moving about, upstairs, in my father's studio. I was about to turn and run. A head appeared above me from the window. *'Na?'*

All my Greek came back. All the words in my mouth I keep swallowed.

*'Kali mera. Me lene Anna, kapote zousa etho. Afto itan*

*to spiti mou.'* My name is Anna. I used to live here. This was my house.

A man, much the same age as myself, held the key. I saw in his face he was going to let me in.

'Of course!' he said in perfect English. 'Can you come back in twenty minutes? I've only just got up.'

'*Na, na. Efharisto poli. Efharisto poli.*' My hands instinctively made a sign of blessing against my chest.

'*Yasso,*' he said, closing the window. I turned and walked back down the lane.

With every step my initial exhilaration faltered. My fervour to get through the door left me. I could never pass through that door again.

My hands shook. I felt like I was going to be sick.

In the room of the pension where we were staying Chris and the boys were absent. I went into the bathroom and vomited into the insufficient toilet. Signs warned me not to flush toilet paper into the toilet and to use the waste-paper basket provided instead.

My head felt strange. For a moment I was uncertain of where I was. The past and the present had joined up.

I carefully cleaned myself. I left the bathroom, lay down on the bed, and waited.

I did not have to go back. I did not have to step over the threshold. I did not have to look again upon my loss.

I could wait instead for the arrival of Chris and Alex and Sam. I could wait quietly in the room until I once again joined the present moment.

I saw from the watch upon my wrist that time was still moving. Ten minutes had passed. Fifteen, twenty. I sat and watched the death of time. Then I got up and went towards the house.

The owner opened the door straightaway. I stepped over the threshold. My legs held me up, taking me into the kitchen. My host led me to a chair by our old kitchen table.

He must have noticed I looked pale. He offered water. 'Perhaps you would prefer a Greek coffee?' '*Na, na,*' I said. *Yes.*

As my eyes adjusted to the light I saw the flagstones of the floor, the windows, the new gas oven, the ledges which once held our fruit and vegetables. The man told me he lived in Athens where he ran an antiques business. He bought the house from the man Thanasis had sold it to. He seemed a kind man, wanting to talk about the impact of tourism on Greek culture, the havoc of capitalism, the press of the world upon the island. I listened to him as politely as I could.

I wanted to shout, *Shut up, you vlaca.*

After a while he rose from the chair. 'I suppose you would like to look through the house?'

There were stairs where there had been none before, new windows, new toilets, new everything. Then we were in our old bedroom, Lil's and mine. The cupboards that Panayotis built. The same circle of damp on the ceiling above where my bed used to be. 'The foreigners who lived here before were spies,' he said, 'for the Americans.' I suppose he meant my parents.

Then he stood before the door to my parents' bedroom. Where our mother had cradled us in bed, where Dad once memorably brought us breakfast of the worst pancakes in the world made of flour, condensed milk and duck eggs.

The man opened the door. *And there was nothing there.* No mother, no father, no sister. No one. The room was empty.

The whole house was empty. Every room an empty shell from which the living essence had been sucked.

I wanted to sink to my knees for want of a ghost. For want of the merest breath of life.

But there was nothing. Nothing.

Just the carcass of time.


It has taken many hours to read my mother's journals. There have been moments when I felt I could not go on. Before I started I thought they might contain some message. Some answer she had failed to provide.

I see now that instead of answers my mother asked a question.

She asked the future whether her long struggle was worth it. Whether the books she made were worth what it took to make them.

Mother, here is your answer: a poem for your face, a book for your life. I came to read your broken book in the hope your breath was upon it still.

How I long to see you old and wise, with whitened hair.

Here I am, your difficult daughter Anna grown old instead, remembering that I once sailed a frail boat with you into the Saronic Sea.

## Acknowledgements

During the writing of this book I learned that a long-awaited biography of Charmian Clift was to be published in Australia. I deliberately chose not to read it, relying instead on my memory of some twenty-year-old newspaper clippings about Clift from the *Sydney Morning Herald*, plus research from various war archives and libraries. However, I have since read Nadia Wheatley's superb biography, *The Life and Myth of Charmian Clift*, and recommend it to anyone wishing to know more about Clift's life.

Thanks and love to dear Les, Caspar and Elliot, Barbara and John Johnson, Molly Cooney, Bill and Helen Webb, Emma Felton and Fiona McCrae.

In London, Emma Mahony and Adam Barker, John Mahony, Katharine and Aidan Elliott, Harriet Griffey, Sheila Murphy, Anna Maclulich and Julian Bull, Debbie Marshall and Mark Stalley, Liz Minter and Ross Tanner provided encouragement, domestic and computer support, car rides and fun. Thanks especially to Victoria Pyeman, Domestic Goddess and deliverer of meals, and to Frances Atkinson in Melbourne, poet and researcher extraordinaire. Kim Knott and Tom Pridham generously gave their time and talent in taking my photograph.

Catherine Drayton in New York was unfailingly supportive. Stephanie Cabot in London was indefatigable. Thanks to Annette Barlow, Patrick Gallagher and everyone at Allen & Unwin.

I am especially indebted to Jamie Grant for help with the poetry.

Without Margaret Connolly there would be no book.